'I cannot ... changed so ... Dinah exclai...

'Yes, you have cha... ...an I could have hoped,' Cobie replied. 'Because you were loved and cared for.'

'*You* have not loved or cared for me.' There was almost accusation in her voice.

'No?' he queried. So much of what Madame had done, had been done because of his instructions.

The new *savoir faire* which Dinah had learned—and was still learning—informed her that, if she wished, she could make him hers at any time, whenever she pleased.

At the top of the stairs she saw the pair of them in a large gilt-framed mirror—and gasped. She was prepared for her husband's splendour. Evening dress became him as nothing else did. But she was not prepared for the sight of herself.

She was his complement in every way. The girl who had hunched her shoulders and bent her head, lest the world look her in the face, had gone.

'Yes,' Cobie said in her ear. 'We go well together, do we not?'

Dear Reader

Some years ago I did a great deal of research on the lives of those men and women who, for a variety of reasons, lived on the frontiers. Re-reading recently about life in Australia in the early nineteenth century, it struck me that an interesting story about them was only waiting to be told. Having written HESTER WARING'S MARRIAGE, it was a short step to wonder what happened to the children and grandchildren.

Hence *The Dilhorne Dynasty*, each book of which deals with a member of the family who sets out to conquer the new world in which he finds himself. The Dilhornes, men and women, are at home wherever they settle, be it Australia, England, or the United States of America, and because of their zest for life become involved in interesting adventures.

Paula Marshall

Recent titles by the same author:

HIS ONE WOMAN*
AN INNOCENT MASQUERADE*
A STRANGE LIKENESS*
HESTER WARING'S MARRIAGE*
THE QUIET MAN

*The Dilhorne Dynasty

THE DOLLAR PRINCE'S WIFE

Paula Marshall

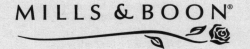

First published in Great Britain 2001
Harlequin Mills & Boon Limited,
Eton House, 18-24 Paradise Road, Richmond, Surrey TW9 1SR

© Paula Marshall 2001

ISBN 0 263 82729 1

Set in Times Roman 10½ on 11¼ pt.
04-0501-86393

Printed and bound in Spain
by Litografía Rosés S.A., Barcelona

DILHORNE FAMILY TREE

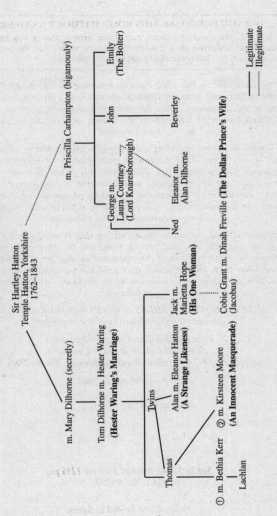

Sir Hartley Hatton
Temple Hatton, Yorkshire
1762–1843

m. Mary Dilhorne (secretly)

m. Priscilla Carhampton (bigamously)

Tom Dilhorne m. Hester Waring (**Hester Waring's Marriage**)

George m. Laura Courtney (Lord Knaresborough)

Ned

Eleanor m. Alan Dilhorne

John

Beverley

Emily (The Bolter)

Twins

Alan m. Eleanor Hatton (**A Strange Likeness**)

Thomas

Jack m. Marietta Hope (**His One Woman**)

Cobie Grant m. Dinah Freville (**The Dollar Prince's Wife**) (Jacobus)

① m. Bethia Kerr

② m. Kirsteen Moore (**An Innocent Masquerade**)

Lachlan

Legitimate ——
Illegitimate ......

Prologue

'What I tell you three times is true.' Lewis Carroll

Early March, 1892, Somerset

Lady Dinah Freville, the unconsidered half-sister of Violet, Lady Kenilworth, who always spoke of her in the most cavalier manner possible, was being equally cavalier in referring to her.

'I really don't want to leave you, Mama. You know how much I dislike staying with Violet—and how much she dislikes having me.'

She was staring through the window of the small dining room in her mother's cottage in Somerset. Her mother, the widow of the late Lord Rainsborough, elegantly dressed in a loose silk Liberty gown of many colours, was busy with her canvas work.

She eyed the flowers she was stitching, yawned, and said gently, 'I know, I know, but you can't stay with me, my love. By my husband's will, now that you're eighteen, your guardianship will pass from me to your brother, and since he is still unmarried he has decreed that Violet will take you over and arrange for you to be presented at court. With luck, she will also arrange a suitable marriage for you. I can't keep you here with me, however much I might wish to do so.'

Dinah's frown grew. 'I don't want to live with Violet, I don't want to be presented at court. I dislike the idea of the whole wretched business. I would much rather live with Faa if I can't stay with you.'

'Oh, that wouldn't do at all!' exclaimed her mother. 'And I do wish that you wouldn't call Professor Fabian Faa. You're not supposed to know that he's your father.'

'I object to that too,' returned Dinah mutinously. 'Such hypocrisy! At least now that Lord Rainsborough is dead I don't have to pretend that *he*'s my father any more.'

'Violet,' observed her mother, 'thinks that you are a docile, spiritless child. I sometimes wish that she knew what you're like when she's absent. Does she really have such a dampening effect on you, my darling?'

Dinah spun round, turning to face her mother at last. 'You don't mind being in exile because you once weren't, because once you had a name and a place, but I'm nobody—no, worse than nobody. I haven't even a proper name, and every time I look at Violet—or anyone else from her world—I always know what they're thinking. "That's the one, the child whose existence ruined Charlotte Rainsborough who bolted with Louis Fabian—and didn't even stay bolted with him once her child was born."'

She suddenly fell silent, half-ashamed of her own vehemence. She looked at her mother's placid face. 'Why don't you stop me when I'm being wicked, Mama?'

'Oh, no, dear, much better to get it out of your system, as Nursie used to say.'

Genuine laughter shook Dinah. 'Why didn't you, Mama? Stay with him, Faa, I mean?'

'Oh, no, once Rainsborough refused to divorce me it would have ruined poor Louis if I had stayed with him. I had no money of my own to keep him. No, Louis and I had our fun, one splendid summer, and then he could go back to being an Oxford don, and I was only too happy to be Rainsborough's exiled wife—much better than having to live with him.'

She fell silent, contemplating that long-ago year when she had had a passionate affair with the young man who had been brought to Borough Hall to tutor her indolent son before he went to Oxford.

No, she told herself firmly, no, I won't think of the life Dinah and I might have had if Rainsborough hadn't played dog in the manger, roaring at me that dreadful day, 'By God, Charlotte, if I can't have you, neither shall he. I'll be damned if I divorce you, and if you still run to him I'll see him ruined, and he shan't have the child, either. He, she, it, will be mine, will take my name, and be damned to the pair of you!'

No, she couldn't ruin Louis, so she had accepted her husband's terms, and her daughter Dinah was now Lady Dinah, who might have been a nameless bastard otherwise. But Rainsborough had taken good care that everyone knew the child's sad history. Both her half-brother, who was always called Rainey, and her half-sister Violet, now married to Lord Kenilworth, but also the latest mistress of Edward, Prince of Wales, were hardly subtle in their constant, unkind reminders that she was only one of them by grace and favour...

Dinah plumped down on her knees and gently took her mother's hand in order to stroke it lovingly. 'The grand passion which only lasted six months. Is that how long all grand passions last, Mama?'

'Yes, if you like, Dinah.' What else could she say?

'But I lasted longer.'

'To my pleasure, yes. And now I must give you up.

And do forget all this nonsense about having no name. Too middle class! My husband acknowledged you. You are Lady Dinah Freville, and the world accepts you as that. You aren't the only one, you know.'

'Yes, I do know that, Mama. And it doesn't comfort me. What would comfort me would be to go to Oxford, to live with Faa and be an undergraduate at Somerville College. But I can't have that, can I?'

'No, my darling, we've had this out again and again. It's imperative that you go to live with Violet, make a good match and be settled in the world. You haven't time to play at being a scholar.'

'Faa says that I could do more than play at it, Mama. He says that I have a good mind.'

'Don't think about that, my dear. You know very well how little money Rainsborough has left—my late husband spent it all on high living—and so your brother can't afford to let me have more than a pittance. You won't even have much of a dowry, and without a reasonable marriage you will be penniless. Just thank God that you're not like some—thrown out to starve—and me, too.'

Dinah began to prowl restlessly around the room, avoiding her own image in the mirror facing the windows. She was ready at last to say the unsayable, the stark truth which her mother always avoided, but which Violet was constantly throwing in her face.

'Who in the world is ever going to offer for me, Mama? I'm not like you or Violet. I have no looks and no light conversation.'

She was only too well aware of her own limitations. She was neither blonde, nor pretty. She was dark and slender, with no bust, she told herself despairingly, and precious little in the way of hips. Nothing about her was at all like the voluptuous women pictured in fashion plates and in the picture postcards of society beauties sold in every newsagent's shop.

'The fashionable clothes of the day aren't meant for me, either. They stifle me. They're meant for buxom, blue-eyed girls with ringlets, not a thin brown girl with raven hair and dark eyes.

'And since I shan't have a decent dowry, either,' she ended ruefully, 'there's no fear, at least, that anyone will want to marry me for my money!'

'Dear, dear,' yawned her mother. 'We have had this conversation so many times before. Sing another song, darling.'

'Oh, I know I never sing the right one—and certainly I shall never be able to sing one which will please Violet. Please God that now that she's taken up with the Prince of Wales she won't have any time for me.'

'Naughty thing,' said her mother, laughing.

She looked thoughtfully at her daughter. For a moment there when she had spoken of Violet and the Prince her face had become animated, had glowed, had suddenly revealed quite a different person, a person of character and passion. It was as though the Dinah of the future had been superimposed on the Dinah of the present before disappearing again.

If she could look like that more often, then perhaps the child might attract someone who could see beyond the obvious, beyond the fashion plates and the picture postcards of society beauties, might even recognise her bright spirit, free it, and allow it to soar into the heavens.

Charlotte Rainsborough shook herself. Goodness, what brought that on? She said prosaically to her daughter, 'One last thing, my dear, you will be careful when Violet takes you into society. There are those who prey on young things like yourself.'

'Oh, no need to worry about that,' replied Dinah, her

face alight with amusement. 'I'm sure that I'm most unlikely to attract either predators or pussy cats. As well imagine I could seduce the Prince himself—or any other of her lovers—away from Violet, or attract any of the men around them. Besides, you're always telling me that men don't like women who argue with them, so I shall know how to put off anyone whom I dislike.'

That last statement ended their discussion. Her mother shook her head at her, tea came in, and visitors, and for a time Dinah was able to forget her future. A future in which she would be sent off, like a parcel, to Violet's grand home, Moorings, to be groomed for the Season where she would be inspected, and almost certainly passed over, before she could retreat into private life again.

Chapter One

'No, really, Cobie, no one should look like you, it isn't decent,' exclaimed Susanna Winthrop, wife of the American Envoy in London, to her foster-brother Jacobus Grant, always called Cobie.

In reply he offered her his lazy smile over the breakfast table—which was sufficient to exasperate her all over again.

It wasn't just the classical perfection of his handsome face, nor his athletic body, nor even the way in which he wore his clothes, or his arrogant air of be damned to everybody which all combined not only to fascinate and to charm, but also to arouse a certain fear, even in those who met him briefly, which was enraging her. No, it was the whole *tout ensemble* which did the damage, so many remarkable things combined together in one human male.

She was so fierce that he could not resist teasing her. He said provokingly, 'Well, nor am I decent. So what of that?'

For a brief moment the sexual attraction between them, long dormant on Cobie's part, had been revived.

'That's what I mean,' she retorted, still fierce. 'To

answer me like you do! You've neither shame nor modesty—and you only believe in yourself.'

His brows lifted, and like Susanna he felt regret for the love which had once existed between them, but was now lost. Alas, that river had long flowed under the bridge, and would not return again.

'Who better to believe in?' he asked, and his grin was almost a child's, pure in its apparent innocence.

'Oh, you're impossible!'

'That, too,' he agreed.

Susanna began to laugh. She could never be angry with Cobie for long. She had loved him ever since she had first met him when he was a fat baby and she was nearly ten years old. He was the supposed adopted son of Jack and Marietta Dilhorne—in actuality their *own* son, made illegitimate by the machinations of Marietta's jealous cousin Sophie. Susanna was the daughter of Marietta's first husband and, as such, no blood relation of Cobie's.

Ten years ago their affection had blossomed into passionate love, but Susanna had refused to marry him, seeing the years between them as a fatal barrier. His calf-love for her had inevitably died, but she was still agonisingly aware that her passion for him was still burning strongly beneath her apparent serenity. Susanna had thought she knew him, but ever since he had arrived in London she had begun to realise exactly how much Cobie had changed—and how little she had.

Eight years ago he had returned from two years spent in the American Southwest and the man he had become was someone whom she hardly knew: a man quite unlike the innocent and carefree boy whom she had refused. She had married in his absence, and had spent her life alternately trying to forget him, or wishing that she had married him, and not her unexciting husband. Her annoyance with Cobie this time was the consequence of what had happened the night before at a reception which she and her husband had given and which the cream of London society had attended.

Inevitably—and unwillingly—Susanna had been compelled to introduce Cobie to that society's most notorious beauty, Violet, Lady Kenilworth, the Prince of Wales's current mistress. She had known only too desolately well what would follow when such a pair of sexual predators met for the first time.

Belle amie of the heir to the throne Violet might be, but she could not resist the challenge which Apollo—as she had instantly named Cobie—presented to her.

'Half-sister?' she queried after Susanna had left them.

'You might call her that,' Cobie replied in his society drawl, which was neither English nor American but something carefully pitched between the two.

'Might you?' Violet was all cool charm. 'You're not a bit like her, you know.'

'No, I'm not,' Cobie replied to this impertinent remark which broke all society's rules—but Violet, like Cobie, always made up her own. Then, with a touch of charming impudence, 'And are you like your sister, Lady Kenilworth?'

Violet threw her lovely head back to show the long line of her throat, her blue eyes alight beneath the gold crown of her hair. 'God forbid!' she exclaimed. 'We are quite unlike in every way—to my great relief, she's the world's greatest bore—and call me Violet, do.'

Despite himself Cobie was intrigued. What in the world could the sister be like who inspired Violet to be so cuttingly cruel? Nevertheless he merely bowed and said, 'Violet, since you wish it. For my part I wish that I were more like Susanna.'

'I don't,' said Violet, full of provocation. 'Not if it involved you turning into a dark young woman. I much prefer tall, handsome, blond men.'

Seeing that the Prince of Wales was neither tall nor blond and was certainly not handsome, this riposte amused Cobie—as it was intended to. Before he could reply, Violet was busy verbally seducing him again.

'You are over from the States, I gather. Is it your first visit? I do hope that you will make it a long one.'

'It will be my first *long* visit,' he replied, his mouth curling a little in amusement at her naked sexual aggression barely hidden beneath the nothings of polite conversation. 'I have made several short ones before—on business.'

'Business!' It was the turn of Violet's mouth to curl. 'Forgive me, but you seem made for pleasure.'

The buttons were off the foils with a vengeance, were they not!

'A useful impression to give if one wishes to succeed in business—' he began.

'But not this visit—' she said sweetly, interrupting him—so for *quid pro quo* he decided to interrupt her with,

'No, not this visit. I have been overworking and I need a holiday.'

'The overwork is truly American,' pronounced Violet. 'The holiday part is not. I thought that Americans never rested, were always full of—what is it?—get up and go!'

'Ah, another illusion shattered.' Cobie was beginning to enjoy himself. 'The first of many, I hope. It all depends on what kind of get up and go we are speaking of.'

'All kinds, I hope,' murmured Violet, lowering her eyes, only to raise them again, saying, 'Now we must part—to entertain others. Before we do so, may I invite you to visit us at Moorings, our place in the country. We go there in ten days' time to spend a few weeks before the Season proper starts.

'In the meantime, allow me to inform you that I am always at home to my true friends from two o'clock. Pray don't wait until four-fifteen—only the bores visit then.'

Cobie bowed, and she moved away. He was aware that he had become the centre of interest. He was, Susanna told him later, socially made now that Violet Kenilworth had taken him up. Not all the eyes on him were kind, among them those of Sir Ratcliffe Heneage to whom Arthur Winthrop introduced him later.

Sir Ratcliffe's eyes raked him dismissively. He was everything which an American thought of as a typical English aristocrat. He was tall, dark, impeccably dressed, authoritative, well built with a hawk-like face. He was a junior Cabinet Minister, a noted *bon viveur*, was part of the Prince of Wales's circle, and had once been an officer in the Guards.

The assessing part of Cobie, however, which never left him, even when he was amusing himself, told him that, disguise it as he might, Sir Ratcliffe was on the verge of running to seed. His face was already showing the early signs of over-indulgence.

'Related to Sir Alan Dilhorne, I hear,' Sir Ratcliffe drawled condescendingly to this damned American upstart, only able to enter good society because of his immense wealth—made by dubious means, no doubt.

'Distantly.' Cobie's drawl matched Sir Ratcliffe's— he made it more English than usual. 'Only distantly.'

'Getting old, Sir Alan—giving up politics, I hear. That's a dog's life, you know. Can't think why I went in for it. Who wants to sit around listening for division bells and all that? Gives one a certain cachet, though. You in politics back home?'

'Not my line,' said Cobie cheerfully. 'Too busy earning a living.' He wondered what had caused the waves of dislike emanating from the man opposite. 'Takes me all my time to survive on Wall Street.'

And, oh, what a lie that was!

Sir Ratcliffe's lip curled a little. 'In business, are you?' he asked, his tone showing what he thought of those who worked for a living rather than played for it. 'Sooner you than me, old fellow. Miss it while you're over here, will you?'

'I've come to enjoy myself,' was Cobie's reply to that. The man's patronising air was enough to set your teeth on edge, he thought.

'Plenty of that on offer—if you know where to look for it. Shoot, do you?'

'A little,' lied Cobie, who was a crack shot with every kind of weapon, but for some reason decided not to confess to that. There were times when he wondered whether he would ever be permitted the luxury of telling the truth, the whole truth, and nothing but the truth!

'A little, eh? Don't suppose you get much chance to shoot anything in Wall Street, hey! hey! Or anywhere else for that matter.'

'Exactly,' drawled Cobie, suppressing a dreadful urge to tell the languid fool opposite to him that there had been a time when Cobie Grant, then known as Jake Coburn, a six-shooter in his hand, had been a man to fear and to avoid.

On the other hand, if Sir Ratcliffe chose to think him a soft townie, then it was all to the good. It usually paid to be underestimated.

At breakfast that morning, Susanna explained why Sir Ratcliffe disliked him so much.

'He saw Violet was taken with you, didn't he? She was looking at you as though you were a rather delicious meal laid out for her to enjoy. He's been after her for months—with no luck. He's made an ass of himself over the Prince's favouring her. On top of that, the rumour is that he's in Queer Street financially, and there's you, an enormously rich Yankee, fascinating Violet without even trying.'

Of course, Sir Ratcliffe had been right to be jealous—and so had Susanna, which was why she was reproaching Cobie for being the man he was and not the man he had been.

Susanna had been only too well aware that Cobie would take up Violet's two o'clock invitation at the earliest opportunity—which he promptly did, that very afternoon. At the Kenilworths' town house in Piccadilly he enjoyed, for what it was worth, what a famous actress and beauty had once called the hurly burly of the *chaise-longue* rather than the deep peace of the marriage bed. One disadvantage being that one remained virtually fully clothed.

He also, a little reluctantly, agreed to visit Moorings several days before the rest of the guests arrived. Violet had smiled at him confidentially, and drawled, 'As early as you like so that we can enjoy ourselves in comfort.'

Cobie was not sure that he wished his affair with her to be more than a passing thing. Violet had not improved on further acquaintance, and to some extent he was regretting having pursued her at all—but he could not refuse to visit Moorings without offending her—and he had no wish to do that. It was plain that she saw him as a trophy, and was determined to flaunt him before the rest of society. He wondered a little what the Prince of Wales would think of Violet taking a second lover, but she made nothing of that.

'I understand that your nickname in the States is The Dollar Prince,' were her final words to him, 'which means that I now have two of such name.'

He was tempted to say, 'No, Violet, you certainly don't have me,' but he was well aware that it would be unwise to make an enemy of her, so he merely bowed in acknowledgement of her mild witticism when taking his leave before the bores arrived at four o'clock.

Well, at least he would be able to enjoy living for a few weeks in one of the most spectacularly beautiful country houses in England, even if he did have to pay for it by pleasuring Violet!

It was for that reason, but not for that reason alone, that two evenings later he left the ball which she and her husband were giving at Kenilworth House long before Violet wished him to. He had bidden her 'goodnight' with all the charm which he could muster, but it was not enough to mollify her.

'Leaving already!' she had exclaimed, her beautiful brows arching high. 'The night is yet young, and many who are years older than you are will not be giving up until dawn.'

'Alas,' he told her untruthfully, 'I have been busy in the City all day, and such a concentration of effort carries its own penalties—I am sure that Kenilworth will have told you that.'

Cobie had always wondered at the workings of chance, and that it might be unwise to ignore them. Chance had led him to overhear something odd that night, something which had stayed in his memory. It was for that reason only that after leaving Kenilworth House, he did not go straight home to the Winthrops'. Instead he dismissed his carriage and walked down the Haymarket, which was so brilliantly lit that it might as well have been day.

The usual stares at his splendid self from both men and women followed him: he ignored them all and carried on his solitary way until he came to an alley about a hundred yards beyond the Haymarket Theatre. Looking down it, he could see a group of top-hatted men of fashion standing and smoking under a swinging lantern over an eighteenth-century doorway.

It must be Madame Louise's: the brothel where the quality went, where discretion and high prices reigned. The conversation which he had overheard at the Kenilworths' ball had him intrigued enough to consider going in. He had been leaning against a pillar, half-hidden, tired of the nothingness of the whole business, when he had heard two men approach and, quite unaware of his presence nearby, begin a muffled conversation.

'Deadly boring tonight, eh, Heneage? Not that these pre-Season dos are ever anything else.'

Heneage—it must be the pompous dandy whom Cobie had met at Susanna's equally boring thrash.

He was answering his companion in an amused knowing voice. 'I know a better way of entertaining one's self, Darrell, and it's not far from here. Madame Louise's place, in short. You can only visit there if you have the *entrée*—and I have. We could move on when I've done the pretty with dear Violet.'

Darrell—that would be Hubert Darrell, one of the hangers-on to the coat-tails of the great. They were rather like those extras in a play who are always shouting 'Rhubarb, rhubarb' at the appropriate moment. From the turn the conversation had taken Darrell was about to be introduced to some vicious inner circle.

'Bit dull, though, isn't it, Heneage? Just the usual, I take it.'

Heneage laughed patronisingly. 'Oh, you can always find variety at Madame's if you're in the know, are discreet and have plenty of tin. You can have anything you fancy—anything—no holds barred. But mum's the world, old fellow. Are you game?'

'Game for anything—you know me.'

'Then we'll do the rounds here first, and sample the goods afterwards. I heard, don't ask me how, that Ma-

dame has some new stuff on show tonight, very prime.'
Sir Ratcliffe's voice was full of hateful promise.

They moved out of Cobie's hearing, leaving him to
wonder what exactly was meant by 'no holds barred'
and 'good new stuff'—and not liking the answer he
came up with.

Curiosity now led him to enter Madame's gilded entrance hall and to bribe his way past the giants on guard
there since he came alone and unrecommended. This
took him some little time. He thought, amusedly, that
he might have been trying to enter a palace, not a
brothel, so complicated was the ritual.

He agreed to hand over his top hat and scarf to a
female dragon at the cloakroom, but insisted on carrying
in his all-enveloping cape—which cost him another tip
for a sweetener. There were reasons why he wanted to
retain it. He then made his way into an exquisitely appointed drawing room.

Everything in it was in the best of taste. There was
even a minor Gainsborough hanging over the hearth.
Men and women sat about chatting discreetly. Among
them he saw Sir Ratcliffe Heneage. He had a brief
glimpse of a man being led through some swathed curtains at the far end of the room and could have sworn
it was his brother-in-law, Arthur Winthrop, who had
also left the Kenilworths' ball early, pleading a migraine.

Madame Louise was tall, had been a beauty in her
youth and, like her room, was elegantly turned out. Her
eyes on him were cold.

'I do not know you, sir. Since you have arrived without a sponsor or a friend, who allowed you, an unknown, to enter?'

'Oh, money oils all locks and bars,' he told her with
his most winning smile, 'but should I require a friend I
have one here—Sir Ratcliffe Heneage. I am sure that

he will confirm that I am Jacobus Grant, the brother-in-law of the American Envoy, and a distant relative of Sir Alan Dilhorne, late of the British Cabinet. Does that make me…respectable?'

Sir Ratcliffe, who had been watching them, was smiling with pleasure at the sight of the Madame of a nighthouse putting down the Yankee barbarian who had succeeded with Violet Kenilworth.

'Yes, Mr Grant is who he says he is. We have been introduced.'

'There!' said Cobie sweetly. 'What better recommendation could I have than one given me by Sir Ratcliffe? I may stay?'

'Indeed. It is my custom to give a new guest a glass of champagne and ask him, discreetly, of course, what his preferences are. You will join me?'

Cobie bowed his agreement, secretly amused at her using the word guest instead of customer. A footman handed him his champagne and Madame asked him, discreetly again, 'Are your tastes as unorthodox as your mode of entry, Mr Grant?'

'Alas, no. I am distressingly orthodox in all I do, if not to say uninventive.'

He looked as pious as a male angel in a Renaissance painting when he came out with this lie, invention being the name of every game he played. He was not yet sure what game he was playing at Madame Louise's, but he hoped to find out soon.

'A beauty, then, and young.'

Cobie bowed again, 'Quite so—and with the appearance of innocence. I am tired and do not wish to exert myself overmuch.'

He was taken at his word, and after he had handed over to Madame a fistful of sovereigns he was allowed to go upstairs—through the swathed curtains—with a young girl dressed in the latest fashion. She was lovely enough to have graced a Mayfair drawing room.

'Her name is Marie,' Madame had told him carelessly.

The bedroom she led him to was as exquisite as the room downstairs. She hesitated a moment before she stripped herself after he had sat on the big bed and thrown down the cape he had been carrying. Even then he made no attempt to touch her.

When she was finally naked, and Cobie had still said and done nothing, but continued to sit there, fully dressed, she walked towards him, her pretty face puzzled. She had not quite reached him when he lifted his hand.

'Stay where you are, Miss Marie, just like that. On second thoughts, unpin your hair, and then begin to restore it to what it was.'

Her look of puzzlement grew, but she did his bidding—as she had been taught. When she finally stood before him, quite still, her shapely arms above her head, he murmured, 'Now, don't move, remain exactly as you are.'

'You're sure?' she blurted at him. 'Is this really what you want me to do?'

He nodded agreement while fetching from an inner pocket of his cape a sketchbook and pencil. He began, rapidly, to draw her, his full attention on every line of her beautiful body. For all the emotion he showed he might have been drawing a still life, not a glowing and vibrant human being.

A moment later, the sketch finished, Cobie showed it to her—to hear her say in her true voice, the cockney in it plain, 'Garn, you're a painter, then. That's me all right!'

He shook his head, 'An amateur, merely. Now, sit down and let me draw you again in a different position.'

'You've only an hour,' she told him, as sharp as he had been.

'I know.' He nodded back at her, his hand moving rapidly over the paper.

'And is this all you want me to do—or do with me? A fine upstanding feller like you. One of *them*, are you? Don't want no one to know, is that it?'

Cobie, unoffended, laughed. 'No, not at all. Idle curiosity brought me to Madame Louise's but I could hardly visit her, and not appear to sample the girls. Keep quiet about your modelling session—no need for Madame to know of it—and I'll see you well rewarded. Let her think that we pushed the boat out together, eh?'

Mischief shone on her pretty face. The mere idea of tricking Madame pleased her, even if it were a shame not to have a tumble with such a handsome fellow.

'If you say so,' and then, anxiously, 'It's not that I don't please you?'

'No, I find you very pretty, Miss Marie. Look over your left shoulder at me, now.'

She obeyed him, only to look over *his* left shoulder after he had finished drawing her, and exclaim, 'That's good, but you're an odd one, and no mistake.'

'Yes, that's what most people who really know me think,' he replied gravely, handing her the sketches he had made. 'There, you may have them. Best not show them to Madame, eh?'

'What the eye don't see, the heart can't grieve,' she told him impudently, rolling the papers into a cylinder and thrusting it into a drawer in a Louis Quinze dressing table.

'This is your room, then, Miss Marie?' he asked, apparently idly, to have her reply,

'Yes, but only when I entertain customers. I live, like the other girls, in one of the attics.'

The anger and the pity which Cobie felt for all exploited men and women was strong in him when he contemplated the minimal state of the world in which Marie lived.

Hypocrite! he told himself fiercely, since you exploit the corrupt world in which you live and do nothing for such poor lost souls as these. He wondered how long she had been on the game, and how long it would be before she lost her apparently virginal freshness and Madame turned her out onto the streets to replace her with someone younger.

'And the other entertainments,' he asked, still idly, 'Where are they, Miss Marie?'

Her face became shuttered. She stared at him and said, 'You told me you weren't like that. Were you lying?'

'No,' he said.

'Then you don't want to know where they are, do you? But if you *are* lying, then ask Madame.'

She was done with him: the brief and strange moment of rapport which they had shared was over. Cobie sighed—he might have known that he would learn nothing from her.

Suddenly and strangely, she leaned forward and said, in a fierce whisper, a whisper which was almost wrenched from her, 'You called me Miss Marie several times—to most men I'm a body, not a name. If you don't want to go out through the salon, you can leave by going down the backstairs—through the far door on the landing outside.

'At the bottom of them there's a hall which opens on to a courtyard and an alley which leads to the Haymarket. At the other end of the hall there's another flight of stairs which leads to the attics—and nowhere else. That's all.'

Cobie rose and said, 'I'm for the backstairs, then. Goodnight, Miss Marie. You made a good artist's model. Here's your reward for that—for keeping quiet—and for helping me.'

She took the money he offered her, her face lighting up for a moment—and then she shrugged her shoulders at him and turned away, before making herself ready to go downstairs again. The odd little interlude was over.

Cobie found the backstairs at the end of a corridor. He had replaced his cloak—then remembered that he had left his hat and scarf with the dragon in the entrance hall. No matter, he had others, and he did not particularly wish to return to claim them.

Running lightly down the uncarpeted stairs, he found himself in another world, where soft luxury did not exist, where the light flared from unshielded gas jets, and where the floor of the corridor which led to the back door and to the Haymarket was bare boards, no rugs or mats to soften it.

At the bottom of the staircase was the small hall, from which another set of stairs rose—Marie had directed him correctly. A large free-standing mahogany wardrobe stood beside the back door, which was tightly shut. Cobie had just wrestled it open when he heard rapid footsteps running down the stairs.

He turned at the sound, to be struck amidships by a small body. High above them he could hear male voices, shouting in anger, and then footsteps thundering down.

The owner of the body was a little girl, no older than ten by the look of her. Scarlet in the face, she was panting hard. When she saw Cobie, looking like a golden angel sent to rescue her, she fell on her knees before him, to clasp his, wailing, 'Oh, Gawd, mister. Save me. I don't want to be hurt like poor Clara was. Don't let him have me.'

Her face was filthy, and streaked with tears. Her dress, a garish pink thing, trimmed with silver tinsel, like a circus performer's tutu, had been ripped from the neck to the waist. The marks of a man's fingers were plain upon her throat and thin shoulders.

Inside Cobie something shrieked incontinent. The red rage with which he had lived since childhood was on him. It came unbidden when he was faced with cruelty or injustice, particularly to the helpless. In it he could kill; to control it took all the strength of his iron will. Its passing left him feeling empty and ill.

He controlled it now with difficulty even though his face remained impassive. The child heard the footsteps, shrieked, 'Oh, Gawd, he'll catch me for sure. Oh, mister, don't let him hurt me. Please, don't let him.'

As was usual when he was in a tight corner Cobie acted with lightning speed. He picked up the child, hissed at her, 'Not a sound, mind,' and, whirling around, he half-threw her onto the flat top of the wardrobe, where she lay concealed by its elaborate wooden and gilt rail. That done, he leaned against the wall, blinking owlishly at the world as though he had drunk too much of Madame's indifferent champagne, and spent himself too much with Marie.

By now the owner of the footsteps, a hard-faced man in workman's clothing—one of Madame's bouncers, no doubt—had arrived in the small hall, to stare at all that was to be seen. A half-cut toff and no girl-child in sight.

'Have you seen a little girl running away from here? Which way did she go…sir?'

This last came out in belated recognition of Cobie's undoubted wealth and superior station.

Cobie decided to be more owlish than ever. 'A small…girl,' he enunciated with great difficulty. 'What…? What…?' He had no time to finish the sentence before another actor arrived on the scene.

'You're taking a devilish long time to catch the little bitch up, Hoskyns,' exclaimed a voice which Cobie immediately recognised. 'Damme, she nearly bit my finger off.'

It was Sir Ratcliffe Heneage, in a state which might have surprised those who only knew him in the salons of Mayfair. He was barefooted and wearing trousers and a shirt open to the waist. Unbuttoned, was perhaps the best description of him, Cobie thought. He decided to run a little interference.

'Oh, Sir Ratcliffe, there y'are. Wondered where you'd got to.' His hiccup at the end of this was particularly artistic.

'Damn that, man,' exclaimed Sir Ratcliffe, 'Did anyone leave while you were here?'

Cobie swayed, thought for a moment, leaned forward and grabbed Sir Ratcliffe by the collar of his shirt, stifling the desire to strangle the beast before him. He had no doubts at all about what had been going on in one of Madame's discreet attic rooms, and wondered how much the bankrupt swine before him had paid for the use of the girl-child cowering on top of the wardrobe above the three of them.

'Just saw a girl go by, old fellow, through the door there, running like a hare. I got lost in the backstairs, don't you know.'

He finished with Sir Ratcliffe, and turned his drunken gaze on Hoskyns. 'Help me to find my way out. Left m'hat with the doorkeeper. Don' want to catch cold.'

He knew that he was risking having Hoskyns take him at his word, and that he might show him out through the main entrance—which would mean leaving the abused child behind on top of the wardrobe.

The risk had been worth taking, however, for Sir Ratcliffe roared, 'Find your own way out, Grant. Hoskyns, go after the little bitch. She can't have got very far. And you, Grant, get Madame to call you a cab.'

He turned on his heel to make his way back up the

stairs to whatever hell-hole he had come from, where
the special and curious tastes of depraved gentlemen
were catered for. Hoskyns, shrugging his shoulders and
mentally damning the demanding nature of the powerful
in his world, did what Sir Ratcliffe bid him.

Cobie heaved a great sigh and straightened up when
he found himself alone again. He turned towards the
wardrobe, called up softly to the waiting child, 'Little
'un, put out a hand, and I'll try to get you down and
away from here.'

It took some manoeuvring before she was beside him
in the hall again; it was much harder to get her safely
to the ground than it had been to throw her up.

Once down, the child seized his hand and covered it
with kisses. 'Oh, thankee, mister, thankee, for saving
me.'

'Not saved yet,' said Cobie shortly. 'Thank me when
you are. We can't leave by the easiest way, we might
meet Hoskyns coming back. Now, how strong are you?'

'As strong as you want me to be, mister,' she said
fervently. 'Only, I ain't got nowhere to go, that's all. It
were me stepdad what sold me to this place.'

Cobie, wondering what further disgraceful revelations the night held for him, threw back his cape, and
asked, 'If I lifted you up, and sat you with your legs
around my waist and your arms around my chest and
your head on it, and I arranged my cape around us like
so, could you stay there, quiet like a mouse, while I
walk us both out of this miserable pigsty?'

She nodded vigorously, and as speedily as he could,
he hid her beneath the voluminous folds of his cape.
She clutched him in a grip as strong as death. He was
grateful that he wasn't wearing his usual overcoat, but
had decided to play the dandy on his first night alone,
out on the town.

Finding the way back to the entrance wasn't difficult.

He made idle chat with the gorgon, and left her a large tip so that she might contemptuously think him yet one more American visitor with more money than sense.

He used his good left hand to take his top hat and scarf, keeping his right hand and arm inside the cloak to steady the girl, once again grateful to the fate which had made him ambidextrous. This time his unusual skill was not going to save his own life, but might save that of the child he was carrying.

Cobie could feel her breathing, and she had been right when she had told him that she would be as strong as he wanted. Her grip continued vice-like, and he walked indolently along, apparently unencumbered. He was grateful that Madame's doorkeepers were tired and incurious, only too glad to get rid of him now that he had finished spending his money with them.

Once outside and walking along the Haymarket, still a sea of light although it was now well past midnight, he continued to carry the girl beneath his cloak. He dare not let her down, for a man of fashion walking along with an oddly-dressed girl-child at one in the morning would be sure to attract unwanted attention, even in the Haymarket.

Particularly in the Haymarket, where he knew that all the vices in a vicious city were available for those who had the money to pay for them.

He paused and thought for a moment. The Salvation Army, of course. Susanna was one of a group of society women who were involved in helping the poor and unfortunate. She had once told him that the Salvation Army had shelters where the wretched might find succour, even in central London.

He had been mildly interested, he remembered. Susanna had mentioned that there was one not far from Piccadilly. He made sure that the child was still firmly gripping him and set off to find it.

Chapter Two

At the shelter, which had originally been a small church hall, the Salvation Army was giving tea and comfort to a group of derelicts. They included a battered tramp, and a prostitute who had been brutally beaten by one of her clients and had staggered in to the Sally Ann's Haymarket refuge for help just before Cobie walked in.

He was so unlike their usual customer that everyone stared at him and his physical and sartorial splendours. The man who was busy bandaging the tart's wounds, and the two young women who were looking after the tea were as bemused by him as the down and outs whom they were tending.

For the moment he kept the child hidden beneath his cloak.

'I am told that you save souls—and bodies—here,' he drawled, looking around him. 'I need your help and I see that I was told aright.'

'That is true,' said the Captain, walking forward. A middle-aged man of undistinguished face and figure, he had been seated at a desk at the back of the hall, writing in a ledger. 'What may we do for you? We are always ready to help a soul in need.'

'Oh, your help is not required for me, sir. At least, not this time. In fact I fear that I may be unsaveable at any time. But I do need advice of the most delicate nature, and if there is a room where we may speak privately, I should be grateful if we might retire there.'

The Captain looked at Cobie, at his easy air of authority, his aura of wealth and power. What advice could he possibly be in need of?

'Very well. Come this way, please.' So saying, he led the way into a small room off the main hall.

'Now, what may I do for you?'

Cobie smiled—and unfurled his cloak.

'I repeat, not for me, sir. It is this poor child for whom I need your assistance. You understand that there are few places where I may take her without suspicion falling on me.'

By now the little girl in her tawdry and unsuitable finery was fully revealed. She slid gratefully down Cobie's long length to sit on the floor.

'Coo-er, mister, that were hard work, that were.'

'You see now why I asked for somewhere a little more private, Captain,' Cobie said. 'This is not a pretty story, and neither of us would welcome publicity—even though it is a mission of mercy on which we are engaged.'

The Captain nodded. He offered the little girl a chair, but he and Cobie remained standing.

'Now,' he said, 'Tell me your story—although I think that I can imagine the gist of it.'

'The trade in children being neither new nor rare, I am sure that you can. I believe that some years ago the Salvation Army found itself in trouble when it tried to reveal the facts to a disbelieving world.'

'That is so,' agreed the Captain, surprised a little by the knowledge of the arrogant and handsome young man before him—even more surprised to find that he had seen fit to rescue a child from the slums. 'You are referring to the Stead case, I take it, sir, when those who were trying to save exploited children were sent to prison and those who exploited them escaped punishment. You are saying that you have knowledge of something similar?'

'Oh, come.' Cobie's voice was as satiric as he could make it. 'You are not about to pretend that, living and working where you do, near to the Haymarket, you are unaware of what goes on—'

He was rudely interrupted by the little girl standing up and tugging at his hand, 'I'm hungry, mister.'

To the Captain's further surprise the young dandy before him went down on one knee, took a large handkerchief from an inner pocket of his immaculately cut jacket, and carefully began to clean the child's face.

'So you must be,' he told her gently. 'Do you think we could ask this gentleman to find you something to eat while he and I talk about what to do with you?'

She nodded, and then suddenly grasped his hand again. She kissed it, gasping, 'Oh, Gawd, mister, you won't send me back, will you? Let me eat in here. I feel safe wiv you.'

'No, I won't send you back, I promise. I'll find somewhere safe for you to go.'

He stood up again, and thought, My God, and now the rage is making me rescue slum children, when all I want is a night's sleep!

He said brusquely to the Captain, 'You can feed her?'

The Captain went to the door, and called to one of the women, who presently came in with a bowl of soup and a buttered bread roll.

'What's your name, little girl?' she asked the child, who took the bowl from her and began drinking greedily from it without using the spoon.

'Lizzie,' she said, 'Lizzie Steele,' and then, to Cobie, 'What's yours, mister?'

Cobie began to laugh, stopped, and asked her gravely, bending his bright head a little, 'What would you like it to be?'

He felt, rather than saw, the Captain look sharply at him. Lizzie, slurping the last drops of the soup, said through them, 'Ain't yer got a name, then?'

'Not really,' Cobie told her, which was, in a way, the truth. He had no intention of letting anyone at the shelter know who he really was. Caution was his middle name, although many who knew him would have been surprised to learn that.

Now that the child was safe the rage had begun to ebb. It was leaving him empty—except for his head, which was beginning to hurt. Soon, he knew, his sight would be affected. But he could not leave until Lizzie's immediate future was assured.

She was still watching him, a little puzzled.

'Everyone has a name, mister,' she finally offered him.

'Of sorts,' Cobie agreed gravely.

The Captain took a hand. Lizzie, starting on her roll and butter, continued to watch them, or rather to watch Cobie, who seemed to be the magnet which controlled her small universe.

'I think,' the Captain said, 'that we ought to ask my aide, Miss Merrick, to find Lizzie something more suitable for her to wear. You and I must talk while she does so.'

To Cobie's amusement Lizzie, pointing at Cobie, chirped, 'I ain't goin' nowhere wivout 'im, and that's flat.'

Again the Captain was surprised by his manner towards Lizzie. Cobie spoke to her pleasantly and politely after the fashion in which he would address Violet Kenilworth, Susanna, or the Queen.

'You're quite safe here, Miss Steele. You will be well looked after, I'm sure. Nothing bad will happen to you whether I am present or not. You have my word.' He took her grubby hand and bowed over it.

Her eyes were still watchful. She had been betrayed too often to believe that he would necessarily keep his word.

'You promise?' was all she said.

'I promise.' He was still as grave as a hanging judge.

He was aware that the Captain's shrewd eyes were on him, trying to fathom him. His whole interest centred on Cobie, not on the child. He had doubtless seen many like her—but few like him, someone apparently unharmed by the world's wickedness.

The rage revived for a moment, to die back again. God knew, if no one else did, how near Cobie Grant had once been to dereliction, violation, and death!

The woman who had brought Lizzie the soup was called in once more, to take away both the empty bowl and the child, with orders to find something respectable for her to wear—after she had been washed.

Lizzie demurred a little at the notion of being washed, until Cobie said, his voice confidential, 'Oh, do let them wash you, Miss Steele. I like washing, I assure you, and do it a lot.'

She stared at his golden splendour for a moment, before saying, 'Yus, I can see yer do.' To the woman leading her from the room she said, ungraciously, 'I'll let yer wash me so long as yer don't get soap in me eyes!'

'To be brief,' Cobie said to the Captain, 'I stole her from Madame Louise's and then brought her here because I had heard that you were in the business of saving such lost souls. By good chance she had succeeded in escaping from the man who would have violated her. She owes her safety, if not her life, to her own wits.'

'And to you.' The Captain's face was as impassive as he said this as that of the strange young man to whom he was talking. He was taking nothing on trust, not even the child's rescuer. He was also showing little of the humble subservience usually offered in England by those of the lower classes to their superiors.

'I was an instrument, merely,' drawled Cobie, 'there to see that she was not caught again.'

'You were one of Madame's clients?'

'After a fashion, yes.'

Cobie was languid, unapologetic. 'Now let us speak of her disposition. She told me that her stepfather had sold her to the house.'

Since he was a good Salvation Army man, the Captain could neither curse nor blaspheme, but the sound which escaped from him could have been construed as either.

'Exactly,' agreed Cobie. 'The vile business is run from the top floors of Madame Louise's sumptuous house—I'm sure you know that without me telling you.'

'Yes—and I can do nothing. Evidence which would stand up in court is impossible to find. I cannot even do as much as you did tonight.'

'Which is little enough. So many sparrows fall. I was privileged to save one—not more. Now, what shall we do with this one poor sparrow?' Cobie was pleased to see by his expression that the Captain took the Biblical allusion.

'Whom God has permitted you to rescue.'

The Captain was rebuking him, no doubt of that.

'God.' Cobie raised his beautiful eyebrows. 'Ah, yes, the All Powerful. Who allows so many to fall into the pit...so many sparrows to fall...and who put Lizzie in the way of her captors. No matter, I will not refine on theological points with you—only ask what may be done for her.'

Cobie's smile was cold, not really a smile at all. 'Money is not a problem, sir.'

He put his hand into his jacket pocket, pulled out his purse, and opened it. A cascade of golden sovereigns fell onto the dirty deal table which stood between him and the Captain.

'This is merely the beginning, a token of good intent.'

The Captain said, 'Who, and what, are you buying? God, salvation, me or the child?'

Cobie answered him in his most sardonic mode. 'All of them, sir, all of them. Everything is for sale, including salvation, and may be bought either by money—or by love. If your conscience will not allow you to help such a sinner as I am, then I shall take the child elsewhere to find those who are not so particular, but who will offer us assistance.'

The money was back in his purse and he was striding to the door. Oh, the damnable, monstrous arrogance of him, thought the Captain—but Lizzie's rescuer had said 'us', associating himself with the child, and he would be failing in his Christian duty to refuse her succour because of the nature of the man who was asking for it on her behalf.

He thought that the stranger had a contempt for the whole world—himself included. He must not allow that to sway him. There were two souls to save here—not one. In some fashion it was not the child who had the greater need.

He said to Cobie's back, 'Wait one moment. There is a home where I may place her temporarily, where she will be safe. We have a shortage of permanent accommodation.'

'More fallen sparrows than you can deal with?'

'If you like.'

'Then I will make you a proposition. Take Lizzie Steele into your permanent care, and I will give you enough money to buy, equip and maintain a house large enough to give shelter for up to twenty such, where they may be schooled and cared for until they are old enough to make their own way in the world.'

'Dare I believe that you mean what you say, sir?'

'No one,' Cobie told him, and his voice was deadly, 'has ever had reason to doubt my word, whether what I promise be good or ill.'

'I must know your name, sir.'

Cobie considered. He had no wish to tell the Captain the one by which high society knew him, but he had never hesitated to use another when it seemed more profitable, or safer, to do so. He did so now.

'I told Lizzie that I have no name. I was born without one. You and she may call me Mr...'

He hesitated; some freakish whim was urging him to give his true father's name, Dilhorne. He compromised, finished with a grin, '...Mr Dilley. John Dilley.'

The Captain thought that he knew that he was being lied to. He watched Cobie fling the purse back on the table and pull his sketchbook from the poacher's pocket in his cape.

Cobie began to write in it. He looked up and said, 'Your name is...?'

The Captain said stiffly, 'Bristow, Ebenezer Bristow.'

'Well, Captain Ebenezer Bristow, my man of business will call on you tomorrow. At what time?'

'I am here from four in the afternoon.'

'At four-thirty, then. Have some of your financial advisers present. My man will arrange with you whatever needs to be done. The money will come through him. Should you wish to contact me, you will do so through him. You will not attempt to trace me—if you do, you will forfeit what I am offering you. You understand me? I have a mind to be an unknown benefactor.'

He laughed the most mirthless laugh the Captain had ever heard. 'That is what you will tell your superiors— the money comes from an unknown benefactor.'

He tore out another sheet, wrote on that and thrust it at the Captain.

'That is for you to keep. You will give it to my man when he calls tomorrow. Now you may tell me where you propose to place Lizzie for the time being—so that I may call on her, and satisfy myself that she is being well treated.'

Stunned by this unexpected bounty, the Captain picked up the paper.

'Why are you doing this, Mr Dilley?'

'A whim. Nothing more.' Cobie was short.

'And the others? What of them?'

'What others?'

'The others mistreated at Madame Louise's house. Those not so fortunate as Lizzie.'

Cobie's smile was wolfish. 'Oh, you must see that I cannot rescue all of them. But those who run the trade there, and those for whom they run it, will I assure you, pay, in one way or another.'

The Captain could not quite believe him. In his world golden young men did not arrive from nowhere, playing at being Nemesis on behalf of stricken children.

'You must be rich,' he said at last.

'Oh, I am,' Cobie was affable. 'Most enormously so. Far more than you, or most people, can conceive. Neither Midas nor Croesus could compete with me. And all my own work, too!'

'Does it not frighten you? Make you unable to fear God, since you can dispose so easily of his creatures?'

'Oh, no one does that, Captain. No one is disposed of easily. No, I never dispose…I simply give events a push, or a shove. Avalanches start that way. As for fearing God, I gave that up eight years ago when I began to prefer people to fear me... Now I will say goodnight to Lizzie, after you inform me of her destination.'

'She will be going to a man and wife I know in Bermondsey who care for homeless children. At 21 Sea Coal Street.'

He hesitated. 'You will be careful with her, I trust. It would be unkind of you to give her expectations beyond the station in life to which it has pleased God to call her.'

'Believe me, I wouldn't do that, Captain Bristow, sir,' Cobie told him, 'even if God was pleased to place her in a pervert's power, you may trust me not to do so!'

'But He sent you to save her.'

The Captain was determined to have the last word, but Mr Dilley was of a different mind.

'Oh, but think of all those whom He does not save!'

Ebenezer Bristow gave up. Whatever his private thoughts about the man before him, he must not forget that he was offering the Salvation Army a splendid prize.

Cobie saw that Bristow was struggling with his principles. Self-disgust overwhelmed him. It was brutally unfair to taunt a man who had dedicated his life to serving others, particularly when he, Cobie, was dedicated to serving no one but himself.

For the life of him he could not explain the impulse which had led him to snatch from the feral clutches of Sir Ratcliffe Heneage the child who was now being cared for in the other room. Once he had done so, could he live with the knowledge of what was happening in the upper rooms of Madame Louise's splendid house?

For no reason at all he shivered, shook himself, pulled out his magnificent gold watch, and snapped it open.

'The hour grows late, I must leave you. Remember, my man will be here tomorrow, so be ready for him. Goodnight to you, sir.'

He turned on his heel and prepared to take his arrogant splendours away with him.

Captain Bristow, possessed by he knew not what, said to Cobie's retreating back. 'I bid you have a care, Mr Dilley. Those who fly too near the sun may have their wings burned away. God is not mocked.'

Cobie swung his head round, showed the Captain his splendid teeth, and said softly, 'Oh, no, Captain, I never thought he was.'

Moorings Halt was exactly as Dinah remembered it: warm in the early afternoon sun, its flower-beds flaming below the enamel notices advertising Mazawattee tea and Swan Ink. The station cat was curled up on one of the green-painted benches. Sanders, the porter, sat in his little sentry-box.

He rose and helped Dinah and her maid, Pearson, to lift her luggage on to the station platform.

'I'm sorry, Lady Dinah, but we didn't know that you were coming and the Big House hasn't sent the dog-cart for you.'

'Oh, I'll wait here, Sanders. It's a splendid afternoon for sitting in the sun, isn't it. I'm sure that it will be along soon.'

She wasn't sure at all, but some twenty minutes later, thank goodness, the dog-cart arrived with one of the grooms driving it.

'So sorry, Lady Dinah, but m'lady forgot to tell the stables that you were arriving this afternoon. We have an American gentleman with us, though, and it seems that he found out that you might be stranded at The Halt, so he arranged for me to come.'

It was just like Violet to have forgotten her—and how

strange to be rescued by an American gentleman! Dinah wondered who in the world he might be. She knew that a number of rich Americans had been taken up by society. They were usually middle-aged or elderly. Perhaps he had been feeling fatherly enough to make up for Violet's carelessness in leaving her eighteen-year-old sister stranded in the middle of nowhere. She must be sure to thank him prettily when she met him.

Not surprisingly, there was no Violet to greet her when she finally reached Moorings. Mrs Greaves, the housekeeper, informed her that Lady Kenilworth had been called away suddenly, and in the rush had forgotten to notify anyone that Lady Dinah was due to arrive that afternoon.

Fortunately, she had told the American gentleman, Mr Grant, who had arrived before the rest of the house-party, that Dinah was expected and he had immediately arranged for her to be collected when he had discovered m'lady's oversight.

There had been something odd in Mrs Greaves's expression when she had spoken of Mr Grant. Could he be one of Violet's admirers? Surely not—she preferred young and handsome men.

Chesterman, the butler, arrived to say, 'You would like some tea after your journey, I am sure, Lady Dinah, before you change out of your travelling costume. May I express my regret for the oversight. Mr Grant was most…exercised by it.'

Yes, Lady Dinah would like tea. And why were Chesterman and Greaves being so mysterious about the American? It was bad enough working out what to say to a house full of Violet's cronies without wondering how she ought to address an odd, old American, who had arrived early. Why?

Later, after she had drunk her tea, she allowed Pearson to dress her in a little girl's frock of white-dotted

Swiss with a blue sash, her long dark hair tied back by a blue velvet ribbon. It was an outfit which Dinah glumly decided made her look about fifteen, but which would certainly protect her from unwanted masculine attentions!

What to do now in this great empty barracks? She decided to visit the library and spend a happy hour there, forgetting Violet and at the same time avoiding elderly American gentlemen who would not be likely to find the library at all attractive.

Her notebook and her pencil-case in her hand, she made her way towards it down the main staircase. On the way she walked past the portraits of Lord Kenilworth's predatory-looking ancestors—he must be a great disappointment to them, she decided. Her mother always spoke of him as a pussy cat who allowed Violet far too much of her own way.

Finally she reached the library's double doors—to discover that she was mistaken. Someone was already there. A someone who, improbably, was playing the guitar. Equally improbably what was being played superbly was a piece written for it by Vivaldi, which she had once heard at a concert in Oxford she had attended with Faa.

For a moment Dinah hesitated, thought of retreating, and then, clutching her notebook and pencil-case to her, she made a decision which was to alter her life forever. She opened the door and walked into the library in order to discover who the unknown musician was...

He was seated on a long, low bench in a huge bay window facing the door, his head bent over his guitar. He lifted it to look at her whilst continuing to play...and Dinah stopped dead at the sight of him.

He was, quite simply, the most beautiful man she had ever seen. So beautiful that she swallowed unbelievingly. He was like the statue of the Apollo Belvedere, a copy of which she had seen at Oxford. He possessed the same classic perfection of both face and figure. His eyes were blue and the hyacinthine curls of his hair were of the palest gold.

His clothes were perfect, too. He made Dinah feel untidy. It wasn't fair that he should look like that—and to be able to play so well—she thought in anguish. No one person should possess so much when so many possessed so little.

His amazing eyes were steady on her while the music began to wind in on itself to reach its ending, which it did in a cluster of phrases of the utmost purity. What was more amazing was, that although the complex series of notes flowed from Apollo's fingers with such divine accuracy, there was no music before him.

It was over. He rose, placed the guitar on the bench, and walked across to where she stood, mesmerised, registering his height and his compelling presence.

He said, bowing, 'You must be Lady Dinah Freville, Violet's sister. You will forgive me for remaining seated and continuing to play when you entered, but the music demanded my homage, and yours, too, I hope.'

He took her unresisting hand, kissed the back of it, and relinquished it gently. He retreated a little but still continued to speak, since he appeared to realise that she had been struck dumb by shock.

The moment that he had taken her hand in his, Dinah had suddenly been transported out of the library and into a vast open space, with a multicoloured sky above it, banners of light weaving in the warm air. He was there beside her—how?

Then, when her hand became her own again, they were back in the library, and she was listening to his beautiful voice.

'Allow me to introduce myself. I am Jacobus—

Cobie—Grant from New York. Lord and Lady Kenilworth have kindly invited me to Moorings. We meet unconventionally, but I hope that you won't hold that against me.'

So this was her Yankee rescuer whom she had supposed to be middle-aged and odd!

So strongly did his mere presence affect her that Dinah felt as though she were under a spell, or had been hypnotised. She suddenly knew why the servants had spoken of him as they did. He was an enigma...yes, that was it. An enigma—and Violet's latest lover: she was sure of that, too.

She almost croaked at him. 'Indeed, I don't, seeing that you did me the kindness of making sure that the dog-cart was sent to rescue me at Moorings Halt. Besides, I don't mind unconventionality, and oh, how beautifully you play!'

Unable to stop herself, she added, 'But why in the library, Mr Grant?'

Her reply amused Cobie. She was so unlike Violet, so unlike anything which he had expected after listening to Violet's cruel descriptions of her. She reminded him of the young Susanna. There was the same quality of vulnerability about her, something in the defensive way in which she held herself. But Susanna had always known that she was valued—and this girl knew that she wasn't.

Besides, Susanna had always been beautiful, and Dinah plainly thought that she wasn't. She was still unformed, half a child, but Cobie judged that the promise of beauty was there.

He answered her gravely in order that she might think that what she had just said was important enough to deserve a reasoned reply. 'It seemed a convenient place, Lady Dinah. Few appear to use it—or so the butler told me—which meant that I was unlikely to be disturbed.'

'You were playing Vivaldi, weren't you? I like Vivaldi. I always think…'

Dinah hesitated, not sure whether to continue. He might laugh at her behind her back: she knew that Violet often did when she was foolish enough to reveal her inward thoughts to her…but…but…she decided to go on…

'His music always reminds me of a fountain playing. The water is rising and falling, spreading and narrowing, until finally, just before it ceases altogether, there comes a great burst when the last drops fall into the basin… Only…only…those last notes still remain with you—unlike the water drops.'

She must have been mad to offer her secret imaginings to a Yankee barbarian—which was what her brother Rainey always called them—and one of Violet's confidants into the bargain. Only he had played the Vivaldi concerto so beautifully that he must have had some real feeling for it.

If Cobie was surprised by what she had just said to him, he didn't allow it to show. Instead he picked up the guitar—it was Violet's—and still standing, holding it high and upright against his left shoulder, he began to play the concerto's coda again.

This time with even more feeling so that the last few notes seemed to hang in the air even longer—like the drops of water of which she had spoken, slowly falling into the basin of which she had spoken.

He said nothing, simply raised his beautiful eyebrows questioningly.

Dinah shivered.

'Yes, like that,' she finally achieved. 'I wish that Faa could hear you play.'

Cobie inclined his head. He didn't ask who Faa was, but he could guess. Violet had told him her half-sister's sorry story earlier that day as though it were something of a joke. He was more than ever relieved that he had discovered Violet's careless treatment of the poor child. She had allowed her half-sister to be abandoned at Moorings railway station as though she were an unconsidered package.

Well, be damned to that. He had not gone to rescue her himself, but had caused her to be rescued by others because Violet had always spoken of her so dismissively that he had feared that it might not be tactful for him to do any such thing.

For the same reason, he did not see fit to tell Dinah that her sister's neglect of her had been deliberate. Violet's behaviour towards her sister was making him regret his decision to have an affair with her. Cobie liked his women to be honest, and he tried to be honest with them—or as honest as he ever was with anyone.

Now that he had met Lady Dinah, he wished that he *had* gone to Moorings to collect her. Her shy and drab exterior concealed a lively and original mind—a present from her unknown father, no doubt.

'It is kind of you to praise my playing,' he said. 'I fear that I am somewhat of an amateur, unlike my foster-sister Susanna who could have had a career as a concert pianist. If women were encouraged to have them, that is.'

Once again Dinah was to surprise him—and not for the last time. 'You didn't sound like an amateur, Mr Grant, nor do you sound very much like an American— if you will allow me to be impertinent—even if you did say that you come from New York.'

'No, I don't consider you impertinent,' he said, smiling at her eager face and her transparent pleasure at being allowed to speak freely.

'Allow me to thank you, Lady Dinah, for both your compliments, especially since I have been somewhat remiss since you arrived. I did not ask you whether you had been offered tea after your journey, which I believe was a long one. Shall I ring for some?'

'Yes, and no,' said Dinah merrily. 'Yes, I have had tea, and, no, I do not wish to drink any more.'

There was something about him which made her want to talk to him. He held himself, she thought, as though he were prepared to listen to her. She wondered for a moment what it would be like to be as beautiful as he was and to possess such perfect manners into the bargain. He even made Violet look a little frantic. What did being such a *nonpareil* do to you? Would she have his effortless calm if she were ever to become his female equivalent?

Later she was to laugh to herself for having such an absurd thought. Of course, she could never be like him. Pigs might fly sooner, her old nurse had once said of a similar piece of nonsense of hers.

'Well, that disposes of tea as a subject of conversation,' returned Cobie equally merrily. 'Now, how about the weather? Shall we have a go at meteorology as a topic? It seems to be a favourite one over here. For example: Do you think it will continue fine, Lady Dinah? Or would you rather allow me to ask you a personal question along the lines of: Why are *you* in the library?'

'That would be a fair one to ask,' answered Dinah gravely, sitting down so that he need no longer stand, 'seeing that you were kind enough to answer my question about the library earlier. I thought that I might do some work. Faa, that's Professor Fabian, told me that the last Lord Kenilworth but one had accumulated a superb collection of memoirs and papers of all the most important statesmen of the last three centuries. If I'm ever allowed to read history at Oxford, it would give me a flying start to have gone through them carefully, making notes.'

So, Lady Dinah Freville took after her real father and, all in all, she was proving to be a very unlikely cuckoo in the Rainsboroughs' nest. Cobie doubted very much whether Dinah would ever be allowed to go to Oxford. Violet, for one, would never agree to it.

'A most sensible notion,' he said approvingly. 'There is nothing like reading those documents which have come down to us from the past to give us a true idea of it. I congratulate you, Lady Dinah: not many scholars have grasped that.'

Goodness, Rainey's Yankee barbarian sounded just like Faa when he was talking to her seriously! Did he treat Violet and Rainey to such learned and erudite discourse? These were Faa's words for what went on in academic tutorials and the dons' discussions. She rather doubted it.

'Do many Americans think that, Mr Grant? Are American statesmen like ours, do you know? Have you met many politicians over there? I suppose that New York is not much like Washington.'

'Indeed not,' he said, turning his amazing eyes on her again, something which, oddly enough, made Dinah feel quite dizzy. To amuse her, for he found her eager interest strangely touching, he began to tell her some comic stories of what politicians got up to in the United States, which set her laughing.

'I suppose the only real difference between yours and ours,' she volunteered, 'is that yours are more straightforward and ours are more hypocritical. I was always told that the First Lord Rainsborough—his name was Christopher Freville—was given his title for some grand diplomatic work he did for King Charles II at the time of the Dutch Wars.

'Only Faa told me one day that that was all a hum, and he also told me where to look in the papers to find the true story. He had discovered it the year he came here to be Rainey's tutor, and had begun to catalogue our archives before he ran off with Mama. So, the last time I came, I found the papers—and Faa was right.

'Christopher, whose ancestral home was Borough Hall, was a boon companion of King Charles II,' she explained, her eyes alight with amusement. 'He was a King whose habits we are all supposed to deplore, although he doesn't seem to me to be so very different from the present Prince of Wales.'

She would never have uttered this last piece of heresy in front of Violet, but the man to whom she was talking seemed to provoke her into making such lively indiscretions.

'He was just a nobody about the court, you understand, a mere gentleman-in-waiting. One day the King went for a walk—he was a great walker, Faa said—and it began to rain heavily. He was only wearing a light coat and Christopher was wearing a thick one. He saw that the King was wet, and offered him his own in exchange.

'That night, at court, they all drank too much, and the King told Christopher that he could have any favour he wanted as a gift for having lent him his coat. Christopher told the King that he could keep the coat—provided that he agreed to make him an Earl in exchange for it. Instead of condemning him for his impudence, the King laughed and said, ''Since you saved me from the rain I shall call you by its name—you shall be Lord Rainsborough.''

'Christopher was a pretty frivolous fellow. He was never a diplomat or statesman as his descendants have liked to pretend. Making him an Earl was just one of King Charles II's jokes—he was very fond of them, Faa says. Please don't tell Violet the truth—she wouldn't find it at all amusing.'

To be sure she wouldn't, Cobie thought, while thank-

ing Dinah for telling him of this comic piece of unwanted family history.

A little later he was to discover that Violet wouldn't
find anything amusing about her half-sister. After a
happy hour's conversation the library door was flung
open by an imperious hand, and Violet entered, resplendent in an old-rose tea-gown.

She stared at Cobie and Dinah laughing together over
the chess set which stood permanently ready on a mar-
quetry table in front of yet another window. Dinah was
finding that Mr Grant played an even better game of
chess than Faa. Violet, however, approved of neither
the game, Mr Grant, nor Dinah.

She particularly didn't approve of Dinah.

'So there you are, Cobie,' she said unoriginally, sailing over to them like some galleon strayed from the
high seas, 'in the library. Of all odd places to find you!
Have you had tea?'

She stared down at the chess game where Cobie's
Black Queen and Knight were pinning Dinah's White
Queen. She drawled mockingly, 'What a hole you are
in, darling,' and, throwing out a careless hand to wave
at Dinah's pieces, she knocked them all flying.

'Oh, sorry,' she exclaimed, still mocking, 'but really,
Dinah, no need for you to carry on with *that*. Now, why
don't you go upstairs and find something suitable to
wear—that thing you have on looks more fitting for the
nursery than the dining room. Oh, and thank Mr Grant
prettily for taking the trouble to entertain you.'

She spoke as though Dinah were a fractious three-
year-old, and Cobie was her elderly uncle.

Cobie, caught between red rage at Violet's casual
cruelty, and wry amusement at the way in which she
was expressing it, was unhappily aware that anything
he might say to comfort the poor child would only give

Violet the opportunity to cut her up even more savagely, said nothing.

Dinah, her face flaming scarlet, rose and prepared to retreat upstairs to change—although into what she did not know. She was well aware that she possessed nothing of which Violet would approve. Violet had always had the power to make her feel ugly, clumsy and stupid—particularly stupid.

The happiness which she had been experiencing over the last hour had flown away quite. She now felt that Mr Grant must have been concealing his boredom skilfully, whereas until Violet had arrived she had thought him to be enjoying their impromptu tête-à-tête as much as she had been doing.

'Y...y...yes,' she began to stammer miserably. She bent down to rescue the White Queen which had rolled under the table and, when she rose with it, found that Mr Grant was gently taking it from her to replace it on the board.

'We must resume our game another day,' he told her gravely, his amazing blue eyes hard on her. For her sake, he dare not say any more than that. He would offer Violet no ammunition to use against her.

Violet's eyes were boring holes in her for some reason which Dinah couldn't understand.

She said disjointedly, 'No need, thank you...Mr Grant... I'm not really a very good player...mustn't bore you.'

Cobie was quite still: a danger sign with him if either of the two women had known it. 'Oh, you didn't bore me, Lady Dinah. I enjoyed my hour with you.'

Violet tapped her foot on the ground peremptorily until Dinah, blushing furiously and unable to answer Mr Grant coherently, left them.

The door had barely had time to shut behind her before Violet said nastily, '*I enjoyed my hour with you!*

Really, Cobie, there was no need for you to go quite so far to keep the child in countenance—a quiet ''thank you'' would have been more than enough.'

Could she conceivably be jealous of Dinah? And why? Until Violet had walked in, Dinah had been a happy and interesting companion, but it had become immediately apparent by Dinah's subsequent behaviour that this was not the first time Violet had treated her with such cold cruelty. All her charming composure had been destroyed in an instant.

Cobie's dislike of Violet was growing at the same speed. He made an immediate resolution to try to protect the unloved child. She reminded him strongly of another whom, long ago, he had also tried to protect but had failed to do so through no fault of his own. The memory of her death would haunt him all his life. Pray God he could do more for Dinah, if only while he was at Moorings.

Nothing of this showed. He was charm itself to Violet, but she was shrewd enough to notice that he never mentioned Dinah to her. She could not have said why seeing Dinah laughing with Cobie had flicked her on the raw. Perhaps it was because, at nearly forty, she was approaching the time when no one would think of her as 'that great beauty, Violet Kenilworth' but instead she would be spoken of as 'Violet Kenilworth—who had once been a great beauty'.

And Cobie was only twenty-nine to Dinah's eighteen.

Chapter Three

That part of London society which had been invited to
the Kenilworths' house party and a large number of the
more important folk in the county of Warwick were
assembled in the Great Hall at Moorings for a reception
being given by the new Lord Lieutenant of the county,
Lord Kenilworth, to mark his accession to that honour.

South Africa had been looted of diamonds to hang
around beautiful necks and to depend from beautiful
ears. It would not be exaggerating to say that the women
present were wearing a king's ransom between them—
except for Lady Dinah Freville, of course. She hid herself in a corner and watched them walk to and fro, waving their fans like the lovely peacocks they were.

Among the guests who made up the house party was
one who had only recently been introduced to the Kenilworths by the American Envoy and his wife, who were
also present. They were, indeed, apart from his hosts,
the only persons in the whole vast Hall whom he knew.

He was, as the saying had it, yet another rich Yankee
robber baron, Mr Hendrick Van Deusen, who had made
himself a fortune in Chicago, having appeared there
from nowhere some years ago. He was a heavy-set man

in his early forties, resplendent in his new English evening dress from Savile Row.

Violet had flung an invitation at him on hearing of
his immense wealth and that he liked to play cards for
money. Her poverty-stricken brother, Rainsborough,
must be given the chance to win some of his loot from
him at Moorings.

Like Lady Dinah, whom he had not yet met, he had
hidden himself away in a small ante-room which
opened off the Hall where he could both see and hear
the passing show, but could not be seen himself. A wise
man ought to know more than other people wished him
to. He soon gained his reward for his cunning.

A pair of society women, resplendent, but flimsy, but-
terflies, both came and stood near him, gossiping loudly
about their hostess.

'I see that Violet Kenilworth's Apollo is one of the
party,' drawled the prettier of the two, amusement on
her face and in her voice. 'I hear that she granted him
the privilege of arriving before the rest of us.'

'Now, now, Emily, don't be jealous—there's no point
in it, none at all. There's only one at a time for him,
they say, and at the moment it's Violet. And she's got
her hooks into him well and truly.'

'I can't say that I blame her. I'd have had my hooks
in him well and truly if I'd had the good luck to meet
him first. Tell me, is it true that he's the American Envoy's brother-in-law?'

'By proxy,' chuckled her friend, 'only by proxy. Her
half-brother, so they say. Not much alike, are they?
Apollo is as blond as she's brunette.'

This conversation intrigued its unknown listener who
decided to go and find Apollo. Anyone who could entrance two such hard-bitten beauties must surely be
worth looking at.

Mr Van Deusen strolled forward, looking around him

for a tall, blond man: he had decided that Apollo must be tall—and there was a tall, blond man standing with his back to him, talking to his hostess. He suddenly turned his golden head and Van Deusen caught his breath at the sight of him. It wasn't Apollo's perfect profile, nor his athletic body which intrigued him, but something quite different.

It couldn't be! Surely not! Not here, not the US Envoy's brother-in-law! Not the darling of London society! For Mr Van Deusen had last seen this man, or one very like him, nearly eight years ago in Arizona Territory, America's Southwest. He had been a man you could not forget and Van Deusen had never forgotten him—but he had never thought to see him again, and particularly not as an honoured guest at an aristocrat's house party.

He was older now, but, as always, every feminine head turned to look at him when he walked away from his hostess, holding himself with the arrogance which Mr Van Deusen remembered only too well—and which had infuriated everyone who met him.

Could it really be the man he had known? If he were, under what name was he now going? And did the effete fools here know what sort of tiger was living in their midst? No one present could conceivably guess at the life which respectable Mr Van Deusen and Apollo had once shared.

Mr Van Deusen gave a long, slow grin. Well, he would soon find out if he were mistaken, and if he were, he would apologise. After all, he had never seen his man spotlessly clean, perfectly groomed, and the current lover of the Prince of Wales's mistress!

He was behind Apollo now. Hendrick Van Deusen grinned again, showing strong yellow teeth. He bunched his right hand into a fist with two of his fingers sticking out from it. He jabbed them into the small of Apollo's back, as though it were a revolver he was thrusting there, and said in a thick Texas drawl, 'Hi, there, Jumpin' Jake, fly at once. All is discovered.'

Mr Van Deusen felt Apollo stiffen, every muscle tensing before he turned to face his accuser. That face was an impassive mask, showing none of the emotions which one might expect, given the abrupt shock he must have felt on hearing a voice sounding from out of his disreputable past when he had been an outlaw in the Territory.

Yes, his man was Apollo, by damn, and no doubt about it, and Apollo was speaking to him, his voice beautiful, with no hint of an American accent, let alone the thick Texas drawl which Jumpin' Jake had affected.

'Do I know you, sir?'

'You should. Because I know you, and I owe you— and that is enough for me to know you.'

Cobie's smile was one which no one in English society had ever seen. It was deadly—and proved to Mr Van Deusen how little he had changed.

'I only ever knew one man who owed me anything— but that debt was cancelled long ago—which you should know.'

It was a tacit admission of who he was—or who he had been, and Cobie saw that the man opposite to him knew that.

'I didn't accept that cancellation,' growled Mr Van Deusen. 'No man saves my life and goes unthanked, unrewarded. You saved my life twice. I paid you back only once. That second debt still stands.'

Cobie's smile at this was so charming that Mr Van Deusen could see why the women about him were watching them with such hungry eyes. He took Mr Van Deusen by the arm, led him, in silence, out of the ballroom, through the small drawing room along a corridor and into the library where he shut the door behind them.

'Now,' he said, 'we may talk in peace. Where were we? Ah, you were reminding me that I saved your worthless life, and that you wanted to recompense me for doing so. Well, you are hardly likely to be able to return that last favour here. We are a long way from San Miguel—or Bratt's Crossing.'

'So you *do* know me.'

'But do you know my name?'

'You were Jake Coburn in San Miguel, and Cobie Grant in Bratt's Crossing. I would bet that you are Cobie Grant here.'

'Jacobus Grant—and you would win your bet.'

Cobie looked at Mr Van Deusen, at the beautifully cut suit which clad the thickly powerful body, at the cared-for hands and massive head and face. 'I doubt that I could guess your name—Professor—or, in Western slang—Perfesser.'

'Nor you could. I now use my own. I am Hendrick Van Deusen, a respectable financier, if that is not a contradiction in terms.'

Cobie threw back his head and laughed.

'Ever the old Perfessor! Even if I would wager you are not now known as Schultz. Can you stand this effete life?'

'The question is, can you?'

Cobie thought that he couldn't, but he didn't think that he wished to return to Arizona Territory and be a boy of twenty again, either.

'Life is what you make of it,' he said at last.

'A truism—but looking at you, I don't think that you have changed much...other than that you are now clean.'

Cobie's smile was sweet. 'Yes, I hardly think that I looked like this eight years ago.'

'No, indeed. But the man inside is the same, I'll be bound. Is London safe while you live in it?'

Cobie thought of the night on which he had rescued Lizzie Steele—and began to laugh.

'Perhaps, perhaps not. But I don't pack a pair of six-shooters on my hip whilst walking down Piccadilly, more's the pity.'

'What exactly are you doing to stir up the assembled nobility and gentry? I would wager that there are easier pickings here than at San Miguel.'

Cobie offered him his most winning smile.

'Nothing.'

'You're doing nothing? Now that I don't believe.'

'Ever the sceptic. Believe what you like.'

Mr Van Deusen also smiled. Cobie knew that smile. He had seen it on the face before him in more than one tight corner. He decided to provoke in return.

'And what exactly are you doing here, Mr Van Deusen? It's odd, you know, but I find it hard to think of you as other than Schultz, the Perfesser who packed a mean gun.'

'The Perfesser and Jumpin' Jake are long gone,' remarked Mr Van Deusen smoothly, 'and no resurrection awaits them, I think.'

Cobie remembered the boy he had been, laughed and added, 'You hope, rather. You remember the old saying, "Truth will arise, though all the world will hide it from men's eyes."'

'By God, I hope not,' said Mr Van Deusen fervently. 'I am a most respectable and wealthy citizen of Chicago, thinking of running for the US Senate in the next elections.'

'The Perfesser in the Senate would only be matched by Jumpin' Jake marrying into the British aristocracy.'

Cobie paused, and then, as though some ghost, some premonition, had walked through his head, asked himself, Now, why did I say that?

'I thought that Lady Kenilworth was already married,' remarked Mr Van Deusen slyly.

'So she is, but I have English cousins. Best to tell you, knowing you, you'll soon find out. Sir Alan Dilhorne, the noted statesman, now retired, is by way of being a relative. He is the elder brother of my foster-father, Jack Dilhorne.'

Van Deusen whistled. 'Dilhorne of Dilhorne and Rutherfurd's and Dilhorne of Temple Hatton, Yorkshire?'

When Cobie, his mouth twisted derisively, nodded assent, he exclaimed, 'By God, young sir, what were you doing wandering around the West, stealing peanuts when all you had to do—?'

Cobie cut in, his voice quite different from the one he had been using. Instead he was speaking in the harsh Western drawl which had driven the respectable and the unrespectable mad in Arizona Territory.

'Ah, yes, when all I had to do was take foster-Daddy's handouts, get him to destroy Greer and all my enemies for me. Say pretty please, Uncle Jack and Uncle Alan, and let them run my life for me.

'Oh, Perfesser, I thought you knew me better than that! Besides, the peanuts I stole from Bratt's Crossing and San Miguel became the wealth of the Indies when I lit out from the West and arrived on Wall Street and began to trade with it. What did you do with your pile, Perfesser, sir?'

'The same as you. Made myself richer. Returned to the bosom of my remaining family, began a career in politics for the hell of it—no illusions there—Republican infighting is merely San Miguel writ large.'

'Oh, the whole world is merely San Miguel writ large,' remarked Cobie dismissively, 'my father and Sir Alan notwithstanding.'

'Then that being so, shall we pillage it separately—
or together?'

Cobie's crack of laughter was spontaneous.

'Neither, I'm resting. I'm having a holiday which I
haven't done since I last saw you. My foster-sister
wishes me to marry, hence my earlier comment. My
foster-father wants me to settle down. Sir Alan, I suspect, wants me to think of a future in England—the
Dilhorne branch here has become too respectable. He
believes I may be a buccaneer and wants to have the
pleasure of watching one of the family live up to its
somewhat dubious past. My foster-father's father was
transported to New South Wales and made his pile
there. You may judge how legitimately if I tell you that
I am supposed to resemble him somewhat.'

Mr Van Deusen thought that the resemblance might
be stronger than that.

'Your grandfather?' he ventured.

Cobie's grin was nasty. It came all the way from San
Miguel, and belonged to the boy gunman who had terrorised that outlaw township.

'Oh, that would be telling. Now give me your address, both here and in the States, and after that we had
better return to the reception. My brother-in-law sus-
pects me of wanting to escape my responsibilities to
him and his wife, and he is determined that for once I
shall conform.'

'That would be a small miracle in itself,' remarked
Van Deusen thoughtfully. 'Though outwardly you are a
model of the perfect English gentleman, no transatlantic
odour stains your person.'

'Aren't I just,' agreed Cobie cheerfully. 'The original
chameleon, that's me. Now, let us go back, and I will
introduce you not only to the ineffable Violet, who is
temporarily bound to me with hoops of steel, but to
several of her friends who are as accommodating as

Kate's girls in the Silver Dollar, if a little cleaner. We mustn't let your stay in London be disappointing in any respect.'

Oh, I'm sure it won't be that, thought Mr Van Deusen, following Apollo back into the ballroom, not with Jumpin' Jake to entertain me!

Perhaps, ironically, the first person whom they met when they were about to leave the library was innocent young Lady Dinah Freville. Dinah, bored by the whole wretched business of pretending she was enjoying an event where everyone's eyes passed over her unseeingly, was just entering it in search of more agreeable entertainment.

She stared at Cobie and the man to whom he was speaking, or rather, with whom he was laughing. A man whom she had heard Violet describing as 'yet another Yankee vulgarian to whom Kenilworth wishes me to be polite'.

Well, he couldn't be all that vulgar if Mr Grant was enjoying his company so much. She smiled at him, and said, a trifle breathlessly, 'Were you bored, too, Mr Grant? Won't you introduce me to your friend?'

It was true that he was a rather unlikely friend for Mr Grant. He was middle-aged with the hard face which Dinah had come to recognise as belonging to those visiting Americans who had, in society's words, 'made their pile'. Although Mr Grant, reputed to be immensely rich by his own efforts, was not like any of them.

Mr Grant was smiling at her now, and saying, 'Lady Dinah, I should be delighted to introduce you to an old friend of mine, Mr Hendrick Van Deusen. His nickname is the Professor because he is immensely learned. I first met him nearly ten years ago when I took a long painting holiday in the American Southwest, and he was kind enough to look after me—I was such a tenderfoot as they say over there. It was rather dangerous territory, you see.

'We lost touch with one another once my holiday was over, and I am delighted to meet him again in an English country house, and introduce him to my hostess's sister.'

His smile was even more saintly than usual when he came out with this preposterous and lying description of his violent Western odyssey.

Mr Van Deusen bowed to Dinah, registering that she was totally unlike most of the other society women whom he had met in England. He wondered why Apollo was interested in her, something which Cobie explained when all introductions were over.

'Lady Dinah,' Cobie told him, 'is by way of being an amateur historian who hopes to be a professional one. She has been showing me the old letters and papers collected by her ancestors, many of whom, if she will forgive me for saying so, resemble our own wilder politicians more than they might like to think. I should perhaps inform you, Lady Dinah, that Mr Van Deusen is hoping to run for the Senate as a Republican candidate.'

As usual when she was with him Dinah forgot her usual shyness and found herself discussing politics with Mr Van Deusen as though she had been doing such an unlikely thing all her life. Cobie also noticed that when she was away from Violet and her friends she came to glowing life: not only did her face and manner change, but she displayed a light and elegant wit—with which she was now charming Van Deusen.

'But I must not keep you,' she said at last. 'Violet has been looking for you, Mr Grant. She has been trying to make up a whist table for Rainey now that the reception is over, and she gathers that you like to play an

occasional hand at cards. She also mentioned the possibility of poker—do you play poker, Mr Grant?'

'A little,' he told her gravely, which had Mr Van
Deusen giving him an odd look when Mr Grant said
that, but she did not allow it to worry her, particularly
since Mr Grant immediately added, 'If Lady Kenilworth
summons me, then I must instantly obey. You will forgive me if I leave you.'

They both did, and Dinah spent a further happy ten
minutes with Mr Grant's unlikely friend—who proved
to be as learned as he had told her.

It was all much more fun than being a wallflower in
the drawing room.

A week later Cobie was trying not to win at poker.
He was part of a group of men playing in one corner
of the green drawing room at Moorings. A few women,
Violet among them, occasionally wandered over to
watch them. It was already half-past three in the morning, and most of the house party had gone to bed hours
ago.

'Thought you Yankees were masters of this game,'
grunted Sir Ratcliffe at him, as he raked in his winnings.
Cobie had not lost very heavily, but he hadn't won either, not on that night nor any preceding.

The sixth sense which often told him things that he
sometimes didn't want to know—but more often did—
informed him that to appear a bit of an ass at the game
might be no bad thing.

Some of those who knew that he had accumulated a
fortune in dealings on Wall Street had already begun to
believe that his fortune had been made for him by other
men, and that what he was most possessed of was idle,
easy charm rather than the usual Yankee know-how. He
had no objection at all to appearing far less shrewd and
dangerous than he actually was.

On the contrary he had frequently found that it was an advantage to be underrated. People became unwary, and now everyone in society was unwary about Jacobus Grant who had made such a hit with the ladies, was a pleasant fellow to spend an hour with, a bit of a fool, quite unlike most of the hard-headed Yankees who invaded London society and whose one idea was to chase after the almighty dollar.

Not winning, Cobie had often found, was harder work than winning. He had to restrain himself, and when the ass opposite to him, for that was where Sir Ratcliffe sat, made a particularly bad play, it took Cobie all his considerable strength of will not to fleece a black sheep who was so determined to be shorn. Worse than that, though, was his suspicion that every now and then Sir Ratcliffe indulged in some clumsy and obvious cheating—which no one but Cobie appeared to notice.

'Thought Tum Tum was coming to stay, Lady K.,' Sir Ratcliffe drawled at Violet in a pause during the game when the men rose, stretched, refreshed their drinks, and lit new cigars. Violet's brother, Rainey, was leaning against the wall. He was a handsome enough fellow but Cobie had yet to see him sober after seven at night. He was a poor poker player, too. Another piece of knowledge Cobie filed away for possible future use.

'Met Tum Tum, have you?' Sir Ratcliffe asked Cobie in his most condescending manner, offering him a cigar, which he refused.

Yes, Cobie had met the Prince of Wales, but left Violet to tell the Rat—as Cobie privately thought of him since saving Lizzie Steele from him—that the Prince had had to remain in London on official business.

'Don't have much luck, do you, Grant?' Now he was more condescending than ever. 'Cards not runnin' your way?'

Cobie was all ineffable boyish charm, saying, 'No,

never do, you know. Can't think why I play the game. Passes the time, though.'

He offered the Rat his most winning smile. 'You seem to be doing well. Perhaps I ought to take lessons from you.'

He looked up to see Violet's eyes hard on him. No one else, apart from Mr Van Deusen, had taken his words at other than face value, but Violet, he was discovering, was also no fool—it wouldn't do to underrate her. Particularly since he was beginning to annoy her by avoiding her bed ever since Dinah had arrived at Moorings. He thought that she was beginning to see a little of what lay below the mask of innocence which he had worn since he had arrived in England.

He decided to cut the whole pointless business short. He rose, and said, 'Leave my money in the pot, I think I'm ready for bed.'

Sir Ratcliffe said disagreeably, 'Don't like losing, Grant? You Yankees never do.'

'Strictly speaking,' and this came out so languidly that no one could be offended by it, 'I'm not a Yankee. Born in the South, you see. Live in New York, I do admit. Sometimes wonder why.'

He thought he heard a snort from Mr Van Deusen but ignored it, and took his leave. He had hardly gone a yard down the corridor before the door opened again and Violet was with him.

'Cobie!' she shrilled.

'Violet,' he said, and bowed, like the old-world Southern gentleman he had pretended to be, and then, monstrously, he couldn't resist it. 'What can I do for you?'

'You know very well what you can do for me,' she told him, the light of battle on her lovely face. 'What you haven't been doing since Dinah walked into Moorings.'

So, his worst forebodings had come true. Since Dinah had arrived, a fortnight ago, he had watched Violet humiliate her daily, along the lines of that first afternoon in the library. In the last few days he had taken to avoiding the girl to save her from Violet's tongue, where in the beginning he had sought to amuse her.

She touches my hard heart, he thought, wryly. She didn't touch Violet's. Neither did he wish to touch Violet, and again, he regretted ever having become involved with her.

Desolately he knew that Violet's public ill treatment of the child was to punish him, as well as her. Violet brooked no rivals, and ridiculously, improbably, she saw poor Dinah as a rival.

As usual he thought quickly, then offered her, 'I could hardly be your *cavaliere servente* while Kenilworth was hovering, Violet. Not seemly.'

'Kenilworth is not hovering, Cobie. He knows perfectly well why I asked you, as he asked Daisy Masham.' She put out a hand to him. 'You may escort me upstairs. Our rooms are quite near.'

There was nothing for it. He had meant to try to leave Moorings early without offending her—but she was now determined to be offended unless he did what she asked.

Every fibre of his body revolted at the notion. And when, having taken her arm, and he had begun to walk her up to her room for her poor sister's sake, if for nothing else, she said, in a poisonously sweet voice, 'Oh, and by the way, Cobie, there is one more favour you can do me—do the both of us.'

He took her hand and put it to his lying lips. 'Of course, Violet, my darling, and what is that?'

She shook her head, 'Oh, it's Dinah again. Too ridiculous, the poor child obviously thinks that you have a *tendre* for her. All that attention you've given her—

playing to her on the guitar…chess games…talking to her in the library…walking with her in the gardens… encouraging her to think of going to Oxford—has quite turned her head. I think that you ought to disabuse her of the notion that you are interested in her—very firmly. I warn you, if you don't, I will. She really ought to have nothing to do with such as you,' and her eyes were on him, hard and cruel.

He knew immediately what she meant, and the kind of blackmail she was subjecting him to. Somehow, she had read him, seen the pity he felt for her unloved sister, and was threatening that, if he failed to do as she asked, Dinah's public humiliations would continue—might even grow worse. Jealousy is as cruel as the grave, and Violet, astonishingly, was jealous.

For a moment the world reeled about him. Violet had touched some memory in him which she could not know existed. Long ago he had been kind to a waif even more abused than poor Dinah, more even than Lizzie Steele—and his heedless kindness had led directly to her death. Dinah was in no danger of physical death, but she could not, he thought, stand very much more of the treatment which Violet was meting out to her without her inner self being in serious danger.

He had gone quite still again. He stood motionless. He was fighting the red berserker rage which Violet, by her cruelty, had roused in him. He was helpless before her, and she knew it. Sleep with me, humiliate Dinah— and I will leave her alone. All he could do was control himself and offer her what she wanted. At the same time his busy brain was working—after a fashion which would have astonished Violet.

'You ask a lot of me,' he said at last.

'Really, Cobie, really? You surprise me. I had not thought that you favoured children. I thought that you left that to others,' and she laughed.

Like Sir Ratcliffe, Cobie thought, and Arthur Winthrop—and who else?

'She is lonely,' he told Violet gently, 'and not very happy.'

'And you make her so? You take a lot upon yourself. After all, it is *my* sister of whom we speak, not yours. It is I who am concerned about her welfare. It demands that you disillusion her. And be sure that you do it in such a way that I will know that you have done so.

'Otherwise, my dear, otherwise, I shall immediately send her to my deaf, strict and bad-tempered old aunt in the country to be her permanent companion.'

'Pax,' he said, with the sweetest smile he could summon, throwing up his hands like a schoolboy. 'I think that this is all a great pother about nothing, but have it your way, Violet.'

'Oh, I intend to do so,' she told him, mockingly, 'and now we are here, Cobie. Here is the door to my room. Choose, like the man in the story—the lady—or the tiger?'

'Oh, no choice,' he told her carelessly. 'The lady every time.' He pushed her through the door, rather ungently, and told himself, that if one must sacrifice one's principles—not that I possess any—this is as pleasant a way to do it as any. The unpleasant part will come tomorrow, with Dinah.

He was particularly good value that night, Violet thought, unaware that in his mind Cobie was treating her like the whore she was.

Chapter Four

M_r Grant had been dodging her for the last few days, Dinah thought desolately, which was not surprising. After all, he came here to be with Violet. She was sitting in the Elizabethan Knot Garden looking blindly at the flowers and remembering what she had seen that morning.

She had risen early in order to go riding before anyone else was about, and when she had turned into the corridor where Violet had her suite of rooms, she saw Mr Grant quietly closing Violet's door: it was obvious that they had been spending the night together.

Shock kept her quiet, so that he had no idea that she had seen him. She had known, of course she had known, that he had been invited for Violet's pleasure. She had known it since she had first seen him in the library. She had tried to put the knowledge out of her mind in those few, early days when she had walked and talked with him. I like him, she told herself firmly, not because he's beautiful, but because I like talking to him. He's so clever, it's like talking to Faa.

Listening, always listening, because no one ever included her in their conversations, she discovered that he was thought to be something of a charming fool. How could anyone think any such thing? It wasn't simply that he knew a lot, could play the guitar and the piano divinely, but she had grasped at once that even his most innocent remarks frequently carried a double meaning.

Listening, always listening, she noticed that he was particularly good with Sir Ratcliffe Heneage, whom Dinah disliked intensely. He wasn't bad with poor Rainey, either. Dinah knew that her half-brother was dissolute and not very clever. It was not that Mr Grant made fun of his hearers, but that he tailored what he said to what they were. Of course, he did it with everyone—except Mr Van Deusen.

Dinah wasn't sure that she liked Mr Van Deusen. He had an eye which frightened her. An eye which saw into people. She had watched him play at chess with Mr Grant one afternoon before Mr Grant had begun to avoid her, and she had expected him to win.

He had said something odd when he swung the board round to give Mr Grant the Black pieces without even tossing up, or asking him which he wanted, 'Play me properly, Nemo, that's the only condition on which I will give you a game.'

Nemo. Nobody. She wondered why he called Mr Grant that. Mr Grant had laughed his charming laugh, and said, 'If you are sure that is what you want?' Mr Van Deusen had nodded, and said, irascibly, as though he were cross, 'You know dam' well it is.'

After that they played, and Mr Grant had won easily. Once or twice he offered to let Mr Van Deusen replace his piece and make another move because the one he had made was disastrous, and each time, Mr Van Deusen said irritably, 'Oh, be dam'd to that, Nemo. Play properly for once.'

Dinah thought that neither of them had seen her. She was scrunched up small behind a curtain on the window seat near the table where the chessboard was set out.

After Mr Van Deusen, neatly mated, had stared in disgust, first at the board and then at Mr Grant, and snarled, 'Always the same, dammit. You've got better, not worse,' he strode off to commit suicide, or so he said.

Mr Grant had laughed and leaned back, remarking to her around the curtain, 'He doesn't mean that, you know, but chess brings out the worst in people.'

'Only if they lose,' Dinah offered.

'Not invariably,' he replied gravely.

'Is that why you let them win?' she asked him, because that was the only thing which made sense of Mr Van Deusen's remarks. He was telling Mr Grant to play up to his paper, a phrase which Faa had once used.

'It's bad for me to win or lose,' he told her.

'Did you know that I was there all the time?' she asked him.

'That would be telling,' he said, just like a nurse whom she had once had.

'Why did he call you Nemo?'

'That would be telling, too.'

Dinah considered him. It was, she later remembered sadly, the last conversation which she had had with him. After that he had avoided her, and she wondered what she had said or done to make him do so.

'Nemo means nobody.'

'Yes.'

'And you're not nobody.'

'True.'

Dinah gave up. He was laughing at her, kindly and gently. It was at that moment that she knew that she loved him. Not simply because he was kind to her, although that was part of it, and, of course, she must never let him know.

'Would you play chess with me again? I'm not such a good player as Mr Van Deusen.'

She thought for a moment. 'You could teach me. It's more than just knowing the moves, isn't it?'

He taught her that afternoon. Carefully and patiently. She had thought at the time that she might use what he told her against him the next time that they played, but it was to be the last game he played with her at Moorings.

He had just finished explaining to her the importance of protecting her centre when she saw, over his shoulder, Violet looking at them. Dinah didn't like the expression on Violet's face. It was one which meant that she was doing something wrong, and for the life of her she couldn't think what it was about playing a game of chess against Mr Grant which could be wrong.

'Dinah!' Violet called, irritation in her voice. 'I thought I told you not to trouble the guests. Kenilworth particularly wanted Mr Grant to ride out with him this afternoon, but he couldn't find him.'

Cobie swung round. 'My fault, Lady K.,' he said cheerfully, 'not Dinah's. I felt lazy this afternoon.'

Violet had shown him her sweetest smile. 'Oh, you weren't to know. Besides, Dinah ought to go to her room and do her piano practice. I particularly promised Mama that she would do at least an hour every day. I don't think you've done any at all for the last two days. Off with you now.'

There was nothing for it but to leave him, and since then Mr Grant, to please Violet, because she plainly didn't want Dinah to call him Cobie, had hardly spoken to her. He hadn't looked at her, either. All because he was so besotted with Violet that once she had taken him over so completely he had had no time to look at anyone else.

Worse, Violet was being particularly nasty to her these days. And if it went on she would ask either to go back to Mama's, or to Faa. And if Violet said no, she had a good mind to take Pearson, herself and their bags, go to the station and buy tickets to take them to Oxford—and Faa.

She had just reached this point in her musings when she saw Mr Grant walking along the path which skirted the top lawn and led to the garden in which she was sitting. He was wearing a black-and-gold striped blazer with a white shirt and cream flannel trousers, a turn-out which made him look more handsome than ever, and made Dinah in her child's dress of blue-and-white striped cotton feel more of a frump than ever.

He had seen her and was walking towards her.

But he wasn't giving her his white smile. His face was stern and shuttered, as though she and the rest of the world didn't exist.

She remembered that she had seen him looking like that the other day. Violet had just left him and he was standing alone. He had been laughing with Violet, looking particularly handsome, and then, suddenly, he had turned away. Before he had done so, however, she had seen his face change for a brief moment into that stern impassive mask, and she had wondered what had caused such a transformation.

He saw her, and hesitated. She thought that he was about to change the path he was taking in order to avoid her. In the distance, through a gap in the hedge, she could see Violet walking along yet another path, exquisitely turned out, a parasol in her hand, even though the sun was watery today.

Perhaps it was her he wished to join, and Dinah Freville was only an unconsidered nuisance in his way. He must have changed his mind again, for after that infinitesimal pause he was continuing his walk towards her. Dinah smiled at him, a strained smile, not sure of its welcome.

'Lady Dinah,' he said, bowing. 'It is not quite so

warm today, I think. The weather is hardly suitable for sitting outdoors.' And then, after this cold beginning, so unlike the warmth of their earlier conversations, he asked her, still in the same distant tones, 'Were you waiting for me?'

Why, she didn't know, Dinah began to tremble. Had she been waiting for him? Of course she had. Not consciously perhaps, but she must have known that he walked this way each morning, through the Knot Garden, through the wicket gate at the end, and out into the park, going as far as the lake whose waters sparkled in the distance, before he turned back.

Some of the guests had expressed a lofty amusement at this uncharacteristic energy in a man who usually appeared to be languid. 'Perhaps he's a true Yankee after all,' had been Sir Ratcliffe's sneer, 'in that if in nothing else!'

'You shouldn't, you know,' he told her, still in that same bored voice. 'You are still a very young lady, Dinah, and forgive me, but you ought not to appear to be chasing after an older man—that way reputations are ruined. I hope you won't mind my giving you this advice. It is what I would offer you if you were my sister.'

It was not the words themselves which hurt her, suggesting as they did that she had been immodest, but the manner in which he uttered them, so unlike the charming friendliness he had previously shown to her.

Dinah flushed an unbecoming scarlet, which was rapidly succeeded by an ashen grey. She rose, twisting her hands together, and stammered, 'I thought that we were friends...Mr Grant.'

'There,' he said, and the frost in his voice was as plain as though icicles were coming out of his mouth. 'That is exactly it. You are not yet out, your sister tells me, so one must forgive you a certain gaucherie.'

He watched her face change again, both felt and saw,

the pain on it—and cursed the necessity to do what Violet had cruelly ordered. He had to remember that by doing so he was saving the child before him from even greater humiliation—and permanent exile.

Dinah was shaking now and, to make matters worse, she saw Violet bearing down on them, an expression on her face which she had seen before, and which boded no good.

'So, there you are, Cobie,' she exclaimed to his back before Dinah could answer him. 'Is this wretched child *still* pursuing you? She is becoming the talk of the house party. I really must have a word with you, Dinah, about the correct way for a girl who is not yet fully out to behave.'

Dinah, still mute, looked at them standing side by side, impregnable in their beauty. She had never before been so conscious of her plainness and her lack of the *savoir faire* which her sister and her lover possessed in such abundance.

They were both so…handsome.

She found herself saying, rather like her old nurse, 'Handsome is as handsome does,' and was surprised how level her voice was, although she was white to the lips. 'And, Mr Grant, I think that I hate you more than I hate her.'

She waved a shaking hand at Violet. 'She, at least, never pretended to like me. What a whited sepulchre you are…Mr Jacobus Grant!'

'Such melodrama, darling,' drawled Violet mockingly, 'and all because a silly little girl mistook common courtesy for something…more…shall we say…?'

Cobie, hardly able to endure this, agonisingly aware that to defend Dinah would result in an even crueller punishment for her, put a hand on Violet's arm to try to silence her. He would have preferred to put both his hands around her neck and strangle her.

Violet flung the hand off, and stared hard at him to try to compel him to say something more.

'I wasn't having you leave all the dirty work for me to do, darling,' she told him later. Cobie saw the anguish on Dinah's face but there was nothing he could do to staunch it without causing her future pain.

He bowed to the white-faced child, whose very courage in the face of the insults being put upon her were a reproach to him.

'I can only say that I am sorry that you might have mistaken what your sister calls common courtesy for something more. Put my thoughtless behaviour down to my Yankee ignorance…'

He paused, added, his eyes on her, 'It might be useful for you to remember in future that appearances often deceive.'

This last cryptic statement reminded Dinah of some of his other utterances which possessed a double meaning, although what he was trying to say to her—if anything—she couldn't think. He had made his own revulsion at her importunate behaviour sufficiently plain, and the pain he was causing her was making it difficult for her to think clearly.

What was also plain was Violet's scarcely disguised glee at what was happening.

'I think that it would be a good idea for you to go to your room, my dear,' she said peremptorily, as though to a servant.

She had put her hand on Cobie's arm, and was leading him away. Dinah watched them go. Violet's reproaches, crueller than ever, had stunned her. But not so much as his had done. She had fallen in love with him and what a dreadful mistake that had been. She had never known him. That hard face she had glimpsed once or twice was the true Cobie Grant—and when she had become troublesome to him he had not hesitated to rid himself of her, however much he hurt her in the doing.

All the way back to her room Dinah was crying inside.

If he had meant at the end to be so cruel, why had he been so kind to her in the beginning? Far better if he had ignored her as the other guests had done. But she would not let anything show, she would not. She would take what had happened as a valuable lesson, and would never trust anyone again. Nor would she fall in love again, since her first encounter with that emotion had been so disastrous.

She thought of his last words, 'Appearances often deceive.' Well, his appearance and his behaviour had deceived her—but never again.

Cobie excused himself after his brief walk with Violet—much shorter than his usual morning constitutional—was over. He smiled his charming smile, told her that he had received a large budget of business letters that morning and must see to them.

Violet was not sure that she believed him. She watched him go with a frown on her lovely face. He had been as harsh with Dinah as she had hoped that he might be, but she did not feel quite so pleased with him—or with herself—as she had expected.

She walked thoughtfully to her own rooms, unaware that, for once, Cobie had not been lying to her. He had received a large number of letters which he needed to deal with quickly, and on his way upstairs he knocked at the door of the room which his temporary secretary, Rogers, had been given and told him to report to his suite at once.

He was reading a letter when Rogers entered. It was from Ebenezer Bristow, addressed to Mr John Dilley, care of the shabby office in the City which he had hired in that name together with a clerk to run it for him. The letter told him that a suitable house—the one next door to 21 Sea Coal Street—had been bought, and was being furnished and staffed, ready for more abandoned and homeless children.

He also added that Miss Lizzie Steele appeared to be happy in her new home. Her stepfather had not tried to trace her and make trouble, and was probably lying low, fearful of the law.

'Take some dictation, Rogers, if you would,' he said abruptly, and rapidly answered Bristow's letter, before picking up another, and saying, 'I fear that our time here is up. I have a mining expert from the States waiting to see me in London, and news in from Paris which may necessitate me travelling there. Notify my valet that we shall be leaving tomorrow, and make all the travel arrangements necessary for the three of us.'

Rogers raised inward brows. He could have sworn that Apollo, for he was aware of Cobie's nickname, was nicely settled in at Moorings until the Season began, what with Lady K. being so available, and Lord K. apparently a congenial and obliging host ready to turn a blind eye on Lady K.'s interest in the handsome American.

He wondered what had happened to change his new employer's mind.

So did Hendrick Van Deusen, to say nothing of Violet, when Cobie told her his news.

'Oh, really, is this necessary?'

'My dear Violet, wild horses would not drag me away if there were any means by which I could stay. But, alas, I am needed elsewhere. I did not inherit wealth, Violet, I make my own, and dare not neglect my interests lest I end up a poor man unable to visit

Moorings. I shall be back in town for the beginning of the Season, you know. I don't intend to abandon you.'

No, it's only poor Dinah I'm abandoning. But God help *you* if I discover that you have persecuted her further because of my rapid departure, but God help *me*, I cannot endure to stay here longer and see a helpless child suffer because I was foolish enough to try to lighten her life a little.

Violet said nothing more, merely pouted. Mr Van Deusen by contrast, was blunt.

'Had enough of Lady K., have you?'

'Now, what on earth should make you think that?'

'Oh, I know you, Jumpin' Jake. Nothing you ever do is unconsidered. Jealous of the kid sister, is she?'

Mr Van Deusen had seen far too much. He wondered if others had. Mr Van Deusen now did a bit of mind-reading of his own.

'No, my friend, I don't think anyone else has noticed. They don't know you well enough. Reminds you of Belita, does she?'

The face Cobie offered him after he had said that was one which the Professor had not seen since his days as a desperado in Arizona Territory. They were alone: Cobie took him by the lapels of his expensive and beautiful coat and put his savage face into his friend's, his teeth and his temper showing, the rage almost on him.

'By God, Professor, don't take advantage of our friendship by reminding me of Belita. I can only live in peace when I forget what I unwittingly did to her. To satisfy you I'll say this: that, yes, the situation has its similarities, but speak of Belita or Dinah Freville to me again, and I won't answer for the consequences.'

Mr Van Deusen freed himself, and murmured wryly, 'Oh, you've not changed—except to become even less civilised. I'll give you a piece of advice, because I think that you may be about to try to set the world to rights in your own inimitable fashion. Don't fly too near the sun. You've cut a swathe in the States and here which many men might envy, but the over-reacher always goes too far. You fly high, but the higher you go, the greater the fall.'

It was the second warning! The Salvation Army Captain had given him the first. He remembered what Lewis Carroll had said in his riddling rhyme *The Hunting of the Snark*: 'What I tell you three times is true!'

Well, no one was more aware than Jacobus Grant of the dangers of hubris: that in every venture he had ever undertaken he had always followed a narrow path between triumphant success and dismal failure. He would not have it otherwise.

'Don't croak at me, Van Deusen,' he said dismissively. 'Your own life is hardly fit to be a sermon on the charms of cautious rectitude!'

'True, but I don't care for people, and for all your claims to be hard-hearted, Jake, you do. And that makes you vulnerable. Mind your back, is the best advice I can give you. And don't hesitate to call in the debt I owe you, that's all.'

Cobie knew that he had had no right to speak to Van Deusen as he had done. He owed him too much. Whatever his old friend said, the debt was his, Cobie's, rather than the other way round.

'You minded my back more than once,' he told Van Deusen, 'and for that, I shouldn't have reproached you as I just did.'

He said nothing more. Mr Van Deusen shrugged at the apology.

The person Cobie really wanted to apologise to was Dinah, and he thought so even more that evening, at dinner, when he saw her wan face and Violet's satisfied one.

Dinah had heard that he was leaving, and she thought that she was pleased, which was a lie, she acknowledged while she made herself ready for bed. She had thought that all her feelings for him had died, which was also untrue. She hated him now, and wanted him to be there, to be hated.

Only, that night, she had a dream, a strange one. She was wandering in the dark, alone and frightened. A moment earlier she had been a child again in the gardens at Borough Hall, holding Violet's hand, but the hand had been snatched away, and night had fallen.

Terror struck, hard. She was lost and knew no way back to safety. She began to run, calling out Violet's name, and only succeeded in ending up in a place which was so black that darkness itself became something palpable, a garment which she was wearing.

Just as everything seemed lost, someone said her name, and took her hand in his. She knew that it was a man's hand, it was so large and strong. It was warm, like the voice which said, 'Don't be afraid, Dinah, I'm with you.'

The darkness cleared for a moment, and it was Mr Grant—she wouldn't call him Cobie—holding her hand. She could hardly recognise him, he looked so strange and feral. He wore a beard, his hair was long and greasy, tied back from his face, and his clothes were dirty, and odd. Perhaps the oddest thing of all was his hairy filth, he being a man whom she had never seen as other than goldenly clean-shaven and spotless.

Wordless, she looked up into his wild face, asking him a question with her eyes. He nodded, said once again, 'Don't be afraid,' and then, 'Remember this, Dinah...appearances often deceive.'

She tried to snatch her hand out of his, but she couldn't, he held it so strongly, pulling her towards him with his right hand, repeating, 'Remember this, Dinah…appearances often deceive.' Immediately before both he and the dream disappeared she saw that he was holding a revolver in his left hand…

And then she was sitting up in her bed, crying out his name. She lay back against the pillows. The night was not very warm, but she was running in sweat. Her nightgown was drenched, and her hair was wet. She had been crying in her dream before he had appeared to take her hand and offer her comfort, and the tears were wet on her cheeks.

How shameful to dream of him! To wake up, calling his name when he had treated her so dreadfully. Pearson, now her maid, always said that dreams had meanings and were trying to tell you something, usually about the future. She had told Dinah that her aunt was a wise woman, and if she gave you a small pouch filled with herbs and put it under your pillow you would dream of your future husband, see his face.

Well, Dinah, hadn't put anything under her pillow, and she didn't want to dream of Mr Grant, but he had walked into her dream to repeat twice more what he had said to her the other day. Why was he dressed so oddly, nothing at all like the dandy he usually was: the dandy he had been on that dreadful morning, who always put her own drab outfit to shame?

Was the dream trying to tell her something? If you took what he said at face value he was simply saying that she had been mistaken in him, and his meaningless kindness. What else could he possibly mean?

The puzzle was too much for her. She lay down and tried to sleep, and then she sat up again, her heart thumping. Suppose she dreamed of him again?

The thought didn't prevent her from sleeping. When she did her dreams, if she had any, faded with the morning, as so many dreams do, except for the one which she had had of him offering her help and comfort.

It remained as clear and bright as though she had walked out of Moorings and turned a corner to find him there, a smile on his face, waiting for her.

Chapter Five

If Dinah Freville haunted Cobie, then the child he had
rescued from Madame Louise's haunted him, too. That,
and the decision he had made at Moorings before he
had left. Those who used Madame Louise's deserved to
be punished as well. Only then could he decide what to
do about Dinah.

He decided to visit Lizzie Steele at her new home,
claiming to be a relative of hers. He arrived in the late
evening, wearing an ill-cut suit, a cloth cap, and heavy
laced-up boots. Mrs Hedges, Lizzie's guardian, the wife
of the Superintendent Bristow had appointed to run the
refuge Cobie had paid for, stared at him when he told
her that he was Uncle Jack, Lizzie's mother's brother.
She said doubtfully, 'She's never spoken of you.'

'She wouldn't, I'm the black sheep, ain't I.' He was
so busy imitating Lizzie's own broad cockney that he
missed her appearing suddenly at the bottom of the
stairs. She was spotlessly clean. Her dark hair was
screwed back from her face, and she looked quite unlike
the waif he had rescued.

'Here's your Uncle Jack come to see you.'

'Uncle Jack?' Lizzie was doubtful, until she saw him.
Her face suddenly broke into a broad grin. Before she

could begin to speak and perhaps give him away, he said rapidly, 'Come on, our Lizzie. Remember old Jack, don't you?'

Lizzie was no fool. Life had taught her to dissemble. If well-spoken, flash Mr Dilley chose to look and speak like any masher who walked London's East End, that was his business. He had done Lizzie a good turn, and she wasn't going to let him down.

'Thought as how I'd come and see how you was doin'. Happy, are you?'

'Very happy,' she told him. 'Ain't you goin' to come in? Mrs Hedges'd give you some tea, I'm sure.'

'Haven't time,' he told her. 'Jus' came to see that you were happy and well. That stepdad not bothering you?'

Lizzie shook her head and put out a hand to touch his timidly. 'You'll come and see me again, I hope.'

'When I can,' he said. 'I've been away.'

He carried the memory of her face away with him. Also with him was her likeness to Dinah in the early days of their friendship when her face had lit up every time she saw him. He wondered where she was, and what that bitch, her sister Violet, was doing to her now. He had no real hope that she would stop persecuting Dinah once he was not there to see that she kept her worthless word.

He swore to himself, and carried on walking to his next rendezvous, which was with a possibly corrupt copper from Scotland Yard whom an enquiry agent had found for him. He had asked that a meeting be arranged, and the agent had set one up at a pub called the Jolly Watermen, which stood, not surprisingly, near to the Thames.

It was small, dark and full. His man was waiting for him in a corner seat, a glass of whisky before him. He was wearing a brown Derby hat and a crimson tie; a copy of the *Morning Post* lay on the table beside the whiskey—all there to identify him to Cobie. Cobie was now wearing a tartan muffler. He had rubbed ashes from a fire grate into his hair, and on to his hands and face. His dirty appearance was unremarkable and unremarked.

He sat down next to the copper, said, cheerfully, 'I'm Mr Horne, James Salmon's pal. You're…?'

'No one whose name you need know,' said the copper. He was a plain-clothes man, and his face, too, was unremarkable. He was as hard and dour as everyone else in the snug. 'What'll you have?'

'Same as you,' Cobie told him, and waited while it was fetched. He had dropped his cockney voice and spoke an undistinguished English.

The whisky arrived; he drank some of it. The copper, who still hadn't offered his name, watched him with a marked lack of interest. He said after Cobie had put his glass down, 'What is it you want, chum?'

'Information.' Cobie was in his brief business mode. 'And help.'

'I don't know whether I can offer you either.'

'If the cash was right…' Cobie let his discreet murmur die away.

'Depends.'

'We're talking in hundreds, perhaps thousands—all the way up to the top.'

'Pennies or pounds?'

Cobie gave a snort of laughter. 'Pounds, of course. The more information you give me, the more you do as I wish, the more you'll get. Mark me, though, tricked I won't be.'

'Wouldn't dream of it. So…?'

'Children—and the traffic in them. Specifically at Madame Louise's off the Haymarket. Who's behind it, and who is paying for protection. If they're paying you, I'll match their offer—then raise it.'

If the man before him was surprised, he wasn't showing it. 'So, you want to muscle in on the game?'

'Oh, no,' and Cobie's voice was suddenly sweet, more like the one which society knew. 'No, I want to break it, put those who run it where they belong—in a cell.'

He had surprised the copper now, who said, 'Listen to me, I don't—and won't—take their dirty money to help them run a dirty business, but I know those who do. Among them are powerful people—both those who offer and those who take. Who the devil are you to challenge them?'

'The devil,' Cobie said. 'I can't pursue every foul swine who organises this trade, every house where it happens, but I want to break this one—spectacularly. To do so, I need your help. I don't much care whether you have been on the take. Your guilt or innocence leaves me cold.'

'Then why worry? About the children, I mean.'

'Why should I tell you?'

He saw the other man shrug, and said, 'Right, I ran across them at their filthy game. I saved a ten-year-old girl from being violated by a man who in his public life has power, position—and respect. If I can close this one house, then I shall have done something, however small, to redress the balance a little in favour of the unfortunate, the illegitimate and the exploited. Satisfied?'

'Yes, Mr Horne. Which is, of course, not your name. What do you propose that we do?'

'I want you to tell me exactly how much money it would cost me to pay to have the house raided by the police whilst the filthy business is going on in the attics, so that the perpetrators of it are caught red-handed. In other words, I am prepared to pay as much as it takes.

Afterwards, your people can tell those whom they are selling down the river that the scandal had grown too great to be endured, and that an example had to be made. Above all, I want no one warned beforehand. You understand me.'

'You have no idea how much this would cost.'

'Oh, spare me. I have said that I will pay what it takes. Tell me what it might cost me, and then we'll talk about whether I can, or can't, afford it.'

The copper looked hard at the shabby character sitting opposite to him who talked so carelessly of tons of money. He named a price, a high one, and watched his man carefully.

Cobie nodded. 'I'll double it,' he said coolly, 'and half of it will be paid in golden sovereigns before the raid, and half in a bank draft drawn on the account of Mr Horne after it.'

'Oh, come,' said the other man with a smile. 'Why should I believe you?'

Cobie put his left hand in his pocket, and withdrew from it a heavy purse, 'There's a hundred golden sovs for you personally as a sweetener. You may also contact Coutts Bank and ask what lies in the account of Mr John Horne. I'll give you a piece of paper authorising you to do so.

'Coutts will pay out the sovereigns at my order to your messenger after I receive your answer, here, tomorrow night. I shall require you to give me details of the day and the time of the raid. Only then will I hand the first payment over. After that you'll not see me again. Don't be more of a fool than you need be and have me followed. I promise you I'll dispose of anyone who tries to track me down.'

The copper whistled. 'What about your agent? Suppose we put the frighteners on him?'

'He only knows me as Mr Horne, of an address which

I have now vacated. Don't waste your time on him. He's
a go-between—like you.'

'Suppose we take your money and run?'

'Then pray, Mr Policeman, pray. For I know you, and
you don't know me, and my revenge will be swift and
sure—and not only on you. Do we have a deal?'

'I think so. Be here at the same time tomorrow.'

'And no double-cross?'

'No, you offer too much for that.'

So, the deed was done. He had little doubt that he
had offered a sum so large that those in the police force
who had been protecting Madame Louise would snap
his hand off to get at the fortune he was offering. Ever
since he had rescued Lizzie and told Ebenezer Bristow
that those who had thrown her in Sir Ratcliffe's way
would pay—and then Sir Ratcliffe himself—he had
been planning to make them do exactly that.

He thought of the network of bolt-holes he had set
up round London to cover his tracks, and all the way
to the nearest of them where he had a change of clothes
waiting, he was on the *qui vive* for the man whom he
was sure would be following him. He finally made certain of him on Waterloo Bridge and walked off it for
about a hundred yards to wait for his quarry in an alley.
The hunted had become the hunter.

He heard footsteps coming along, the steps which had
followed him from the Jolly Watermen. He laughed to
himself, and when the man passed the end of the alley,
he caught him from behind with his tartan muffler in a
garrotter's grip. It took him only a moment to drag him
against the nearest wall.

He held his victim tightly to him, slipped a razor-
sharp knife from his pocket to hold it with his left hand
under his jaw, whispering, 'I told your superior not to
have me followed. I could cut your throat, but I prefer

to have you go back to tell him how I keep my word. Nod, if you can hear what I am saying.'

The gasping man nodded frantically.

'Good. Tell him I shall kill the next man he sends to follow me, and as an earnest of what I say, you may show him this.'

With one swift motion he cut off half of the man's mustachios, before releasing him, coughing and spluttering, black in the face and clutching his throat. Once he had straightened up, Cobie kicked his feet from under him, and then rolled him, semi-conscious, into the gutter, before running silently and swiftly away in the opposite direction from the one he had previously taken.

He had not the slightest intention of killing anyone—particularly a policeman—but it would not hurt to impress upon those with whom he was dealing that to cheat him might be dangerous.

Later, at the Jolly Watermen, Inspector Will Walker glared at his sergeant who stood before him, hangdog, his hand over his face.

'What happened?' he said at last.

'Somehow, he found out that I was following him, sir.'

Walker's glare grew nastier. It took in his sergeant's bruised face and neck, and the damage done to the mustachios of which Bates was so proud. Sour amusement grew inside him and found an outlet.

'I know that, Bates, you excuse for a man, you incompetent half-wit. Tell me what happened.'

Bates swallowed. 'He was waiting in an alley, just across Waterloo Bridge. He garrotted me—with his scarf, I think—and shoved me against the wall. I thought that my last moment had come.'

Walker remembered Mr Horne's unseasonable tartan muffler and his internal grin grew nastier.

'And?' he prompted. 'Spew it all out, Bates, or I'll finish Mr Horne's work for him. I'm sure there was more to it than that.'

'He put a knife to my throat and said he would have cut it, but that he wanted you to know he's a man of his word...'

'Many words,' cut in Walker wearily, 'and all of them nasty. Go on.'

'He said he'd kill the next man you sent after him, and then...'

'He cut your throat for you, you fat fool.'

'What!'

Bates put his hand to his bruised throat, and discovered the thin, shallow cut which Cobie had made, and which was dribbling a little blood.

'I need a doctor!' he moaned.

'You'd need a grave digger if I had my way. What else?'

Bates moaned silently to himself. He might have known that the swine in front of him would drag every last detail of his humiliation into the open. 'And then he tripped me, and kicked me into the gutter. I caught my head.'

He fingered the lump there gingerly. 'I think that I was out for a few moments, and when I recovered...'

'Don't tell me. He'd gone. Why am I surrounded by fools and ponces, Bates? Tell me that. Would you say that he was a gentleman?'

'A what? A gentleman!' Bates stared at Walker. Had frustration made him mad? 'He didn't sound or behave like one, sir.'

'That wasn't what I asked you, Bates. I asked you whether he was a gentleman because although he was dirty, wore filthy clothes, and his hands were particularly grimy, there was one thing he couldn't disguise. His nails. Beneath the dirt his hands and fingernails were in perfect condition. He either never does manual work—or hasn't done it for years. Does that tell you anything, Bates? Of course it doesn't. Oh, never mind. Do you think that he would kill, or was he just talking?'

Bates said, after thinking hard. 'Yes, I think that he could kill. There was something about him... On the other hand, he might just have been trying to frighten us—he could have finished me off then and there if he'd been so minded. There's another thing, sir. How did he know that I was following him?'

'Mmm.' Walker contemplated Bates's ruined face and neck. 'I think so, too—both as to killing, and to frightening. As to knowing that you were following him, you were probably as noisy as a herd of elephants on the loose!

'What I do know is that I want him found. I'm sure that Coutts won't tell us anything—other than that there is a Mr Horne, with money in his account—a lot of money.

'I don't like being made a monkey of, Bates, even if you're happy to dance round his barrel organ. I'd like to cut *his* throat.'

'Sir...' began Bates indignantly.

'Oh, shut up and go home, man,' Walker ground out wearily. 'You've done enough damage for one night. Get some iodine on that cut.'

He watched his wretched sergeant begin to walk away, then called to him, his voice as nasty as he could make it, 'Oh, and another thing, Bates.'

Bates turned, 'Sir?'

'For God's sake, shave off the rest of your moustache before you report to me in the morning. You look a right fool with half of it gone!'

Cobie couldn't sleep that night. In the small hours he rose and walked to the window to stare out at Hyde

Park in the darkness. Improbably, it wasn't what he had done that day, the risks he had taken, and was taking, which kept him awake, it was Dinah Freville.

How in the world had she arrived from nowhere to walk in his dreams? Her white reproachful face, that last day at Moorings, haunted him. Perhaps it was seeing Lizzie Steele which had done the damage. Or his tormenting of the unwary copper whom the wary copper had sent after him. He was prepared to suborn half the police at Scotland Yard to avenge Lizzie Steele and her fellow victims, but he had done nothing yet for Dinah.

Tomorrow. He would do something tomorrow. Find out, if he could, where she was, how she was being treated, and then decide what to do if Violet's cruelty was continuing. It was as though two images came together in his mind. One was of Lizzie when he had first seen her, the other was of Dinah's stricken face—and the second image was his fault, and no one else's.

The rage took him; he struck his clenched left fist hard into his open right hand, the only action he dared to allow himself. And after he had thought what to do about Dinah, he must see the wary copper, to find out whether his attempt at major corruption had succeeded.

'I can scarcely credit this, Walker. You are sure of what you are telling me?'

'Quite sure, sir. I visited Coutts first thing this morning. They would tell me nothing of Mr Horne—which was what I expected. What they did say after I showed them his note—and they had obviously been primed by him to say it—was that he had an account there. They would release the promised sovereigns to us, tomorrow, when he sent word to them to do so. The same went for the bank draft.'

'You have absolutely no idea who he is, or whom he might represent? I find it difficult to believe that a man who is offering us all this money is wandering around London dressed and speaking like a common thief.'

'No idea at all. I sent Bates after him, to try to trace where he came from, but he muffed it. Our man threatened to kill anyone we sent to trail him. By the way he treated Bates I'm inclined to believe that he might have meant what he said.'

The Commissioner shook his head in disbelief. 'I would have thought that you knew every major villain who lurked in London's sinks and alley ways. But you don't know him.'

'No, but I have a nark at Coutts. A junior clerk. He helps me a little in exchange for the ready. I spoke to him after I had seen the manager. He told me that, by chance, he had overheard something about the Horne account. He thought nothing of it at the time, but now that I was interested he would pass it on—in exchange for the usual, of course. Our man might be a Yankee, he said, that was all, no name.'

'A Yankee?' The Commissioner stared at Walker. 'Not what you described, surely?'

'I know. Frankly, I can't believe it. On the other hand, to be able to dispose of so many thousand pounds suggests a Yankee. More to the point—do we take up his offer?'

'Are you joking, Walker? Of course we'll accept his offer. They've been growing careless at Madame Louise's lately. I've an informer there who told me that some weeks ago one of the…younger…inhabitants escaped, no one quite knows how, and has disappeared completely. A bad business, that. Madame and her runner have grown complacent. Wouldn't hurt to raid them, let it be known that it was because they'd grown careless. We don't want a scandal, do we? It wouldn't be a bad idea to make an example of them—it might frighten the rest into being more careful. We kill two birds that way. Guard our own position and gain our man's massive…sweetener.'

Walker did not inform the Commissioner that he was using almost the same words about the raid as the mysterious Mr Horne.

Instead he said slowly, 'I think, from something he said, that it was our man who made off with the…younger inhabitant. No, I've no idea where she is. And we're no nearer to knowing who he is. So, I'm to meet him tonight, agree his terms, give him the date and time of the raid—shall I have someone try to follow him again?'

The Commissioner thought for a moment before he said, 'I think not. I'd like to know who he is, what game he's really playing, whether he's some Yankee come over to take charge of the underworld here—but for the moment we'll take it that he's telling you the truth. He's doing us a favour, Walker, apart from the money, I mean. No, we'll keep our eyes and ears open and try to identify him, but not tonight. By the by, I can't believe he's a gentleman.'

You mean I'll keep my eyes and ears open, thought Walker sardonically, you'll sit on your backside here and take the credit. And if you don't think he's a gentleman—or what passes for one—I do. I shall make it my business to investigate all the Yankees running round London society at the moment, for I swear I'll have him, if it takes me the next year. No man speaks to Will Walker—or treats his sergeant—as he did.'

He didn't tell the Commissioner of the hundred golden sovereigns which Mr Horne had handed over to him. It was no business of his.

Dinah hadn't seen Mr Grant since she had come to London with Violet for the Season. She had been introduced to many other men, none of whom showed the slightest interest in Lady K.'s younger sister, whose dowry, word had it, would be negligible. She couldn't ask Violet about him, and she had only found out by speaking to Mr Hendrick Van Deusen that he had been to Paris.

'On business,' Mr Van Deusen had said, 'but he should be back any day now.'

Dinah had changed her mind about Mr Van Deusen. He was kind to her, and since Violet had no interest in him, she had no interest in discouraging him from speaking to Dinah.

He was clever, too. He was interested in the things that she and Faa were. After Mr Grant had left Moorings, Van Deusen had played chess with her and talked about whether Gibbon had been accurate in his writings on the Roman Empire. He didn't seem to think that she was foolish to wish to go to Somerville.

One day, sitting in the grounds before the great seventeenth-century fountain which an ancestor of Lord Kenilworth's had brought back from Italy, she said to him abruptly, 'Have you known him long?'

Mr Van Deusen looked up from his book. It was written in German, and looked learned.

'Who?' he asked her, although he already knew whom she meant.

'Mr Grant? I know that you're a friend of his. A great friend. I watched you play chess with him once.'

'Yes. We're friends. I owe him a debt of gratitude.' He stopped—and didn't tell her what it was.

Dinah couldn't prevent herself from quizzing him further. No lady should ever ask anyone personal questions, but she suddenly wanted to know more about Mr Grant. More than that he was a handsome man who had first been kind to her and then cruel. He puzzled her— for she was sure that he was not what he seemed. She also knew, from what he had said in that odd chess game, that Mr Van Deusen was aware of that, too.

'How did you come to meet him?'

Mr Van Deusen considered her gravely for a moment. To tell her the truth was impossible for any number of reasons. Even to him, sitting beside Dinah in this civilised garden, the peace of the English countryside all about them, the truth seemed even more improbable than any fiction he might invent.

'By accident,' he said at last. 'I had lost my way. He put me on the right one,' which was, after a twisted fashion, the truth. 'He was very young at the time.'

He had a sudden flash of memory. He was back in New Mexico, on the edge of the desert. Cobie Grant, who was then twenty-year-old Jumpin' Jake Coburn, a six-shooter in his left hand, was standing over him where he lay wounded. Two men who had been trying to kill him from ambush lay dead in the rocks above them—and Mr Van Deusen's debt of gratitude for their deaths, and his salvation, was still not fully paid.

'Oh,' said Dinah doubtfully, trying to visualise the circumstances in which Mr Van Deusen, who seemed commendably capable of finding his way in any circumstances you might care to name, needed to be helped to do so.

'Was that when you played chess together?' and then, 'Have you ever managed to beat him when he cared to play properly?'

Mr Van Deusen told Dinah the whole truth this time. 'I don't think,' he said, 'that I could ever beat Mr Grant at anything he was playing properly. Nor could many others.'

'I thought so.' Dinah's tone was melancholy. 'He doesn't wish to let people know that, does he?'

She had surprised him, but he didn't let it show. 'No, but it's clever of you to have grasped that.'

That was the end. She had already broken too many rules of conduct and she could not bring herself to break any more by questioning him further. The whole conversation made her feel melancholy. For why should such a man as she dimly saw Mr Grant to be, feel any need to trouble himself about anyone as insignificant as Dinah Freville?

If she had surprised Hendrick Van Deusen a little by the nature of her questions and her response to his answers, it was his turn to surprise her a little by saying negligently, before he returned to his book, and she to hers, 'You know, Lady Dinah, that he's a man *you* can trust, although I can't honestly say that many others would be wise to do so.'

'Oh, no,' she said sadly, 'I don't think you're right there, Mr Van Deusen.' She was thinking of that dreadful three-sided conversation she had had with him and Violet on the day before he left Moorings.

'Nevertheless,' he said gently, and this time he did begin to read again, but Dinah's book lay neglected on her knee. She was too busy pondering about the unlikely turn of events which had made two such different people as firmly friendly as she was suddenly sure Mr Van Deusen and Mr Grant truly were, to take any interest in the events surrounding the murder of Elegabalus in the very long ago.

For the first time events in the here and now seemed much more important than those in the lost past. Particularly those events which surrounded that elusive and enigmatic scoundrel Mr Jacobus Grant—for some reason her talk with Mr Van Deusen had made her sure that that was exactly what he was!

Mr Van Deusen was nearly as elusive as his friend. She was thinking this while she prepared to go to a reception at Harrendene House where she knew that Mr

Grant was due to be present, because Violet had told her so.

She had also said, pinching Dinah's arm to make sure that she was attending, 'And don't make a fool of yourself over him, mind. Remember what that got you, last time.'

Dinah had nodded mutely, and now, putting on her childish dress, which wouldn't attract any man—let alone him—for Violet always chose dowdy things for her to wear, she wondered what she would say to him, if he chose to speak to her, that was. Which wasn't likely.

When she did see him, however, in Harrendene House's huge ballroom, she didn't want to speak to him, for the anguish which she had felt so strongly at their last meeting swept over her once again. It was really hate that she felt for him, she told herself, untruthfully.

Somehow it made it worse that, as usual, he looked so absolutely splendid in evening dress. The black and white of it suited him to perfection. By her behaviour Violet thought so, too. The only thing to do was find a dark corner to sit in, surrounded by the companions of other young girls who, unlike Violet, were prepared to push the charms of their charges at the eligible young men who made up so many of those present.

What a pity we don't live in the time of Henry VIII, before the Reformation, Dinah thought morosely, and then Violet could shut me away in a nunnery and forget about me. Not that I should have liked that. But I might as well be in a nunnery for all the notice that Mr Grant, or anyone else, takes of me.

Unknowingly, she wronged him. Cobie had seen Violet and her husband enter, Dinah walking a little behind them, and had been shocked by her appearance. Her dress was so unsuitable; it hid what few charms she possessed, and being designed to make her look younger than she was, emphasised her coltishness even more.

He knew why she was dressed so badly, and looked as she did, quite ill, her face white, her eyes enormous, with pale blue shadows under them, and her manner so defeated. It was the bitch-goddess Violet Kenilworth at her unsavoury work. All the world knew of the great disparity of age between herself and Dinah, and to reduce the toll of her own years she was making Dinah look more babyish than she was—and extinguishing her in the process.

While Cobie laughed and talked to Violet who, in her usual proprietory fashion, monopolised him, he watched Dinah, hidden in her corner. He registered the sad sag of her head, the weary droop of her shoulders, the fact that she sat alone, and that Violet made no effort to find her partners.

It was plain that the plan which he had been considering for several days, 'the matter of Dinah Freville' he had dubbed it, needed to be put into operation once tonight's business was over. To have too many irons in the fire at the same time was not a good thing.

Arthur Winthrop came over to ask a favour of him: Susanna was one of a party of women who were entertaining the Princess of Wales. The Prince was already installed in a salon off the ballroom, surrounded by his courtiers, friends and assorted toadies who accompanied him everywhere.

'Ah, Cobie. I wonder if you would do me a kindness? You seem a little at a loose end tonight.'

He means that Violet isn't paying me too much attention tonight because she doesn't want to arouse the Prince's jealousy, but never mind.

'Yes, Arthur, what can I do for you?'

Arthur answered him looking surprisingly coy for a fifty-year-old man. 'It's not very lively here tonight, is it? A group of us thought of looking for better entertainment. Thing is, could you take Susanna home for me? Shouldn't like to neglect her. I've told her that business calls me away, and that you'll look after her.'

Time to think on one's feet and quickly, too. The little entertainment would, of course, be at Madame Louise's and on this night of all nights would not be little at all! It was imperative that Arthur, the American Envoy, should not be caught in the police raid there, due to take place shortly after midnight.

Not only must Susanna never know what villainies her husband had been getting up to, but he also had to consider what the revelation that the American Envoy had been caught in the company of children at a notorious night house would do in the way of scandalous damage to Anglo-American relations!

''Fraid not,' he said, and his smile had never been more innocent. 'I was coming along to ask you to make up a four at whist with myself, Van Deusen, and one of his friends, Bellenger Hodson, a crony of the President's who most particularly wants to meet you. Knowing my relationship to you, Van Deusen relied on me to arrange it tonight. Short notice, Arthur, but I know you won't let me down. Duty always comes first with you.'

He saw Arthur hesitate, and thought wryly, if he refuses, then, by God, I shall not hesitate to blackmail him, and threaten to tell Susanna the truth about his perversions if he doesn't do what I ask of him. He'll love me even less after that—but I can't tell him the truth about the raid, too risky.

'Oh, very well.' Arthur was sulky. 'I'll tell Gascoigne and the others that I'll have to give it a miss tonight. Duty and all that, must come first. I never thought I'd hear you using the word.'

'Never thought I'd use it myself.'

Cobie, having got his way, was cheerful. 'You do that, Arthur, and I'll tell Van Deusen and Hodson the rubber is on.' He couldn't help adding, 'I promise you, you won't regret it!'

Mr Van Deusen stared at him and groaned when Cobie, having cornered him, hissed in his ear, 'For the friendship you bear me, Professor, agree to do what I ask, and tell Hodson to say nothing which would contradict the lies I've just served up to Winthrop.'

'Oh, Jake, what dubious tricks are you up to now, that you need to ask me to play whist with a stuffed shirt and a redneck from the backwoods! You can have Hodson for a partner, I refuse to sacrifice myself to your whims completely!'

Cobie's smile had never been sweeter. 'You'll regret that, Professor, but you're on. Be in the blue drawing room in ten minutes, and dodge the Prince while you're at it. I want nothing to stop me from well and truly cornering my worthy brother-in-law!'

The game was as boring as Mr Van Deusen had feared it would be, and Cobie kept his promise that he would regret refusing to have Bellenger Hodson as a partner. He and Hodson ran out consistent winners, with Arthur inwardly moaning that he had lost his fun in order to be fleeced by his brother-in-law and a hick from the sticks who had happened to make a large fortune with which he proposed to assist Arthur's party, and must therefore be kept happy.

About half-past one, the evening, which had been as dull as such grand affairs usually were, became less so. One of the Prince's bodyguard who had been on duty outside, came in and demanded to see his Royal master—a matter of some urgency, he said.

A little later the whole company was abuzz. Hodson, who was finding whist small beer after poker, waved his cigar at his companions, and asked, 'What's up, gents?'

Cobie, who knew perfectly well what was causing all the excitement, shook his head. 'No idea, Hodson. The Prince is ready to go, perhaps?'

Hodson, who was watching a small group of highly connected gentlemen talking excitedly together, corrected him. 'Oh, no, Grant, something is definitely up.'

He laid his cigar down, and called over to the group, his mid-west accent particularly strong, 'Say, gents, what the hell's going on? Let us in on the secret, eh!'

Annoyance at being accosted by someone no one knew, was succeeded by the usual desire to spread bad news. Rainey came over to salute Cobie, Arthur Winthrop and Van Deusen, whom he knew, and to stare at Hodson, whom he didn't.

'Haven't you heard? The police raided Madame Louise's...establishment off the Haymarket not long ago. They netted several of Tum Tum's friends who were here earlier, a High Court judge, a leading actor, and what's worse, they found in the attics a number of small girls and boys being held prisoner...'

He stopped, needing to say no more.

Arthur Winthrop's face was a picture. He looked across at Cobie, who was staring interestedly at the ceiling which depicted the young Iphigenia being sacrificed, with Jupiter hovering on a thunder cloud, about thirty feet above her, a lightning bolt in his hand. Quite suitable under the circumstances, he thought.

'A High Court judge?' Arthur asked dazedly. 'Was that Gascoigne to whom I was speaking earlier?'

Rainey nodded. 'He was making up a party to go there, I do know. I refused. Madame's been too ripe for me lately.'

This wasn't the real reason, which was, as Cobie already knew, that Rainey could no longer afford Madame's prices.

'Thank God you asked me to play this rubber with you,' said Arthur fervently to his half-brother-in-law. He had never liked him so much. Meantime Bellenger Hodson treated M'lord Rainsborough—as he called him—and the rest to a pious sermon on the decadence of the aristocracy and judiciary in Britain while Mr Van Deusen looked across the table at Cobie. His friend now wore an expression so innocent that he could have stood in for Saint Anthony being tempted in a medieval painting, and resisting it nobly.

Arthur, still inwardly congratulating himself on his narrow escape, left the game to find others to exclaim with him about the exciting news.

'You knew, you slimy devil, you knew,' the Professor hissed at Cobie in return for Cobie's hissing earlier. 'How the devil did *you* know?'

'I?' Cobie's expression grew even more saintly, if that were possible. 'How should I know of such a thing? I've spent the whole evening with you, quietly minding my own business...'

'Oh, yes, and what about the evenings you've spent not minding your own business, but quietly minding other people's? You went out of your way to stop Winthrop from going to Madame's tonight. I know you did, he complained about it to me between rubbers. I hope he realises that he, and the President and Congress, owe you a debt of gratitude for saving them all from a nasty scandal. Who did you bribe, what did it cost you—and what's more, why did you do it?'

'Really, Hendrick, you credit me with more than I deserve...'

'Oh, no, Jake, never that. You deserve all and more that I credit you with. Who and what were you after? No, don't tell me, I don't want to know. Then I don't need to lie when the police come after you. They're not like ours at home, you know. They're not so corrupt here.'

'Oh, Hendrick, how wrong you are. They're exactly like ours at home. Which isn't to say that I admit to anything. As to being after anyone...' He shrugged.

What he really wanted to know was whether Sir Ratcliffe had been caught in the net. If he had, it would save him from pursuing the man further. He rather thought not. Such a tit-bit would have been round the company in no time.

Dinah, sitting in her corner, was aware that something had happened, something exciting, and certainly scandalous. But, of course, no one would tell her what it was. When she asked Violet why everyone was so up in the air, her sister replied dismissively, 'Nothing for little girls to know about. Fetch your cloak from the cloakroom and meet me in the hall. Kenilworth wants to go home.'

She was walking to the cloakroom when she came across Mr Van Deusen and Mr Grant talking together. Mr Van Deusen was laughing in an angry kind of way. There was nothing that she could do to avoid acknowledging them.

They saw her, and stopped their urgent discourse—how did she know it was urgent? but she did—and they bowed to her, as one.

She couldn't help herself, the words flew out.

She said to Mr Van Deusen, ignoring Mr Grant who was looking at her rather keenly—was her petticoat showing?—'Oh, Mr Van Deusen, pray tell me why is everyone in such a pother suddenly—if you feel able to, that is. Has the Prince been taken ill?'

It was Mr Grant who answered her, as smoothly as though they had not parted such dreadful enemies. 'Well, the news might have distressed him, but it is not that, Lady Dinah. I think that you are old enough to know that some distinguished personages were caught by the police in—what shall we say?—compromising circumstances.'

Dinah was not so young and innocent that she didn't get Mr Grant's drift.

She answered him immediately, while trying to forget the last, dreadful, occasion on which he had spoken to her for, if she were to allow herself to remember it, she could not have spoken to him at all.

Like Mr Van Deusen, she could not help noticing how singularly innocent Mr Grant looked tonight, like a saint in a fresco in a church. She didn't comment on that, of course, although she would have liked to have done.

Instead, she said, rather dismissively, 'Oh, Mr Grant, I'm happy to learn that you now consider me elderly enough not to have my reputation ruined by being told such a thing by a gentleman so much older than I am. You recently told me that appearances often deceive—something which tonight's events seem to prove. They also confirm that you are, as usual, accurate in your judgements—or, perhaps I ought to add, some of them.'

Mr Van Deusen laughed aloud. Mr Grant was more discreet, although his grin was a broad one.

He bowed again. 'So happy to learn, Lady Dinah, that you treasure every word I say so carefully. I wish that I could say the same of all my friends.'

Here was her opportunity, and Dinah took it. She bowed back at him, walked by him, and turned just before she entered the ante-room, to say, 'You are far from being my friend, Mr Grant, and I don't so much treasure your words as use them to make darts of my own.'

She might have guessed that nothing anyone could say to him would ever put him out of countenance.

He bowed again, put his hand on his heart, and said, '*Touché*, Lady Dinah. I can only suggest that you do what I always do, and sharpen your darts before you use them again—never waste anything being my motto.'

What could she do but ignore him, take her cloak from the maidservant, and bow again when she passed them.

Behind her, Mr Van Deusen said, almost beneath his breath, 'By God, Cobie, my friend, that girl's a treasure. Now, if she only had the looks to match her brains...'

The stare Cobie gave him was a freezing one, and for once, it froze Van Deusen. 'Oh, but she will, Professor, she will. Just you wait and see.'

Chapter Six

For a few days all London society found nothing else to talk about but the police raid on Madame Louise's night house and the big fishes who had been netted there. Oh, not openly, in front of the children as it were, but behind female hands and in the clubs where only men gathered.

Pearson smuggled in one of the low newspapers which Dinah was never allowed to see, and there she had read what was openly written and of which Mr Grant had told her, oh, so discreetly.

The Commissioner found himself explaining his actions to a small grey man who was a very important person indeed.

'Oh, no,' he said earnestly, looking the man in the eye as candidly as he could. 'No, this is not a general move against all such houses. It was necessary because Madame and her people had become indiscreet. You wouldn't want a scandal, surely. A child escaped—think of that! Think of what would have happened if it had become openly known. Besides, it keeps the others in order.'

Naturally he said nothing about dubious characters

who handed over a fortune as though it were marbles to be played with in the street.

The grey man said something in the order of, 'I trust that you remembered my wish that if such action were necessary then a few discreet warnings—in certain quarters—might have been in order.'

The Commissioner looked out of the window, and said smoothly, 'I am sure that you understand that some warnings were given—otherwise the scandal would have been...unsupportable—the government might have fallen...'

He let his voice trail off, smiling brightly at his interlocutor...who looked away.

He didn't say that Sir Ratcliffe Heneage, that minor minister, and Madame's most faithful customer, had been one of the few who had come home to find a letter marked URGENT and PRIVATE AND CONFIDENTIAL on his desk, and had opened it to find a characterless copperplate message inside for him.

'It would be as well to avoid visiting a certain pleasant rendezvous this week. Discretion is the better part of valour.'

The coded message, previously agreed, had told Sir Ratcliffe all that he needed to know. He made himself particularly visible at all the places he had visited for the next few days, giving a little dinner party for a few highly placed friends on the night of the Harrendene dance and reception. He displayed suitable shock when the news broke, shaking his head and deploring the loose habits of those who should know better.

Downstairs, Walker and Bates were sweating over a *portrait parlé* of Mr Horne. It was a French method of identifying a criminal by carefully recording all of his major physical characteristics, which the Yard had recently begun to employ.

Walker had written it out on the morning after their

second meeting. Told by the Commissioner to rattle his hocks and find the mysterious Mr Horne at the double, Walker was trying to improve it, racking his brains to remember anything significant.

Bates, called in to help—'Surely, you can remember something, Bates, which might give us a handle'—said slowly, smiting his forehead, 'Of course, he was left-handed!'

Walker snarled at him, 'Now, a week later, you tell me that! Are you sure, Bates, or are your wits wandering again?'

Eyes closed, Bates said slowly, 'Yes. He held me with his right hand and arm while he used the knife with his left hand. I knew there was something odd about him.'

'Being left-handed isn't all that odd, Bates, but it does tell us something—which is a sight better than nothing.'

Walker tried to recall Mr Horne, and he, too, remembered that left hand snaking into his tattered coat to pull out a purse full of sovereigns. He realised, mournfully, that his own cupidity had been so great that he hadn't done his job properly.

Left-handed, he wrote, then, 'His hair, Bates? See anything of his hair?'

'Saw nothing of anything, guv, you know that.' Disrespectfully he added, 'Didn't see much yourself, did you?'

'I saw a pair of bright blue eyes—which isn't much help, I know, seeing how many are blue-eyed—but better than nothing, Bates, like him being left-handed, better than nothing.'

Cobie Grant, in the privacy of his room, juggling before a mirror, keeping three, then four, small balls in the air at once, a trick no one knew that he could per-

form—other than Hendrick Van Deusen, that was—
could have told Walker differently. His ambidexterity
was something he rarely displayed publicly, other than
to confuse on certain special occasions, tricking the authorities being one.

He had seen Dinah twice more in the fortnight since
the raid and each time he had merely bowed in her
direction. She had responded so coolly that her reply
was almost the equivalent of a snub. What she didn't
know was that 'the matter of Dinah Freville' was now
in train…very much so…

Earlier that week, Professor Louis Fabian, seated in
his pleasant room in his lodgings at Balliol, a room
which looked out over the Quad, had been told by the
porter that he had an unexpected visitor, a man of whom
he had never heard.

'A Mr Jacobus Grant, sir, says that he wishes to see
you immediately on an urgent personal matter.'

Professor Fabian sighed. He had been looking forward to a pleasant morning examining a rare codex, and
the last thing he needed was small talk with a stranger.
He couldn't imagine what he could have to say on personal matters to a man of whom he had never heard.

Nevertheless, a certain curiosity piqued him, and he
agreed to see Mr Grant, if only to find out what he
wanted. Some useless heir, perhaps, who needed to be
coached before being let loose among Oxford's dreaming spires. Professor Fabian was unique in being mor-
dantly cynical about certain aspects of his position as
one of the more learned dons at Oxford's most prestigious college.

The man who entered his pleasantly cluttered study,
where a fire burned in the grate even though this day
in early May was not cold, was not at all what he expected. His classical learning had Professor Fabian asking himself whether Mr Jacobus Grant more resembled

Antinous or Apollo, brought up to date and wearing clothes of the most exquisite cut—clothes which did nothing to hide the athletic perfection of his body. He appeared to be in his late twenties.

His voice was beautiful, too, as well as his manners. He thanked Professor Fabian for consenting to see him at such short notice, and refused a chair.

'For what I have to say, sir, I prefer to stand,' he said coolly, which had Professor Fabian standing as well, but never mind.

For his part, Cobie thought that Professor Fabian was everything which he might have expected of Dinah's father. He was a handsome, middle-aged man who had once been a handsome young one. He had suspected that Dinah took after him, not the Frevilles: another insult on top of her birth, there to annoy them, and he had been right in his suspicion. Professor Fabian confirmed Cobie's belief that a little more time, plus some loving treatment, might result in Dinah becoming a rarer beauty than her sister.

He began without preamble.

'You do not know me, sir, but I hope that I may remedy that situation shortly. Briefly and bluntly, I have come to ask you to give me permission to marry your daughter, Lady Dinah Freville. Before you reply, I ought perhaps to inform you that I am well able to support her. I am a citizen of the United States of America, my foster-father is Mr John Dilhorne of Dilhorne and Rutherfurd, one of my country's premier corporations. He is the brother of Sir Alan Dilhorne, of whom I am sure you have heard—he has been a member of the Cabinet for many years. My own fortune is greater than that of either of them.'

Louis Fabian said, taken aback for once, 'Why ask me, sir? I have no legal standing where Lady Dinah

Freville is concerned,' and he leaned ever so faintly on
the word Freville.

'Oh,' Cobie said, almost carelessly, 'I understand that
you are her true father. I have no wish to approach
either Lady Kenilworth, or her brother, who is her
guardian, in the normal way, for they would each, for
their own selfish reasons, refuse to allow me to marry
her. If I were to propose to Lady Dinah as I ought, she,
too, would refuse me. She dislikes me very much, for
reasons which I will shortly explain. I wish to marry
her because I need a wife, and because I respect her as
a person and as an intellect, and because I believe that
we could make one another happy.

'That being so, I fear that I must resort to an under-
hand trick to win her. I am determined to do so for her
sake as well as mine. Her position in her sister's house-
hold is intolerable, and anyone her sister is likely to
arrange for her to marry will almost certainly not only
be unsuitable, but likely to make her life even more
grossly unhappy than it already is.

'I am sure that, as her father, you would not wish her
to be doomed to the kind of misery to which she is at
present condemned.'

He paused, and smiled his winning smile.

Professor Fabian said slowly, 'You have not mentioned the word love, sir. Do you love my daughter?'

Cobie raised his eyebrows after a fashion which Dinah would have recognised.

'Love, sir? What has that to do with marriage? You,
of all people, should understand that. No, I respect your
daughter, I wish to rescue her, and would do my best
to make her happy once we were married. If you agree,
I will tell you what I propose to do. I hope that you are
sufficient of a realist to understand why I am acting in
this way. Coercion is not pretty, but is sometimes the

only way to force the resolution of an intolerable situation.

'I am here because I need some moral support from a man whom my investigators inform me is not only of a towering intellect, but is known for his downright common sense—something rare in the academic world, as I am sure you are aware.'

Louis Fabian had rarely been so surprised by anything he had read or heard that he was deprived of speech—but he was now. He was silent for some moments, looking out of the window at the view of the quadrangle across which two of his colleagues were walking, heads bent in earnest conversation, black gowns flying out behind them, before he answered his unusual visitor.

'You intrigue me, sir. Either you are the most consummate scoundrel, or the most remarkable philanthropist, I have ever met. Certainly your pragmatism is great enough to astonish even myself! Pray continue. I thought that this was going to be yet another predictably dull morning—I see that I was mistaken!'

'Oh, splendid, sir.' Cobie's smile was now warm, as well as winning. 'I can see that we shall deal well together—particularly if you accept me as a scoundrel! Now, allow me to tell you what I propose.'

'Only after you have taken a chair, Mr Grant, and a glass of some rather good sherry. It is not every day that a man is asked for the hand in marriage of the daughter whom he may not acknowledge—and after such an intriguing fashion, too.'

'Willingly, sir.' Cobie accepted both the offered chair and the sherry before beginning to unfold his plan of campaign to the sardonic man before him.

Louis Fabian was laughing when he had finished. 'And you are sure that you can bring this off?'

'Oh, absolutely, sir. Quite sure. The beauty of it is that everyone benefits in the end, particularly me.'

'Yes, of course. Particularly you. And you guarantee to be kind to Dinah, whom I dearly love, and you are right to respect her. She wished to go to Somerville, but of course, they wouldn't allow any such thing. If you marry her, she still loses that, but she gains her freedom from the pack of them—which is all I care about.'

He put down his glass of sherry, leaned forward and said gravely, 'I am human enough to wish you to succeed if only to pay them back for what they did to Charlotte and me nineteen years ago. The late Lord Rainsborough agreed to divorce her so that we might marry when he found that she was expecting my child. I was prepared to throw up my academic career, seek another, I had a little money, enough to keep us in modest comfort.

'He tricked us. I left the Hall, as he asked, and then Rainsborough refused the divorce, and put poor Charlotte out to grass. I wanted her to leave him, live with me, but she said no, he had promised to ruin me if she came to me, and she couldn't have that on her conscience. I, God forgive me, let her persuade me to agree. It was not she and I who suffered, but poor Dinah who became the scapegoat for our sin.

'Now you say that you will rescue her, care for her, and do it in a fashion which humiliates them. Yes, I agree, and you will stay for lunch to allow me to become acquainted with my daughter's future husband.'

It had all gone better than Cobie had dared to have hoped, and now he could go back to London and win Dinah with her father's blessing.

After his early weeks in London, and then his stay at Moorings it was an understood thing in London society

that Cobie Grant, whatever else, was an easy mark so
far as playing cards was concerned.

In the week after he had met Louis Fabian and in
doing so had found a new friend, he did particularly
badly, both at the clubs where gambling took place, and
in those Mayfair drawing rooms where the men retired
to amuse themselves after their wives had gone to bed.

One person who did particularly well out of him was
Gerald Rainsborough, although Sir Ratcliffe Heneage
ran him a close second. So well did Rainey do that he
thought that he might even be able to recoup the Freville family fortunes by fleecing the rich Yankee who
seemed so happy to lose his money to him.

'Luck's a variable mistress,' Cobie moaned late one
night, paying over his dues to Rainey and Sir Ratcliffe,
'and the devil's in the cards for me these days.'

'Can't have it every way, Grant,' offered Rainey,
kindly and a trifle patronisingly, 'and your luck in other
quarters has been astonishingly good, or so I understand.'

He winked meaningfully at Sir Ratcliffe who, having
failed with Violet Kenilworth, was happy to see that the
man who had not was paying for it in another fashion.
He was given to saying, 'Grant ought to remember that
lucky at cards, unlucky in love, and vice versa. At the
rate he's going, he'll make a rich man out of Rainey.'

'Paying for Violet K. after another fashion,' was yet
another unkind *bon mot* he started on its way around
society.

Rainey, light of head as well as light of heart, decided
that next time he played Grant he would go for broke,
and make his fortune for good and all. It was obvious
where the skill—and the luck—lay, and it was not with
Apollo.

Cobie, who had been using Sir Ratcliffe's marked
cards and other dubious ploys to lose money instead of

win it, had decided on quite another conclusion for Rainey's little drama. He had, he thought, paid out enough rope and it was time to pull it in. Marked down as a fool at cards who was unlucky into the bargain, it would be easy to lead Rainey so far down the garden path that he would finally lose his way in the dark which it led to.

His mark had grown careless, and now, after a chaste little dinner party given by Sir Ratcliffe who was abjuring all such establishments as Madame's these days—it was too risky to visit them until the latest brouhaha had died down—Rainey, half cut and confident, had decided to go for Apollo's jugular, with Sir Ratcliffe's help.

'Let's up the stakes we put into the pot,' he demanded when the cards were set out for poker, and the port was arranged alongside them. He named a figure which had Cobie raising internal eyebrows and deciding that, yes, tonight was the night of which he had spoken to Louis Fabian.

He appeared to drink heavily, with the accent on appeared, but remained virtually sober, coldly aware of all that was going on around him. His belief that he could use Sir Ratcliffe's cheating on his own behalf grew when the evening turned into early morning, and he allowed his luck to begin to change. When he drunkenly insisted that they raise the stakes in the pot yet again, he had Rainey, who saw financial salvation smiling at him, enthusiastically agreeing.

It didn't take long to break Rainey's heart and put another dent in Sir Ratcliffe's fortune. The other players in the game exclaimed at his good luck, which had, he announced tipsily, changed after weeks of non-success. They stayed on to stare when Cobie turned his cards over to win yet again—thanks to his ability to use Sir Ratcliffe's marked ones.

Cobie had had difficulty in refraining from telling Sir Ratcliffe that if he had carried out his clumsy cheating in a saloon in Arizona Territory he would have taken great pleasure in calling him out and shooting him down. Instead he had flattered the man he intended first to fleece at cards, and then to ruin socially, and was at present using to break Dinah's brother.

Rainey drank more and more as he lost more and more. Cobie's only fear was that he would be under the table before he could administer the *coup de grâce*, which he did at four in the morning with the sun shining through the curtains and the dawn chorus sounding outside.

Worse, Rainey had lost everything which he had taken from Cobie in over two months, and much more besides. He was ruined and knew it. But the luck must surely turn again—and soon.

After the damned Yankee had begun to gather up the cards and the pile of Rainey's IOUs, announcing 'I've had enough, old fellow, call it a night, I mean, of course, a day,' Rainey leaned forward to say,

'Damn you, Grant. You've won all night, your streak of luck can't last forever, and I'll prove it.'

Cobie's tipsy smile grew. 'How?' he said pleasantly, and then, 'I'm tired, old fellow, I meant it when I said let's call it a day.' He wanted no man to say that he had pushed Rainey into the final act of folly which he saw coming as surely as the milk cart would arrive that morning at Sir Ratcliffe's kitchen doorway.

'One more hand, jus' one more hand. Give a fellow a chance to win back his losses, Grant.'

Cobie appeared to ponder, then finally lifted his head to say, 'True, Rainey, true, but I'm not taking any more of your IOUs, mind, if you lose.'

His victim leaned back, satisfied. 'Shan't need to

write any more, Grant. My turn now, you'll see. Your turn to deal, isn't it?'

'Under the circumstances, since we were the only two left in at the end of the last hand, and I don't want to take any advantage of that, I propose that we all cut the cards for the honour of dealing, Rainey, how about that?'

Murmurs of approval at this sporting gesture greeted Cobie's words. Rainey graciously agreed. They cut, and Rainey, the last to do so, to his delight won, which wasn't surprising, Cobie thought, having rearranged the cards to Rainey's advantage.

He did the same, laughing to himself when they began to play at the sight of Rainey's artless and visible pleasure at the hand he had given him. Who wouldn't be pleased if they had been dealt a Running Flush, King High—a hand which was an almost certain winner? The end was as predictable as the beginning had been.

The other players, Sir Ratcliffe included, fell out one by one. His face one grin Rainey, having continually raised the stakes, finally called on Cobie to show his cards, his last contribution to the pot being a piece of paper on which, his money having run out, he had promised to forfeit Borough Hall and the estate surrounding it if he lost—which he was certain he wouldn't.

Cobie turned his cards over, to reveal that he held a Royal Flush, Ace High, the only hand which could beat Rainey's. Rainey stared at them as though if he did so they would dissolve into a more suitable combination.

'I've lost,' he whispered.

Cobie gave a giant yawn.

'So it would seem. My luck held to the end tonight. All my bluffing came off for once.'

Had he been speaking the truth he would have said that the hardest thing he had done since he had arrived in England had been to lose so consistently when winning would have been so much easier. Until this evening he had played honestly and with the utmost care to avoid any chance of being accused of cheating when the time came for him to win.

Like his unacknowledged uncle Alan, and his grandfather Tom, whom he so greatly resembled, Cobie had no compunction over cheating cheaters, and using their cheating to his own advantage, as he had just succeeded in doing. If Dinah were to be saved, then foolish Rainey must be his victim as well as the guilty Sir Ratcliffe—whose losses had also been huge. Also, like Rainey, he had no chance of recouping them.

He scooped up Rainey's paper. Rainey, his face now ashen, said, 'I'm ruined, Grant. You've ruined me. What the hell am I going to do now? All that paper—I can't pay any of it. And the Hall. It's our home, been in the family for generations. What the hell am I going to do now?'

The last phrase became a litany which he continued to repeat.

Cobie looked at his winnings and appeared to think deeply. He asked Sir Ratcliffe, 'Is there anywhere that Rainey and I can be alone? We ought to settle this before I leave. Better so.'

Sir Ratcliffe agreed. The news would be all around London by the next evening, and he was not sure how happy he was that Rainey had been ruined in his drawing room, and by a Yankee who had been losing for weeks.

'My study's next door. Use that.'

'Right. Is that agreeable to you, Rainey?'

'Anything. Anything's agreeable. No, I mean nothing is. But yes. I'll talk to you, though what good that will do, I don't know.'

'Privately.' Cobie was firm and half-pushed Rainey,

whose losses had temporarily sobered him, into Sir Rat-cliffe's study.

Once they were alone, Rainey said feverishly, 'Damn it, Grant. I can't pay you any of that—the money-lenders have given me up—and if you take the Hall, I've nothing left. I must have been mad. Oh, God, it's a debt of honour and I can't renege.'

'Nor would I ask you to.'

Cobie was brisk, sweet reasonableness rode on his shoulders. 'I've no wish to break you, Rainey, far from it. I am well aware that even before tonight ruin and bankruptcy stared you in the face. I can only suppose that that is why you gambled so wildly in an attempt to recoup your losses. What I'd like to do is to offer you a permanent way out of your troubles. Will you listen to me?'

'Anything, Grant, anything. Though what *you* can have to propose to me, I can't imagine.'

'No? Take a seat, and I'll tell you,' which he proceeded to do, at some length. Rainey sat there, nodding agreement at the end of each sentence. Finally he said fervently, 'If that's what you want, Grant, then I'll guarantee you that that's what I'll do, or my name isn't Gerald Freville!'

There was a conservatory at the back of the Kenil-worths' home in Piccadilly and Dinah had been helping the gardener to plant out seedlings, an occupation which Violet only grumblingly allowed.

She had heard Rainey arrive some time earlier, and was pleased to avoid him. He never seemed happy about her these days. Like Violet, he considered her a millstone around the family's neck. She retied the strings of her brown Holland apron which had worked loose, and tugged back an errant strand of hair. She wished that she could look for once as spectacularly neat and tidy as Violet always did.

The Kenilworths' butler put his head around the glass door. 'Your brother would like to see you in his Lordship's study, Lady Dinah. At once, he said.'

See Rainey at once! Here! What in the world could he think that she had done now? She almost ran down the corridor to find Rainey sitting at Lord Kenilworth's desk—and where was he?—looking serious, quite a departure for him, she thought unkindly.

What did surprise her was that Violet was present, even more magnificently dressed than usual, and with an expression on her face which could only be interpreted as baleful. What on earth could be the matter that both of her persecutors should be confronting her together?

Rainey waved her to a chair in the manner of one dealing with a recalcitrant servant. He was holding a piece of paper in his right hand. Before he began to speak he looked aggrievedly at her gardening apron which she had not thought to remove.

'My dear Dinah,' he began portentously. 'I've had a communication from Mr Jacobus Grant, or Mr Cobie Grant as he is more commonly known.'

He paused. Dinah was fascinated by his pomposity. It was so unlike him. His manner was usually flighty and feckless to a degree, even though he was now nearly forty, that for him to behave as though he were an elder statesman was so out of character that she suppressed a desire to giggle.

She made no attempt to reply to this remarkable piece of news, only wondered inwardly what a message from Mr Grant could conceivably have to do with her.

Disturbed by her silence, Rainey began again, Violet throwing him an impatient glance.

'In it he asks me if he may have my permission for

him to ask you for your hand in marriage. Most proper of him, seeing that I am your guardian, of course.'

Dinah stared at him. She felt herself growing white. Was she hearing aright? Was she dreaming? Had she run mad?

'Cobie Grant wants to marry *me*?' she said incredulously. 'You must be joking. I certainly don't want to marry *him* of all people. No, not at all...'

Unable to think of anything more useful to say in the face of this extraordinary proposal prevented her from adding anything further to this downright refusal.

Astonishingly Rainey was going white, too. Shock that she was refusing Apollo, she supposed—which seemed a bit of an extreme response.

'Come, Dinah,' he said severely. 'You haven't even given the matter proper thought. This is a most serious offer, I assure you. A magnificent offer. Grant is one of the richest people on earth.'

'Well, I *am* being serious,' Dinah said, her face flooding with colour. 'I don't want to marry anyone yet. Least of all him. For all his riches I wouldn't have him if he were the last man in the world.'

It was Rainey's turn to flush crimson.

'Why ever not?' he demanded belligerently. 'You can't surely be objecting to the fact that he is as rich as Croesus. He's what passes for an aristocrat in America, as your sister has often said, and I understand that all the women in society are wild about him. They seem to think that he's an uncommonly handsome man—eh, Violet? You should count yourself lucky to have attracted such a splendid offer—not dismiss it out of hand.'

Dinah looked at the floor before replying. 'Well, Rainey, I'm sorry. What you say may be the truth. I suppose that I ought to be flattered, but I'm not. I can't imagine why he should want to marry me of all people.

It's not so long ago that he was barely civil to me—
you know that, Violet.'

'Yes.' Violet's face and speech were both ugly. 'Nor
can *I* understand why he wants to marry *you*. But he
does—and Rain-ey is right. You'd be a fool to refuse
him.'

No, I can't be hearing this! Dinah was dazed. It's not
very long since Violet could barely allow me to speak
to him, or have anything to do with him, and now she's
urging me to marry him! On top of *that* remarkable
volte-face she and Rainey are in agreement over this,
which is a miracle in itself since they've always previously agreed never to agree about anything. There's
something odd going on here.

What if I told her I particularly don't want him because he's been her lover!

Her treacherous memory supplied her with a picture
of Mr Grant in the library on the day when she had first
met him, laughing at her over the guitar. Would she
have agreed to marry him then?

'He frightens me,' she said, suddenly, and truthfully,
making a judgement which came out of nowhere, but
which she knew to be true, all the same.

'Frightens you!' they both said at once, Violet adding, 'What a child you are!'

'He's dangerous,' Dinah said stubbornly. 'Can neither of you see that?'

Was it her imagination, or did Rainey look away?

'Oh, I know that he's a tiger in bed,' drawled Violet
tastelessly, in view of everything, 'but I hardly think
that he'd be so with you! Not at first, anyway.'

'I don't mean *that*.' Dinah was firm. She hesitated.
'Besides, I have other plans.'

'Other plans?'

It was Rainey's turn to be incredulous. 'What on

earth can you possibly mean? What plans can *you* have?'

Dinah wondered why he sounded so desperate.

Violet intervened, saying nastily, 'She means she wants to go to Oxford and live with that man and play at being a scholar. I'm right, Dinah, aren't I?'

She nodded, gulping back her tears. Rainey said, now as cross with her as Violet usually was, 'You must be mad. After all we've done for you, Lady Dinah,' and he trod hard with his voice on her title.

'I'm not,' she said. 'Not Lady Dinah.'

'Oh, yes, you are.' Rainey's expression was nearly as ugly as Violet's. 'My father is legally your father.'

Astonishingly, his voice failed him. 'We've kept you all these years, the cuckoo in our nest, and now you won't even help us out.'

'Help you out? By marrying Cobie Grant? Whatever can you mean?'

Impetuously she rose to her feet to defy them. 'I shall go to Faa, I shall, and ask him to help me. You can't stop me...you can't.'

'Oh, tell her.' Violet was all impatience. '*He* told you to tell her the truth about his proposal, and he was right. Tell her why she must marry him, why she's got no choice.'

'Why?' asked Dinah, staring at them both, at their desperate faces. 'Why must I marry him? Why have I no choice?'

'To save us,' Rainey told her, his face twisting. 'I owe him. Thousands upon thousands lost to him at play. Everything will go if I have to try to pay him, the Hall, the estate, everything. We shall be ruined, homeless. But if you agree to marry him, he'll waive all my debts...'

'Everything,' said Dinah, stunned. ' You've lost everything. However much?'

'I said everything and I meant everything. I was already heavily in debt, virtually bankrupt, before I…wagered the Hall. Losing broke me…us. I only plunged so deeply because I hoped to win heavily and believed that my luck was sure to change for the better, and that if it did I should escape ending up in Queer Street.'

'And that was his condition? That he would help you if you helped him to buy me? Why do you think that he has never approached me as a decent man would, to ask me to marry him? He knows that I wouldn't say yes, that I loathe him. Did he do all this simply to get me to marry him? Did he? Yet, in the face of that, you insist that he's not dangerous. Are you all mad to want to marry me to someone so despicable? Why he should want to marry me at all is beyond me…'

'Oh, he's not despicable—or not completely so. And he's enormous fun in bed. You don't know how lucky you are.' This was Violet's desperate contribution to Rainey's attempt to 'bring Dinah round' as he had earlier described it to her. She had already guessed when Rainey had told her that one of Grant's conditions was that she should be present when his proposal was made, that she was being indirectly punished for having made him be so unpleasant to Dinah.

She was torn in two. On the one hand, she didn't want to see Rainey, and the Frevilles, lose everything; on the other hand, the thought of Dinah marrying Apollo was gall and wormwood to her.

Dinah said helplessly, 'Lucky! I still think that you've all run mad. To make me give up everything to save you and Rainey and the estate. How soon before you gamble it away again, Rainey?'

'I can't,' he muttered mournfully.

Dinah was exasperated by her half-brother's weakness, now so openly displayed. 'What do you mean? You can't?'

Rainey was dejected. 'If you agree to marry him, he'll set up a Trust for the Hall and the Estate. He'll give me an income, let me live there, and bring in his man to run the Trust. It will be as though I never lost it. *Now*, do you see why you must marry him?'

'He's a devil,' said Dinah to this, her eyes brilliant with unshed tears. 'It's blackmail that he's practising. Blackmail to get me to marry him. Why did he go to such lengths? Knowing him, I'm sure that in some way he cheated you.'

'Who knows?' This was Violet. 'But he gains a lot, if you think about it: a peer's daughter for a wife, respectability, position, a place in society. Of course he gains by marrying you.'

'Respectability? But he *is* respectable. Sir Alan Dilhorne is his uncle. You can't be more respectable than that.'

'Not his real uncle,' said Violet impatiently. 'He's an adopted nobody, they say, not even legitimate. If we accept him by allowing you to marry him, he's socially made.'

'And that's why he's doing this?' asked Dinah sceptically. She thought of the brilliant face and the devious mind she knew lay behind it. 'I don't believe that for a moment. He doesn't give a fig what anyone thinks of him. Society or anyone.'

'So you have been thinking about him,' said Violet shrewdly, while Rainey made impatient moaning noises at them both.

'One could hardly not.' Dinah was glacial now. 'He's so different from everyone else. Wanting me for a wife proves that! Is *he* mad, too? He could have had all the beauties of the year and all the heiresses sitting around London ballrooms if he had cared to raise so much as a finger. Why buy me? He's a devil. He knows I can't refuse him, that I won't see Rainey ruined. He knows that if he'd asked me straight out, I would have said no.'

She thought for a moment before saying sadly, 'This way he wins. He *makes* me marry him. Rainey says that he's rich. How did he make his fortune? Cheating people?'

Dinah was remembering his odd conversation with Mr Van Deusen which she'd overheard the day that they had played chess. Mr Van Deusen had been twitting him with his duplicity, hadn't he?

'Oh, fudge to that,' said Violet rudely. 'What can it matter how he made his...pile. Merely that he made it—and wants you—us—to share it. I agree that he's mad to want *you* of all people. But that's his business.'

'It appears that mine is marrying him,' said Dinah, not knowing whether she felt happy or sad at the news.

She rose to her feet, walked to the window and gazed unseeingly at the Kenilworths' small lawn. She was to lose her freedom, her possible chance that Violet would tire of her and would, in the end, let her go to Faa. Instead she was to marry a man of whom she was more than a little afraid, to save her half-brother and sister who had never wanted her, and had never loved her.

'Oh,' she said, 'he leaves me no choice, no choice at all. He knew what I would say and do if he had proposed to me properly, and that is why he has arranged it this way.'

She whirled towards Rainey.

'Tell him that he may call on me.'

Rainey's face was transfigured. 'You'll do it?'

'Yes,' said Dinah. 'I'll marry him.'

Bates entered the little cubbyhole at Scotland Yard which he shared with Walker, in a lather of excitement.

'I think I've found our man, guv…sir.'

Will Walker didn't need telling which man Bates thought he'd run down. Ever since Mr Horne had kept his word, and had seen that payment had been promptly made after the raid on Madame Louise's, Walker had burned to discover him—to do what? He didn't know. Why had Mr Horne angered him so? That was another mystery.

Even his fat share, and Bates's, of the money which had been carefully portioned out according to the rank of the recipients hadn't altered Walker's determination to smoke out his quarry, whom he now thought of as 'that man'. Who knew what other wickednesses he might get up to? Forewarned was forearmed.

He sighed. Bates's enthusiastic discoveries so often turned out to be mare's nests. What spavined creature had he found this time?

'Well?' he said discouragingly, 'Out with it, Bates.'

'Last night I found out that Jem, my cousin the footman, recently took on a post with a rich Yankee new come to London. He has a little pad in Half Moon Street. Guess what his name is!'

'I am not playing child's games with you, Bates,' Walker told him through his teeth. 'Either you tell me, straight, or I throw you out, unheard. Which is it?'

Gawd, that man had made Walker more of a beast than he usually was! Bates resignedly offered his superior what he wanted to hear. 'His name's Hendrick Van Deusen. He comes from Chicago—and we all know what goes on there. He's been a bit of a bruiser once, Jem thinks. Not totally on the square, perhaps. Jem says that he's no real evidence of that, but he's a nose, has Jem. He's given us good tips afore.'

That was true enough. Before Walker could question him further Bates was roaring on. 'There's more, sir…guv… Seems this Van Deusen's throwing some sort of do and asked Jem whether he knew of anyone who could act as a bodyguard, or bouncer like. He's a hard man, Jem says, he trusts no one, not even the nobs. Jem thought I might like the job, bit of extra tin. I could suss Van Deusen out for you. See if he's our man.

'Natcherly I never said a word to Jem about him,' he finished piously.

Van Deusen, a Yankee and a bruiser, by way of being a gentleman! It all seemed too easy, but Will Walker was never one to refuse any tip, whether likely or unlikely.

'Right, Bates. We'll follow it up. But I'll be this Van Deusen's bit of muscle, not you. I saw him, you didn't.'

So here he was, standing glumly by a pair of big double doors, wearing some fancy uniform designed to show off his calves, which might have been all right if the whole thing hadn't been a dead loss. He had been taken to see Mr Hendrick Van Deusen by Jem, having told him, untruthfully, Bates couldn't come, 'Otherwise engaged' and he'd turned up in his place.

It only took one look at him to decide that Mr Van Deusen, despite—or because of—his likely name, wasn't his man. His eyes were a dirty brown-gold, not blazingly blue. He was strong and well built, but about four inches shorter than the elusive Mr Horne—and he wasn't left-handed.

Consequently he was doomed to stand about pretending to be a bodyguard who was pretending to be a flunkey, and the pay was hardly enough to compensate him for his disappointment and his boredom.

He enlivened his time by taking note of Mr Van Deusen's guests, and wondering whether any one of them was amusing himself by wandering round dirty hellholes like the Jolly Watermen and bribing honest policemen to raid night houses which exploited children.

Mr Van Deusen was coming towards him, his hand

on the shoulder of a man Walker had seen enter a few moments ago. Walker had blinked at the sight of him. He was exactly the sort of splendid gentleman he disliked most. Togged out to kill, bland, arrogant, weary looking, superior, with a face and body like something out of the British Museum's antique gallery which his wife had once dragged him along to admire.

Mr Van Deusen winked at him, then said loudly to his friend, 'Looks to the manor born, don't he? But he's a sham. Bit of local muscle I fetched in to guard the silver.'

'Don't trust anyone, do you, Hendrick?' drawled my fine gentleman in exactly the sort of cut-glass voice Walker disliked most, because it put him firmly in his place, somewhere near the bottom of the social heap, but doomed to look after the interests of such creatures as this.

'Now, you, Cobie, lad, should know that better than anyone,' and Mr Van Deusen, chuckling, waved his cigar at his friend.

His handkerchief, precariously and unmodishly, tucked into his sleeve, fell out on to the superfine carpet when he did so. Firmly in character as copper, turned mercenary bodyguard, turned footman, Walker bent down to retrieve it, exactly at the moment when my fine gentleman did the same thing.

For a second, raising their heads, they looked one another full in the face. Walker found himself gazing into a pair of blazing blue eyes, and some primitive instinct which had served him well in the past, and of which he had never spoken to anyone, told him that he had found The Man!

He straightened up, and began to hand Mr Van Deusen his handkerchief, looking again at his friend, whose eyes were now hooded and who wore such an expression of bland disdain at Walker, life and everything that

Walker thought, No, I'm mistaken. I'm so determined to find him that I'm seeing the swine everywhere.

'Allow me,' drawled my fine gentleman, taking Van Deusen's handkerchief from Walker, and using his right hand to do so—which was a definite minus, Walker dismally admitted.

'Put it in your breast pocket like the rest of us,' he advised languidly. 'Wearing it in your sleeve is a kind of brand.'

'Oh, I'll defer to you on all matters of etiquette,' was Mr Van Deusen's lazy reply and the pair of them drifted away, leaving Walker to try, frantically, to remember what Mr Horne had looked like. Height right, eyes right, body right, hand wrong, everything else wrong.

He watched his man like a hawk. He noted that the ladies thought he was God's gift come down on earth— and that men found him good company, too.

A few moments later, Jem walked by. 'Who the devil's that?' Walker hissed at him, pointing out the blond Apollo.

'Him? He's Van Deusen's pal. Name of Grant, Cobie Grant. Another Yankee. Richer than Van Deusen, would you believe, rolling in it, they say.'

A Yankee! And rich! It all fit. Only the hand was wrong. Well, one thing was certain, Walker would have Mr Cobie Grant followed and tracked until he was certain that either he was The Man, or he wasn't. A good night's work after all.

Chapter Seven

Cobie had never doubted that Dinah would agree to marry him. Rainey's letter, delivered by a footman, telling him that Lady Dinah Freville would be happy to receive Mr Jacobus Grant at Kenilworth House on Wednesday afternoon at three of the clock, was no surprise to him.

It was much less of a surprise than seeing the wary copper tricked out as a footman at the Professor's home in Half Moon Street, and staring straight at him! Had he been recognised? He thought that he had, and the thought amused him. He had underestimated the man, and he thought again of the warnings he had been given about overreaching himself.

Have I been so successful that I am growing careless? I was a fool to have antagonised him so much. Is Walker aware that Mr Horne is a Yankee, and if so, how? Who gave me away? If I were given away, that is. I shall have to be careful—and the thought excited him.

He put Walker away for the time being in the box he kept at the back of his mind where he stored those matters which he could not attend to immediately, whilst he dealt with Dinah. He dressed himself with more than usual care, and thought hard of what he might say to her.

It was going to be even more difficult than he had thought, because he must try not to hurt her. At the same time he could hardly pretend that he had been smitten mad with desire for her, and given that, if he had made a proposal to her without strings attached to it, she would most certainly have refused him, he couldn't pretend that she madly wanted to marry him, either.

He handed his hat and cane to the butler who told him that Lady Dinah was waiting for him in the drawing room at the back of the house, where he was duly led.

She was seated on a sofa, and someone, Violet probably, had dressed her with a little more care than usual. She wore a rather dowdy gown, but it was a deep blue which matched her eyes, and it was cut rather more elegantly than the frocks which she usually wore. Her hair had escaped from its moorings, though, and she still possessed that slightly *distrait* expression which neglect and lack of loving care had written on her face.

It would be his duty to remove it, and he must remember that.

'Mr Grant.' She rose, and offered him a seat opposite to her.

'Thank you, Lady Dinah, but no. You should remain seated, I think, but under the circumstances, I would prefer to stand.'

Dinah sat down again, puffing her skirts around her conscientiously—something which Violet had probably taught her to do that morning.

'I think that you know why I am here, Lady Dinah.'

Dinah inclined her head.

'Yes, Mr Grant,' she said coldly. 'I am well aware of why you are here—to propose marriage. What I don't understand is why you should want to marry me.'

Her expression was now defiant. Cobie thought that she had been determined to make this declaration, to let him know that he wasn't fooling her. That she knew that he had manoeuvred her into a corner.

'I see that I am a little forestalled,' he said, his eyes mocking her gently. 'You will, I hope, allow me to make my proposal in proper form, all the same.'

'No, Mr Grant, I won't. You have not approached me properly, so why should I do you that honour? Be satisfied that I am accepting your proposal because you, by your actions, have left me powerless to refuse it. To pretend otherwise would be hypocritical in the extreme.'

He bowed to her, keeping his face impassive because he admired the bravery which she was displaying by letting him know that what she was doing was being done through coercion—and for her brother's sake. He must do her the justice of being as honest with her as she was honest with him.

'Because,' he told her, 'I would very much like to start our life together in as proper a manner as possible, after having, I admit, put you in the difficult position in which you find yourself this afternoon.'

'So,' she said, her eyes glowing, giving him a foretaste of the beauty which he thought would one day be hers. If she consented to marry him, he thought that that beauty might come sooner rather than later. 'I take it that you are not about to repent a little, forgive Rainey his debts, and thus allow me not to sacrifice myself to you?'

'Oh, I couldn't do that,' he said earnestly, shaking his head. 'The sacrifice, so far as you are concerned, would be if I did any such thing. Marrying me, you see, frees you. That, Lady Dinah, is what I am offering you, freedom to be all that you might wish to be, instead of being held back by those who do not care for you.

Please accept the humble offer of my hand, be my wife, and make four people, beside yourself, happy.

'Myself being the first, the others being, of course, your brother who at one bound will gain wealth without responsibility, and your sister, who will be delighted to see you so well settled and no longer a charge on her family, and last of all, your true father, who has assured me that he gives my proposal to you his utmost support.'

'My father!' Now he had nonplussed her. 'You have asked my father for my hand?'

'Certainly. I approached him before I approached Lord Rainsborough. Your brother may be your legal guardian, but obeying the laws of nature, rather than those of man, I saw him because I wished to assure myself that your true father would place no obstacles in my way. On the contrary he sends us both his blessing—and you this letter.'

He took the letter from his pocket and handed it to her. 'You may read it when I have gone, but you will find that it is as I say.'

He did not tell her that her father had been told of, and approved, the trick by which he had won her. Some truths, he and her father had thought, should not be revealed.

Dinah took the letter with a shaking hand. She held it to her cheek, and said, 'May I ask you an improper question, Mr Grant?'

He bowed again, his face quite sober for once, and said, 'You may ask me any question you please.'

'You plainly know that I am illegitimate. Violet said that you are, too. Is that true? Don't answer me if you would rather not.'

'Oh, I would rather, Lady Dinah. Yes, I am illegitimate. By accident, my parents always said, and I must believe them, mustn't I? A bond between us, do you think?'

She nodded gravely. He had been so cool and matter of fact that they might have been discussing the Book of Common Prayer, or something equally sober.

'I suppose so. Are you asking me to marry you, Mr Grant, because you love me? I think not, but I should like to know.'

He looked into her steadfast eyes, and decided that only the truth would do.

'No, Lady Dinah, I don't love you. I think that I am incapable of loving anyone. But I like, and respect, you. I need a wife who is a lady and to whom I can talk, and you fill the bill on both counts. Will that do?'

Dinah could only nod, mutely, and nod again, when he said to her, his voice as kind and gentle as he could make it, 'I don't think that you love me, Lady Dinah, rather the opposite, but I promise to be kind to you, and to make you as happy as you ought to be, but have never been. That is a promise.'

Dinah had once thought him kind, and she supposed that now he was showing himself to be so. It was time to give him her answer.

'If you now wish to propose formally to me, Mr Grant, I think that I might be able to give you the reply you want in as proper a way as a young girl is supposed to give such an answer. Our marriage will, as you say, please a great many people, which is, I suppose, as good a reason for getting married as any.'

Oh, bravo, my dear girl, was his inward response, but outwardly he did what she asked, and proposed to her in proper form.

'My dear Lady Dinah, I am here to ask you to become my wife—something which, I assure you, will give me the greatest pleasure. Knowing you, I am sure that we shall deal well together in the future.'

Dinah rose and bowed to him. 'I thank you for the honour you have done me, Mr Grant and inform you that I shall be happy to accept your proposal.'

Cobie bowed back, and thought again that whatever his future wife lacked it was neither courage nor intellect, but his reply to her was as prosaic as he could make it.

'I think, Lady Dinah, that now you have accepted me, I have the right to be seated. By you, if you would be so good as to allow me to do so. We are, after all, formally engaged and may be permitted a little licence.'

The only thing was that when he did sit beside her, his nearness caused poor Dinah to be frightened of him all over again. Sensibly, she decided that he must never know that and listened carefully to him while he told her that he wished them to marry as soon as possible, and with very little unnecessary ceremony.

'I think that you would like that,' he said, adding with a smile, 'After the wedding I shall take you to Paris, and make a fuss of you.'

'How soon?' Dinah asked, thinking that she ought to show some polite interest in her own marriage.

'Next week. I have a special licence in my pocket, see,' and he drew it out to show it to her.

Cobie saw her face change at the sight of it, and cursed himself a little when she said painfully, 'You were very sure of me, weren't you?'

He tried to be as kind as he could, 'Yes, my dear, because I know you to be brave and loving and would want to do your duty, as we all must.'

'And is it your duty to marry me?' she said a little slyly, he thought. He decided to reward her with the truth, although he doubted that she would believe that it was.

'Oh, yes,' he said simply. 'It is my duty to marry you, and it will be my duty to make you happy.'

* * *

Mr Jacobus Grant wrote to his foster-parents, Jack and Marietta Dilhorne, of New York, and Bethesda, near Washington, who were his true parents, and whom he had never really forgiven for having deceived him about his relationship with them for nearly twenty years. He had always been told that he was the son of a war hero and that his mother had died giving birth to him.

Dear Jack and Marietta,
I am sure that you will be pleased to learn that I have decided to marry, and to marry well. My bride, Lady Dinah Freville, is the younger sister of the present, Tenth, Earl Rainsborough, of Borough Hall in Hampshire. She is eighteen years old. By the time that you read this the marriage will have taken place. I regret the haste that will prevent you from attending the ceremony, but for necessary reasons, all too tedious to enumerate, and none of them reflecting discredit on my future bride, the wedding will take place, privately, by special licence within the week.

You have both so often urged me to marry that I am sure that you will forgive me for doing so at such short notice.

Susanna's husband will be my groomsman, and Dinah will be attended by her sister Violet, the Countess of Kenilworth, whose husband is a personal friend of the Prince of Wales. I hope that you are both well, and that my news will ensure that you will feel even better. Give my love also to Jack Junior and the rest of the children.

Your affectionate foster-son, Jacobus Grant.

Jack Dilhorne, still handsome and vigorous in his sixtieth year, handed the letter over with a sigh to his wife.

'A message from Cobie,' he said, 'and absolutely typical, I'm afraid. Yet another *fait accompli*, delivered to us after the fashion of a general in the field writing a despatch to his political masters.'

Marietta sighed, too. She sometimes thought that she knew where Cobie got his barbed tongue from, even though the only time Jack used his was when he was speaking of his wilful son. They had lost Cobie and his love for them ten years ago when her cousin, Sophie Massingham, hatefully and spitefully, had told him the truth of his birth as yet another act of revenge against Jack and herself.

She thought, sadly, that now they would probably never get him, or it, back. The gentle and loving boy he had been before Sophie's revelations seemed to have disappeared for good. He had fled to the Southwest to escape from them, and when he had returned he had changed completely into someone so hard and formidable that it was difficult to remember that he had ever been any different.

'Eighteen,' she said. 'I wonder how the poor thing is going to cope with him. He seems to be marrying into the top drawer—I wonder if that was the object of the exercise, or if there is something more to it.'

'With Cobie,' his father pronounced sadly, 'there is always a double meaning lurking somewhere. Nothing about him is straightforward. And lately he has been treading such a dangerous path in life that perhaps a descent into domesticity will tame him a little.'

They were both silent for a moment, contemplating the unlikeliness of their son ever descending into a tame anything.

Jack finally said, 'I suppose that nothing he does ought to surprise us. He is exactly like my father—except that I'm not sure that he has yet learnt compassion—which my father did when he married my mother.'

'Well, at least Susanna gave the wedding her blessing. Is there a letter from her in this particular budget?'

There was, and it lifted both their spirits a little. 'She is a sweet girl, if shy and rather gauche,' Susanna wrote. 'A lady in every way. I think that she may appeal to his protective instincts. She is certainly quite unlike all the other women he has shown an interest in!'

Since Jacobus Grant's love-life had excited nearly as much Press speculation as his meteoric career on Wall Street, both Jack and Marietta knew exactly what Susanna meant.

There was nothing to do but send him their retrospective blessing, and hope that one day, not too far away, they might meet Lady Dinah Grant.

Years later Dinah was to look back upon her strange wedding and honeymoon with wry amusement mixed with disbelief. A week to prepare for the wedding! Violet threw several fits and expostulated with Cobie, which was, she told the Prince of Wales in the small hours, rather like having an argument with the Rock of Gibraltar.

'Oh, come,' the Prince told her comfortably, for he liked those around him to be happy, 'you're getting the gel off your hands, my dear, and if she's marrying your dollar prince, so much to the good. Some of the loot is bound to stick to your and Rainey's fingers.'

Delivered in his pronounced German accent, this had set Violet laughing, and agreeing with him. She had passed on to him her *bon mot* about Dinah's future husband being a dollar prince by comparison with all the American dollar princesses whose families had bought their way into British society. Forever after he was known as that as well as Apollo.

Cobie knew of his new nickname and was amused by it. Everything amused him, Dinah thought, she being singularly unamused herself. Between rushed fittings for an elaborate wedding dress, white satin with lace inserts, and so many flounces that she felt like a Christmas tree being displayed out of season, the provision of a coronet of lilies of the valley, an elaborate bridal bouquet, and a small trousseau to take with her to Paris, she hardly knew where she was. Particularly since everything she was being laced into was far more suited to Violet's lush face and figure, rather than Dinah's slender and modest one.

'Don't buy too much,' Cobie told her quietly one afternoon when they were taking tea together at Kenilworth House. Violet was acting as a chaperon, and Susanna Winthrop was there to support all three of them.

Not that Cobie needed much supporting, and now he was telling her that she was going to Paris, the couture capital of the world, and he would see that she had a new wardrobe fit for a near-billionaire's wife.

Dinah began to rebel. 'I don't want to be a clotheshorse,' she wailed at him.

'Nor shall you be, my dear,' he told her equably. 'But I should like to see you dressed in something more stylish than your present wear, or the wedding dress which Violet is inflicting on you. It would suit her, I have no doubt, but it won't suit you. Imagine the fuss, though, if I suggested to her what you ought to wear.'

'And what ought I to wear?' asked Dinah, teasing him a little, for she had found that she could do that and he didn't seem to mind.

'Wait and see,' was all he said. 'It will enliven our life after the wedding. Try not to mind all this too much, I don't.'

'You've had more practice,' Dinah moaned gently.

His left eyebrow rose. 'I have?' he murmured, amused. 'I can't recall being married before. Refresh my memory. Because if so, we'd better cancel everything. Bigamy carries a prison sentence.'

Dinah slapped at him, caught Susanna's surprised expression, and blushed. 'You know perfectly well what I mean,' she told him crossly. 'You've lived in the public eye for years, and know exactly what to do. I don't.'

'But you soon will,' he whispered to her, leaning forward confidentially as though they were a real pair of lovers. 'Have another macaroon, you need to gain at least a stone in weight. You don't eat enough.'

She shook her head, saying primly, 'No, I'm not hungry.' She knew that she had become painfully thin during the last year, particularly during the recent weeks of Violet's dominance and that she ought to eat more, but the thought of food was often nauseating.

'Oh, but I insist,' he said gaily, and as though she were a bird he was feeding, he lifted the macaroon towards her mouth, saying, 'Pretty please, Dinah. Your future lord and master commands.'

His expression was so sillily loving that she began to laugh, so he took the opportunity provided by her open mouth to move the macaroon still nearer it. To stop his folly, and for no other reason—or so she told herself—Dinah allowed him to pop it into her mouth.

She could see Violet's stunned and angry expression and, moved by some emotion which she could hardly understand, she made a noise indicative of pleasure.

'More, please,' she murmured, and leaned forward for him to do it again. He obliged her, his blue eyes were wicked.

'I see what it is,' he told her gravely. 'You have grown too weak to feed yourself. We must remedy that.' This time it was a petit four which she took from his fingers.

Violet could stand no more of this.

'Really, Cobie,' she said angrily. 'I wouldn't have believed that you would be so childish as to encourage Dinah to behave badly.' The moment that the words were out, she regretted them.

Neither Cobie nor Dinah responded. Dinah was beginning to feel a wild sense of the freedom which Cobie had promised her when he had proposed.

'I will be good if he's good,' she said like a naughty child. 'I do believe I'm feeling hungry. Are those butterfly cream cakes, Cobie? They used to be my favourite.'

He immediately picked one up from the plate and began unpeeling it from its paper. Cream clung to his fingers. He held them out to her, and said, wondering how she would respond, 'Lick me clean, please, my love, and then I'll give you the rest.'

What wild spirit moved her Dinah never knew. Out came a small pink tongue which scooped up the cream from his hand, and then, when Cobie broke the cake in half to offer her a portion, she said, 'Mmm, nice!' Whether it was the cream, or his fingers which she meant, she wasn't sure.

She was only sure that Violet's jealous expression, and Susanna's astonished one, were giving her a sense of power which she had never felt before.

'And now we must behave ourselves,' she told him severely, 'or Violet will fetch the cane out to make sure we do!'

It was the only light incident of the whole pre-wedding period. The wedding was as sober and dull as a wedding could be, and if Cobie looked particularly splendid, Dinah, in her unsuitable wedding dress, looked quite the reverse and was aware of it. Only Violet was happy that she had succeeded in making the bride look even more dowdy than usual.

The small reception was depressing, too. Everyone made speeches, including the groom, who was behaving so properly that Dinah thought that there must be something wrong with him. The Prince of Wales had sent her, by Violet, a pretty brooch, which was duly pinned to her dress by the groom with a great deal of ceremony. There was rather a lot of champagne, so Dinah drank rather a lot of it—for after the wedding would come— what?

Her mother, who had come out of retirement for the ceremony, murmured to her, 'What a catch, my darling! I told you you would do well, but...' and she had shaken her head. 'He's *formidable*, in every way, isn't he? Such looks—and so rich!'

Which only went to show, Dinah thought, that her mother was a good deal more intelligent than Violet or Rainey if she could see how dangerous he was. She would be sure to ask Faa what he thought of her husband the next time she saw him—*he* was not allowed to be at the wedding, of course.

Sir Alan Dilhorne was there, murmuring what a pity it was that Jack and Marietta could not be present, but, knowing Cobie, he thought that there were probably sound reasons why the marriage had to take place at such short notice.

They were going to the groom's grand new home in Park Lane for the night, and then were due to set out for Paris on the boat-train the following morning. Everyone cheered them when they were driven from Kenilworth House at the end of the afternoon. Before they left Rainey shook hands with his new brother-in-law and made sober noises about the Freville family gaining a benefactor as well as a relative.

Somehow Cobie managed to look suitably modest, a feat no one but himself quite appreciated. Rainey was taking the view of most of society, except perhaps Sir

Ratcliffe Heneage, who had not been invited to the wedding, that Jacobus Grant had had an access of enormous good luck at poker, to make up for all the bad luck which he had experienced since he had landed in England.

The real truth was beyond most people's understanding. Hendrick Van Deusen, who had given the bride a beautiful rope of pearls and a calf-bound edition of Gibbon's *Decline and Fall of the Roman Empire*, was perhaps the only person besides Dinah's father—and perhaps, Sir Alan Dilhorne—who knew what tricks the groom had employed to win his bride.

Not that the bride was worrying about anything but the wedding night, so that when they were at last alone, the butler having retired, and they were ready to go upstairs to the bridal bed, the groom's words to the bride came as a great shock.

He looked at her white face, her poor thin body, and saw how she was shivering, flinching away from his touch. He had made no real decision about how he would treat her when they were at last married, but now that they were he said gently, 'Dinah, my dear, look at me.'

She turned her ashen face towards him. 'Cobie?' and her voice was questioning.

'My dear, I don't think that you are ready yet for me to make you truly my wife, are you?'

Dinah caught her lower lip with her teeth, dropped her head, and muttered, 'I don't know. But I am your wife, aren't I?'

He put an arm around her and pulled her down to sit by him on the sofa. 'Yes, that is true, and I truly want you to be my wife in every way. But I also want you to be happy when I make you so, and I honestly don't think that tonight is the time. You are tired, and unsure of yourself. You don't know me very well, and I think that when you do, we shall know when the time has come, and then we can truly be man and wife. But not yet.

'On the other hand, if what I have said has made you unhappy...' and he left the rest of the sentence unspoken, but she knew quite well what he meant.

Dinah drew a great shuddering breath and said, 'I don't think I'm ready. I hope that I will be soon.'

It was one of the harder decisions he had ever made for he was not sure that he was doing the right thing in delaying matters. He said gently, 'I hope so, too, Dinah, for I not only want you to be my wife, but I think that you will make a good mother for my children.'

She looked shyly at him, 'Really, Cobie, really?'

It was his turn to nod. 'And now we must go to bed. We have an early train to catch, and Paris is waiting. I think that you are going to enjoy yourself there.'

Dinah wasn't sure whether she was pleased or sorry that Cobie and she were not going to...she could hardly say it even to herself. What she did know was that she had felt a sense of relief when he had told her he was prepared to wait.

Paris, now, was quite another matter. From the moment that she saw it, brilliant beneath the early summer sun, she fell in love with it, and remained so for the rest of her life. She and Cobie had separate bedrooms in a big house he owned off the Faubourg Saint Germain, the most fashionable address in Paris, she was to discover. On the first morning they drove to a little eighteenth-century mansion set in a courtyard, behind iron gates.

Inside they went up a flight of stairs and a footman outside a pair of double doors threw them open and shouted their names into an exquisitely furnished drawing room where a woman in her late fifties, white-haired, came to meet them.

'The Marquise de Cheverney,' Cobie told her. 'Bow, my dear, bow.'

She did so, rising to find a pair of shrewd grey eyes assessing her.

'Milady Grant,' the Marquise said to Dinah, and then to Cobie, who stood there watching them both, curiously tense, she noticed with some surprise. 'But she is charming, such promise. And clever, too, you say. But her clothes—atrocious!' and she threw her hands up in mock despair. 'We must remedy that, *immediatement*.'

Dinah wanted to say, I don't like my clothes, either. My sister Violet chose them, I didn't.

Cobie was speaking to them both. His tension had gone. 'Madame la Marquise is to sponsor us in society,' he told her. 'And she will see that you are properly trained to be an ornament of it. Is that not so, Madame?'

The Marquise nodded. '*Vraiment*, mon ami.' She turned to Dinah. 'It is not just your clothes, you understand,' she said kindly. 'It is the hair, the way you walk, stand, talk. Everything must be just so. Oh, but we shall have some fun, you understand, but much hard work, too.'

Her English was good, but heavily accented, and Dinah wondered where Cobie had met her, they seemed to be old friends. Dinah made that observation to him later. He shrugged his shoulders, and said, 'I met her the first time I came here, five years ago. We each did the other some service,' and then softly, 'She was never my mistress, Dinah. I would not do that to you,' and that was all that he would say.

After that the Marquise rang for coffee, and it came quickly: hot, strong and black. 'We cannot start too soon,' she was saying. 'I understand that your time here is short, Monsieur Grant. No?'

'True,' Cobie said, 'but when I go I shall leave my wife with you for a few weeks. I want her education to be completed as soon as possible, you understand.'

The Marquise looked grave. 'You must not try to hurry things too much, my friend.'

'My wife is a quick learner,' Cobie told her. 'I wish her lessons to begin this very morning.'

Apparently beginning meant being driven to a dress-maker with a house in a side street where they were shown into a salon and where girls, brunettes like Dinah, walked about wearing beautiful clothes.

After about an hour, Cobie said, 'This house is too sophisticated, Madame la Marquise, something a little simpler; the simplicity of the very sophisticated is what we are aiming for.'

Are we? thought Dinah, amused. How is it he knows so much about women's clothes? Before she could ask him he was conferring with Madame, and it was decided that on the next day they would visit an even grander house where a special showing would be arranged for them. Meantime, the Marquise told them severely, Monsieur and Madame must rest…

Dinah did. Cobie didn't. He went out that night, doubtless explaining that his young English bride was exhausted, and came back, she thought, very late. How odd it all was. She had never visualised anything like this. Nor had she imagined what would happen in the morning.

This time the salon they went to was a grand one. Cobie and she sat on gilt chairs again, while the Marquise conferred with that great person, the *couturier*—who seemed more enchanted by Cobie than by Dinah.

'An American!' he exclaimed, throwing up his hands. 'Monsieur looks to be a Frenchman to the life.'

He did, too, Dinah thought. He was wearing French

clothes as though he had worn them since he was a child. Black-and-white striped trousers, a black frock coat, high white glossy collar, black cravat, a very, very tall top hat, high black buttoned boots and a cane with a silver top. His French was superb, too.

It came to her that in England he looked and sounded exactly like an English gentleman. She supposed that in America he was totally Yankee. What was the real man like beneath his trappings, she wondered. Which was the real Cobie Grant? Was there even a real Cobie Grant? She had half-thought this before but never quite as strongly as she did now.

After that she had no time to think anything, because the Marquise and Cobie chose clothes for her to wear and she was pushed and pulled in and out of them, the *couturier* murmuring in her ear while he rearranged the folds of her gown, 'You have the perfect figure for the clothes I design, Milady. When I have finished with you, *tout Paris* will be at your feet.' Which was going a bit far, Dinah thought.

When they had bought her a complete wardrobe they all went to luncheon at a very grand hotel, and Dinah found that she was ravenous, which surprised her enormously. Her appetite pleased her husband, or so he told her, and then she was driven to a hairdressing salon, where her unruly locks were tamed at last.

She was allowed to rest a little when they reached home. The Marquise shooed Cobie away, 'Go and amuse yourself, child. We have work to do.'

To Dinah's surprise and secret amusement, he, the man whom she was sure organised and arranged everything, meekly bowed and said, 'Of course. I have work to do, too, and will go and do it.'

'Be not back too late,' the Marquise ordered him. 'It is the Richelieus' reception tonight, and Milady Dinah must be baptised there!'

Well, if baptism is to follow, catechism comes after, thought Dinah wryly, but it didn't: it came before!

After she had been allowed to lie down for about half an hour she returned to the drawing room. There, a large book was balanced on her head—'To destroy your bookworm's slouch,' said Madame de Cheverney severely. She was told to walk up and down the room, curtsy, take a full cup of tea, return it to the Marquise, sit down, acknowledge an imaginary Excellency, converse politely with him, and all without the book falling off!

Oh, but it did: many times.

Each time the Marquise groaned at her. 'And this is to be done, all day and every day—even when you eat,' she was told, 'until your back is straight, your head is just so, and you look the world calmly in the eye. Calm, always calm, my child. I see that you are inclined to be passionate. Save that for your life in private, for *him*. Be calm in public and all will be well.'

After that Madame organised a conversazione—still with the wretched book on Dinah's head—and she was told again, 'Be gentle, my child, when you speak. Do not so much express an opinion as subtly offer it. On some things you must have no opinion at all. You must learn those useful phrases which are the mortar of conversation. At the moment you have too many bricks to offer!'

This made Dinah giggle, and, inevitably, the book fell off. Again!

She was allowed another short rest in her room, and a tisane was sent up.

'To calm your nerves, my child'—a favourite phrase of the Marquise's, Dinah was to discover. Before the tisane had time to work properly, however, the Marquise was back, with Pearson in tow, looking sullen, the

Marquise's lady's maid, and a little French girl wearing a black dress and a pretty white lace apron and cap.

'This,' the Marquise told her tersely, 'is Hortense, who will be your lady's maid in future. Mees Pearson will be her aide to do the sewing, to iron your clothes, and take charge of your wardrobe. Hortense will arrange your hair and dress you. We shall begin now the ceremony which you will follow in England, when you return.'

Pearson threw Dinah a pleading look. The Marquise fielded it and said sternly, 'All this Monsieur Grant arranged in the last week, before you arrived in Paris. To save you trouble, you understand.'

'He said nothing of this to me,' observed Dinah mutinously.

'He is your husband,' the Marquise returned, as though that explained all.

Well, she would speak to Cobie about *that*, rather than brawl with the Marquise before the servants. Without knowing it, Dinah had already begun to learn the lessons which the Marquise was teaching her. Before the afternoon session she would have defied the Marquise and rushed at Cobie when he returned. But she did neither, allowing the Marquise and Hortense to dress her, Pearson assisting.

They had brought home with them from the *atelier* several of the dresses which Cobie had chosen and which fitted Dinah perfectly. One of them was of *peau de soie* striped in pale blue, cream and the most delicate of pinks. It had an oval neckline, descending towards Dinah's slight bosom, with a small frill of cream lace, running around it.

Around her waist Hortense fastened a ribbon from which small pads depended, and over which the dress fell, giving her the air of a woman with a grander figure than the one she possessed, but not overdoing things.

The skirt had been cut to give the dress a beautiful line from her waist to just above the ankle. This allowed her pale blue silk stockings and her little Louis-heeled blue, pink and cream shoes to show their best advantage.

The dress had also been cunningly cut to make her bosom look larger than it was, and before it was reverently eased on to her, she had been laced into a corset which made her tiny waist even tinier.

After everyone had walked around her, exclaiming at her transformation, Hortense went to work on her face. First, she creamed it; next, she applied the merest touch of *papier poudré* and pale pink lip salve, and finally arranged her hair so that it rose high at the back but fell in cunning little tendrils around her face.

To finish off the whole remarkable ensemble Dinah was handed a dear little fan, cream, painted with roses, and told to allow it to depend from her wrist, unless the room grew too hot when she was to use it.

'But not violently, you understand. Nothing must be violent,' the Marquise told her severely as though it were Dinah's custom to go around striking at people— with her fan as well as her voice, presumably.

The whole operation took so long that Dinah thought ruefully that she would have had time to read a whole chapter of Gibbon's great work which Mr Van Deusen had given her, and which, if today was anything to go by, she would never have the time or opportunity to read again.

She was not allowed to look in a mirror, nor to sit down. Instead, the book was placed on her head again, and she walked round the room, Pearson glowering, the Marquise and Hortense applauding when all was done correctly, and looking sad when the book dropped off, or she said the wrong thing.

There was a knock on the door, and in response to

the Marquise crying, 'Enter,' after she had gently pushed Dinah behind a screen, Cobie came in.

Dinah peered around the screen to see that he was dressed for the evening, French style. He looked so magnificent that the very sight of him made her feel nervous, He was carrying a small leather case and a bouquet of tiny pink and cream rosebuds.

'Lady Dinah is ready, Madame?'

'Just,' said the Marquise. 'I think that you will find an improvement, even after this short time. Milady is an apt pupil. Patient and willing to learn.'

She walked to the screen, folded it shut, exclaiming in a dramatic fashion, *'Voila!'* as though she were a stage magician demonstrating her greatest illusion.

Cobie looked at his wife. She bore no resemblance to the girl he had married and brought to Paris. The gown, the careful and discreet make-up, her newly styled hair, and the improvement in her carriage which the afternoon's drill had brought about, had already begun to change her. At this rate Dinah's weeks in France would have her sister Violet eating her heart out with jealousy when she was let loose on London.

'You look enchanting, Lady Dinah Grant,' he said gravely, holding out to her the leather case and the bouquet which he was carrying. 'I think that this will complete your ensemble.'

His compliment bewildered Dinah—but, of course, she thought, he was simply being kind. Cobie saw her disbelieving expression, and said to the Marquise, 'She has not yet been allowed a mirror?'

'As you ordered, Monsieur Grant.'

'Good. Come here, Dinah, my love. Take your present from me, and open it.'

Mortar, Dinah was thinking sardonically, I mustn't forget mortar. She took the case from him and said, calmly, remembering the Marquise's insistence that she must not be passionate, 'Thank you, Cobie. You do me too great an honour.'

She felt, as much as heard, the Marquise purr with pleasure, and knew from the expression on her husband's face, and the slight twitch of his mouth that he was aware that she was mocking them both.

Still smiling, not too little, not too much, after the fashion which the Marquise had taught her earlier, she opened the case, to find there an exquisite necklace of tiny pale pink pearls. This time, her pleasure was genuine. 'Oh, how beautiful, and it goes with my new dress, too.'

All the Marquise's lessons flew away at once. Dinah began to move towards Cobie to embrace him. His mouth twitched even more, but all that he said when he received her kiss on his cheek was, 'Yes, the match of colours was intended, my love. Now you will allow your husband to put it on for you, I hope. The clasp will be a little too difficult for you to manage on your own.'

'Oh, yes,' she said impetuously, and then, eyes glowing, remembering all that she had learned that afternoon, she continued more gently, 'It will be a pleasure.'

Dinah could feel the fingers of his strong and beautiful hands warm on her neck, and without thinking, after he had arranged the necklace to its greatest advantage, she bent her head to kiss them.

Cobie allowed his hands to linger on her neck for a moment, before saying quietly, 'Unshroud the mirror, Madame la Marquise, *s'il vous plaît*.'

Madame obeyed and he swung Dinah gently round to face it, so that she saw her new self for the first time.

Was that Dinah Freville? Had one day done so much to change her?

Where had that graceful figure come from? The dressmaker's art, and the Marquise's instructions to

Hortense and Pearson, together with the torture of the book, had all combined to create an elegant creature who bore little relation to the Dinah Freville who had been married in the dowdy gown which Violet had chosen for her.

Of course, it wasn't Lady Dinah Freville she was looking at. She was Lady Dinah Grant now—and she must never forget it.

Like Cinderella, the Marquise and Cobie took her to the ball that night, but her Prince had already chosen her, her carriage didn't turn into a pumpkin at midnight, and she only had one cruel sister, not two, and no one in their right mind could ever have called Violet ugly.

All the time that she was in Paris Dinah felt that she was living in a pantomime, instead of watching it, which she had once done with her nurse when she had been a child.

Except that in the here and now there was no curtain to fall at the end of the performance, no coat to put on to go through the dark streets back to normal life again.

For to be Lady Dinah Grant, Jacobus Grant's wife, was to be admired and envied: and this, this, improbably was her real life.

Chapter Eight

'He's back from Paris, guv. Without his missis. D'you still want me to follow him?'

Walker knew that his vendetta against the mysterious Mr Horne, whom he was certain, but couldn't yet prove, was Jacobus Grant, was personal, not official, and he really ought to drop the matter and concentrate on the real criminals who surrounded him, of whom he did know. Only yesterday the Commissioner had asked him if he had made any progress in discovering who the mystery man was who had bribed them.

When Walker told him, 'No, but I've not given up hope of unmasking him, sir,' the Commissioner had sighed and said,

'There's more important work on the agenda, Walker. Give it a miss now.'

Well, he wasn't going to give it a miss. Neither Bates nor anyone else need know what the Commissioner had ordered.

'No, not you, Bates,' he told him. 'Not for the time being. He knows your face. Put Alcott on to him. Tell him to be careful, and to report back to me at the week-end.'

Alcott was careful, but not careful enough. After

forty-eight hours Cobie knew that he was being followed. He had a sixth sense about such things, one of his many odd talents about which London society knew nothing. He was not only blessed—or cursed—with total recall, which made him such a masterly card and chess player, but he always knew when he was being watched.

More than that, he invariably knew when he was being lied to, which was the most unnerving accomplishment of all, and which reinforced the profound cynicism with which he viewed his fellow men and women.

So he covertly watched his shadow, and led him a merry dance around Mayfair, while he ambled through its streets and squares in the sun. While doing so, now that he had been unmasked, he decided to baffle and annoy Walker even more—and amuse himself in the doing.

The next day, dressed in his undistinguished clothing, he led the wretched Alcott an even merrier dance. He had learned that the London police were nicknamed rozzers by the criminal element—of whom he was one—so he allowed this particular rozzer to follow him to his dingy office on the edge of the City. There the delighted Alcott, by devious questioning, discovered that he was going under the name of Mr Dilley.

He grinned to himself at the excitement with which this news would be greeted at Scotland Yard. He wasn't wrong. Happy to have succeeded where Bates had failed, Alcott burst into Walker's cubby-hole that afternoon, full of himself, to tell his guv'nor, and a glum Bates, what he had unearthed.

'Well done, Constable,' was his reward from Walker. 'Carry on, and let me know anything further you discover.'

Two days later he returned even more pleased with himself to confront Walker with his latest coup.

'He's an interest in some property down by the docks, his clerk told me. He visits it occasionally. Something odd is going on there, the clerk thinks.'

For one moment Walker thought that this might be all too easy, but dismissed the thought. Alcott was a hard-working fellow, getting good results, and so he taunted Bates, when Bates came in later after a hard day spent trying to put the frighteners on a small fence with a shop off Leadenhall Street.

He would have been right to be suspicious. Mr Dilley was feeding to his clerk each piece of information—which Walker greeted so joyfully—with strict instructions to him to tell his curious new friend exactly that, and nothing more.

He had left Dinah in Paris deliberately, to allow the Marquise time to groom her, but until he had started to deceive Alcott he had been finding life oddly boring without her.

Never mind. He was going to enliven everyone's life before he had finished with Will Walker. That it might only serve to confirm to Walker that he was the mysterious Mr Horne/Dilley worried him not one whit, for the whole business would be a dead-end—he would make sure of that.

Bit by bit Alcott discovered that Mr Dilley occasionally visited his Dockland property. It was two largish eighteenth-century terraced houses made into one. It was shabby and set back from the road, Alcott said, and he could discover little about it—other than that the man and wife who ran it seemed to have a large number of children.

'Children?' mused Walker thoughtfully. 'Some sort of blind, perhaps. What's our man doing with children? You're sure it *is* our man, Alcott?'

'Quite sure, sir.' Alcott could see promotion in the offing.

'Right,' Walker said, 'and he's going there next week, is he, wearing his funny clothes, no doubt.' For Alcott had been allowed to discover the lodgings where Jacobus Grant changed into a dubious-seeming masher wearing loud brown-checked trousers, brown jacket, and brown bowler, the uniform of a lower-class artisan.

'What the hell can he be up to? We'll raid the place, Bates, that's what we'll do. Next Saturday, as ever was. Find out what his little game is. You can come along, too, Alcott.'

He could hardly contain himself that Saturday when he reached the house, Alcott and Bates trailing behind him. Dilley/Horne had been tracked there by Alcott that morning, and hadn't returned to his low-class pad just across the river.

Walker rang the bell. The door was opened by a bent old man.

'Police!' announced Walker. 'I've a warrant to enter this house,' which was a lie, but most of the people he dealt with usually caved in when he said so. 'I want to speak to the owner, or the tenant.'

The old man blinked at them.

'Ain't no one in but me,' he quavered. 'I'm the odd job man here, Parker's me name. Mr Dilley told me to answer the door, he did, seein' as how my sight ain't good these days. They're all at the Church Hall down the road.'

'At the Church Hall? I'll have to come in to check that there is no one but you on the premises.'

Walker and his men shouldered their way past the bemused old man, to find that he had told them the truth. The place was clean, shabby, cheerful and deserted. Upstairs there were beds for twenty children, two to a room.

Walker stormed downstairs. 'Where's the Church

Hall, and what are they doing there? What's Dilley doing here—and there?'

The old man, who had been coached by Mr Dilley himself, quavered, 'I don't know, I'm sure.'

Walker was beginning to have the ghastly fear that this time *he*, with Alcott's help, might have led them all into another mare's nest only to find a beast even more spavined than Bates's usual discovery had been. With Alcott breathing excitedly down his neck, however, and Bates looking sullen, there was nothing he could do but persevere.

'Where's this Church Hall, then?'

The old man gave them directions, and they all set off. Alcott, perennially optimistic, was now the only member of the party not certain that they were heading for some kind of disaster.

They found the Hall easily. It was a wooden building with a corrugated iron roof, from which the noise of shouting and clapping came. A clergyman with a soft, benevolent face stood at the door. He allowed them to enter when Walker grunted 'Police' at him—leaving him to wonder what the police were doing visiting a children's entertainment.

For an entertainment it was. The Hall was full of children, not only the twenty from the house they had just visited. There were a number of adults present, some wearing Salvation Army uniform, and several others, who, Alcott whispered, were from the big house which was connected with Mr Dilley. Along one wall ran trestle tables, set out with children's party food. A dragon in the shape of a grim woman with a mouth like a rat trap was guarding it.

Mr Dilley/Horne/Jacobus Grant was there, too. On the stage. He was wearing his brown masher's suit. His hair, which Walker had seen in Half Moon Street as a mass of carefully ordered golden curls, sleek to his head, had been brushed up on end. He had, after some fashion, extinguished his golden good looks and now resembled every cheap comedian who had ever graced a music hall stage—and his audience was ecstatic.

He was in the middle of a juggling act. After that was over he called a boy on to the stage with him, to begin pulling coloured handkerchiefs from his ears, mouth and pockets. While doing so he saw Walker, Alcott, and Bates, standing there, petrified. He finished playing with the coloured handkerchiefs, returned the boy to the audience, produced a pack of cards, waved them in the air, and shouted, 'I want another volunteer.'

A dozen childish arms waved in answer. Mr Dilley, his grin now from ear to ear, ignored them all.

'No, I'd like a bigger boy,' he announced, and his voice was pure cockney, causing Walker's teeth to grind at his persecutor's accomplishments, and his insolence.

'You, sir, what about you? The one with the big feet at the back.' He pointed at the blinking Alcott, who was beginning to grasp that not all of Mr Dilley's magic tricks were confined to the stage.

'I forbid it,' snarled Walker into Alcott's ear. Alcott shook his head miserably, as all the children turned to stare at him.

'Oh, shame, spoilsport,' Mr Dilley was reproving. 'Would you ruin these little ones' fun? Tell him to come up here, at once, boys and girls. Altogether now, ''Come on, Mister!'''

The children began howling in unison, 'Come on, Mister,' waving and laughing at the three men, glumly incongruous among all the happy faces.

'Oh, for Gawd's sake, get it over, Alcott, and go up there. You got us into this fine mess, and you'd better pay for it.'

Walker's snarl on saying this was nastier than ever,

provoked because he had been compelled to change his mind in order to avoid further embarrassment.

Pay for it Alcott did. Mr Dilley's repertoire seemed endless. His magic tricks with cards were succeeded by his tricks with hoops and coins, all designed to confuse the mark who was Alcott. His performance reached its climax with the production of a rabbit which Alcott had apparently been concealing about his person ever since he had climbed on to the stage.

He was rewarded by being crowned with a paper hat in the shape of a guardsman's busby. All the children cheered at the merry sight.

The performance ended with everyone singing 'God save the Queen', led by Mr Dilley on the guitar. After that the clergyman climbed on to the stage, thanked Mr Dilley—and Alcott—for the entertainment, and announced that it was now tea time. There was a mad rush for the food.

One of the little girls had run to Mr Dilley who, guitar in hand, had climbed down from the stage, followed by a red-faced Alcott, still wearing his busby. He made for Walker and Bates, having first promised the little girl, Lizzie by name, that he would play and sing her favourite song, which turned out to be Marie Lloyd's hit, 'My old man says follow the van'.

Alcott's busby was enraging Walker almost as much as the egregious Mr Dilley was.

'For God's sake, Alcott, take it off,' he roared. 'He's been dancing you round London for the last week, like the fool you are. Why wear a brand to prove it?'

Mr Dilley stared at Walker. 'You only had to ask me, Inspector,' he said mildly. 'I'd have told you that I've been helping to finance a home for abandoned children and orphans. With the assistance of the Salvation Army, and Father Anselm here.'

Father Anselm, who had been standing watching

them, his face not quite so soft as Walker had at first thought, said, 'I am sure that I speak for us all when I say how grateful we are to Mr Dilley. He does not only give us his money. As you have just seen, he also gives us his time.'

'A proper saint, Mr Dilley,' agreed Walker, through his teeth, snidely.

'Oh, indeed. And now, gentlemen, some tea. I understand from Mr Dilley that you are police officers, searching for some miscreant, and that you have been misdirected. Allow me.'

Before Walker could stop him, the deluded and deceived wretch, Alcott, was accepting a cup of tea and a sandwich and Bates was not slow to follow him.

Walker was suddenly alone with Mr Dilley.

'You haven't fooled me,' he told him savagely. 'You gave Alcott the run around, I'll grant you that, and I should have checked his information, not gone off half-cocked.'

Cobie inclined his head. 'True,' he said, lifting his guitar and playing a few chords of a ballad which included the words, 'If you want to know the time, ask a policeman', which he sang in a pleasant, baritone voice.

'Oh, very funny, I'm sure,' snarled Walker. 'But you're a villain, Grant, Dilley, Horne, whatever you call yourself, and I *know* you're a villain. One day I'll prove you are, where there aren't pious fools about who think you're some sort of saint to stop me from throwing you into the slammer.'

'Oh, I do so agree with you there,' Cobie told him earnestly. 'About being a saint. It's very far from the truth. I'm sorry that you didn't like my tricks. My foster-brothers and sisters used to love them.'

'I don't like you or your tricks, whether they're on the stage or on the streets of London, Mr Grant—if that's your real name.'

Cobie played a flourish on the guitar, and said, 'Aye, there's the rub, Inspector Walker. I have no real name, you see. You may call me what you please. Why don't you have a cup of tea and a bun, like your colleagues? You'll feel better after something to eat. I always do.'

'It would choke me,' Walker returned morosely. 'What I want to know is, what the hell is your game, Grant? Tell me that.'

'Life,' Cobie told him with a grin. 'Life's my game, Walker, and I make up the rules by which I play. As you do. Tell me, do your superiors know that you are disobeying them by pursuing me? No, don't answer, your face says it all. You're as bad as I am, Walker, only you won't admit it.'

Walker knew at last why men killed. He swung away, roaring at Alcott and Bates to follow him. His last sight of Mr Dilley was of him singing his promised song to a bewitched little girl who was gazing up at him as though he were Lord God Almighty.

Lady Dinah Grant didn't think that her husband was Lord God Almighty, but she was pleased to see him when he returned to Paris to collect her, after the three weeks he had promised her were up.

An old flame of the Marquise's, the Chevalier de Saulx, had been their escort into French society, and Dinah had entered so many houses on the Faubourg Saint Germain that she had become quite dizzy. No one seemed to think it odd that her husband had deserted her after a mere week's honeymoon. One expected Americans to do such things. He was busy making money, no doubt. Love could come later. They were both young, Milady particularly so, it seemed.

Everyone agreed that Milady Dinah, or Milady Grant as she was mostly incorrectly called, was charming in the most original way. She grew even more poised, even more original as the Marquise's lessons continued daily.

When Cobie arrived, she walked towards him with the slightly swaying gait which the Marquise had taught her, dropped her eyelids over her eyes, held out her hand, and greeted him as coolly as though she were a beauty with a score of Seasons behind her.

Cobie bowed over the hand. 'I must congratulate you, Lady Dinah, on time well spent.'

She answered him in French—she had spoken nothing else since he had left. Those were his instructions, the Marquise had said. 'He wishes you to be fluent: to speak it as easily as you do English.'

Her French had been that of a schoolgirl, but the intellect which would have made her a scholar was now devoted to perfecting it instead of learning Greek.

'Another month,' the Marquise had told her, delighted, 'and you would have been mistaken for a Parisienne.'

She so informed Cobie after Dinah had gone up to change for dinner. They were all due at the British Embassy. The Ambassador was a friend of both Mr Jacobus Grant and the Marquise de Cheverney. He had already been, like many others, enchanted by Lady Dinah Grant.

Lady Dinah enchanted herself. Like the old woman in the song she constantly asked herself, 'Can this be I?' She said as much to her husband when she entered the Embassy on his arm.

Cobie looked at her. She was wearing a gown of the palest turquoise silk, shot with amethyst. He had put a tiny pearl and amethyst tiara on her head, an amethyst necklace around her neck, amethysts in her ears and there was a ring for her finger. He had brought them with him from London. It was a Dilhorne tradition that the men of the family always, at some point early in their marriage, bought amethysts for their wives, in memory of the Patriarch, the dynasty's founder, who had bought amethysts for his young wife nearly eighty years ago, in Australia.

Why he had followed the tradition, Cobie didn't know. Particularly since he never openly acknowledged his Dilhorne blood. He was aware that there was constant speculation wherever he went as to who and what he truly was. This amused him, rather than annoyed him, but for the first time he realised that he didn't want such speculation to touch or hurt Dinah.

Those few who had seen old paintings and drawings of the Patriarch could be in no doubt of Cobie's being a Dilhorne. He was a larger, handsomer version of Old Tom, the name his surviving sons sometimes called him when they weren't acknowledging him as the Patriarch.

'And you are still Lady Dinah Freville inside?' he said, surprising her, once again, by his ability to read her.

'Yes. Very much so. I cannot believe that I have changed so much in a month.'

'Clothes, good food, attention, kindness—all these help to transform a person. Yes, you have changed, more than I could have hoped. As much as I could have wished.'

'You knew that I would.' Dinah's tone was accusing.

'If you were loved and cared for, yes.'

'*You* have not loved or cared for me.' Again there was almost accusation in her voice.

'You don't think so?' he asked her. 'I thought that you were cleverer than that.'

He was right, of course. So much of what Madame had done, had been done because of his instructions.

Her next question wrung his hard heart a little. 'Shall I forget it all when next I see Violet?' she asked him simply.

'No,' he told her. 'On the contrary. For the first time

you will meet her as an equal. Superiority will take a little longer.'

They were walking up a wide stairway now, flunkies bowing them on. At the top they would be received. Once Dinah would have shuddered at the mere notion of doing what she was now doing without thinking. The Marquise and the Chevalier were behind her, both of them lending her their support—but theirs was as nothing, she understood, to that of the man beside her, who was her husband, but not yet her mate.

The new *savoir-faire* which she had learned—and was still learning—informed her that if she wished, she could make him hers at any time and place of her own choice, whenever she pleased. She didn't need him to tell her that now. Once she would have done.

At the top of the stairs she saw the pair of them in a large gilt-framed mirror—and gasped. She was prepared for her husband's splendour. Evening dress became him as nothing else did. His grace, his elegance, were even more marked in it than in any other costume. But she was not prepared for the sight of herself.

She was his complement in every way. Her dark beauty matched his blond elegance. His bright blue eyes made hers seem the darker. The subtle shades of her gown were enhanced by his midnight hues. But in the confidence of their stance, the way they looked about them, there was nothing to choose between them. The girl who had hunched her shoulders and bent her head lest the world look her in the face had gone.

'Yes,' Cobie said in her ear. 'We go well together, do we not?'

She wanted to say, Do you read minds—on top of everything else you can do? But it wasn't necessary for him to read her mind. He had needed only to see them reflected in the mirror, a handsome pair fit to be portrayed by James Tissot, the painter and recorder of aristocratic life.

After that, the night was easy. Dinah had only to pretend that she was in the Marquise's drawing room, the book balanced on her head, making conversation to imaginary aristocrats, ministers, courtiers, and entrepreneurs. At last she was able to convince herself, and everyone else that she had the potential to be Violet's best.

Only when she was alone in the carriage with him, going home, did she allow her shoulders to droop, to become, once again, little Dinah Freville, Violet Kenilworth's unconsidered sister.

Cobie, sitting opposite to her, put a long finger under her chin to push it up. He said briskly, 'Oh, no, Dinah. When we put on a mask, we must wear it until the play is over. It is not over yet. You must sit up, and entertain me.'

'Do you wear a mask?' she asked him bluntly, straightening herself, and doing his bidding.

'Of course. I fancy, though, that I have a larger collection of them than most people do.'

'What have you been doing in London?'

For some reason the line of conversation she had begun was frightening Dinah a little. She hoped that her question was an innocuous one. She wasn't to know that it was very far from being that.

Cobie thought of Will Walker and laughed to himself a little.

He said, 'I have been pursuing my business interests.'

He didn't add that he had not been doing so from Southwest Mining and Associates plush offices in the shadow of Saint Paul's, but from the dingy cubby-hole which Mr Dilley had rented.

Nor did he tell her of something else which was on

his mind. His meeting with his foster-sister Susanna
Winthrop three days ago...

Cobie had gone straight home from his encounter
with Will Walker and his minions. He had changed
back into his usual immaculate clothes at his East End
bolt-hole. He walked into the black-and-white flagged
entrance hall of his Park Lane home to be met by the
butler whom he had hired for the duration of his stay
in England.

'Mrs Winthrop arrived earlier this afternoon, sir. I
told her that I had no idea when you would return, but
she insisted on waiting. She is in the small drawing
room, sir.'

'Have you sent tea in?'

'I was about to do so, sir.'

'See to it immediately. I wish to go to my room before I attend on Mrs Winthrop. Tell her that I shall be
with her in about a quarter of an hour. Send my valet
to me.'

Giles had been Cobie's man for the last five years.
He was used to his master's vagaries, never asked any
questions and kept his mouth commendably shut when
newsmen and others tried to pump him about Mr
Grant's activities, sexual or financial.

He arrived in Cobie's room to find that his master
had his blond head in a bowl of water.

'You couldn't wait for me, sir?' he asked reprovingly.

'No, I couldn't, Giles.' Cobie was brisk. 'I know I
have a visitor, but I need to refresh myself before I go
to her.'

Washing Walker off himself was his internal gloss.
'You may assist me now that you are here.'

His hair was sleekly damp when he joined Susanna,
who was sitting hunched in an armchair, an untouched
tea tray in front of her.

'Forgive me,' he said. She had sprung to her feet on his entrance. 'But I have had a difficult afternoon, and had to ready myself before I saw you.'

This was not strictly true. Intuition had told him that he might not like Susanna's errand. The euphoria of having successfully danced Walker and his men around, and of entertaining a group of deprived children had died away, and left him feeling stale and tired, hardly ready to face another problem.

He was sure that it must be a problem which had brought Susanna to him without any preliminary warning, and had kept her waiting for so long, and had caused her to be so agitated at the sight of him.

'Oh, Cobie,' she exclaimed, and flung her arms around him, hiding her face in his chest. 'You've no idea how relieved I am to see you.'

Her behaviour would have told him that without her words. The Susanna he had known all his life had always been coolly controlled. There was nothing controlled about her now. She was trembling against him.

Cobie held her away, saying gently, 'Sit down, Susanna, pour us both some tea, and then tell me what is wrong.'

'I don't want tea,' she flung at him pettishly, but she sat down all the same, staring at nothing. When he said, 'Allow me,' and began to organise the tea tray as though he had been doing it all his life, she made no demur, but accepted the cup and saucer from him.

She took a shuddering sip, put it petulantly down, and watched him drink his own tea. Had she been more observant she would have noticed that he was not quite so much in control of himself as he usually was.

'What is it, Susanna?' he asked her, still gentle.

She put her head in her hands, lifted it to look at him, her eyes full of unshed tears, and said hoarsely, 'Don't tell me that you don't know, Cobie, you always know everything. It's Arthur.'

'Arthur?'

He put his cup down, and waited for her to continue.

After a moment, looking away from him, she said, 'I think that I've always known that there was something wrong, ever since we were first married. But I've always pretended that there wasn't. I looked away, preferring not to know. Safer so, I suppose.' She stopped, began again.

'Don't ask me for the details, but last night, quite accidentally, I found out the truth I've never wanted to know. All of it. I... can't say it. Don't make me. I'm sure that you know.'

'Yes,' he told her while she looked blindly away from him. 'I've known for a long time. Not always. Not when you first married him, although I never liked him...'

'God help me, I thought that you were simply jealous when you tried to tell me that I was making a mistake in marrying him. God forgive me, I think...that if...he were straightforwardly perverse, I could almost live with it. But children...Cobie...children, like those people at Madame Louise's recently. I know he used to go there...we haven't been man and wife for a long time... Oh, God, what am I to do?'

She stood up, and said frantically, 'I must go home. I shouldn't be telling you this, but I thought...I don't know what I thought.'

Cobie was on his feet, too. He went over to her, put an arm around her to comfort her and began to pet her as though she were a small child.

Susanna shuddered again, at the impersonality of it, remembering how differently he had once embraced her.

'All those years ago I rejected you, because of the

difference in our ages. I wouldn't reject you now, Cobie. I wouldn't refuse you now, not now.'

She pulled his head down to kiss him on the lips. 'Love me, Cobie, and I might be able to survive.'

She looked deep into his eyes, her own tragically brilliant.

He stood transfixed, thinking of how these words would once have moved him, with what joy he would have taken her into his arms, would have married her and bedded her.

To his horror, the very memory of it, combined with the familiar, once so dearly loved scent of her, roused him. For a moment his friendly petting of her became something more, his arms tightened about her, and she turned in them with a little sigh, as though she were coming home…as though she were his wife…

His wife! He thought of Dinah, being groomed for him in Paris. He pulled away.

'No!' Susanna pulled him back, put her mouth to his and began to kiss him. She was suddenly seduction itself. She was his first love, his lost love, so long regretted. He tried to hold the memory of Dinah to him, but even so he felt his body responding…he had gone so long without love, and bedding Violet and the others had been no substitute for love.

Susanna thought that she had won. 'Oh, now, Cobie, now,' she whispered to him, 'after all these years.'

Her voice called him back from the brink which he was rapidly approaching. He turned away from her, his body one vast ache. The piano was open before him. He dropped both hands on to the keyboard and the dissonance of the chord he had created matched that of his mood.

He was in torment. So often in his life he had been confronted with this terrible dilemma: whichever course of action he chose would be wrong. Of two ills, how to choose the lesser? To take Susanna to bed would be to betray Dinah, not to do so would, he was sure, destroy the precarious relationship between himself and his foster-sister for ever. He thought that he knew which evil was the lesser, but he could not be sure.

'No, Susanna, no,' he said, facing her. The tears were pouring down her face, and she tried to clutch him to her. 'Too late, too late. The boy you loved is dead and gone. He died in Arizona Territory, never to be resurrected. And the man who succeeded him knew how right you were to refuse him then, even though it broke his heart at the time.

'Oh, Susanna, I still love you dearly, but only after the fashion that a brother loves a sister. If I took you to bed now, it would not only be celebrating mindless lust, but it would also be an act of treachery to the young wife I have just taken. I couldn't betray Dinah, Susanna, not even to make you happy. She has suffered so much all her short life. She mustn't suffer that.'

'She doesn't love you,' said Susanna, her face an agony of sorrow.

'No, I'm not sure that she does. But I'm not going to take you as a consolation prize, Susanna. I have a little honour left. Not much, but one thing I will not do is betray my young wife before we are a full month married. It was right for you to reject me all those years ago, and now we must live with that rejection.'

'If I hadn't rejected you just after you found out that you were not legitimate,' she said, 'you might never have gone to Arizona Territory, would never have become the man you are, a man I hardly know. I killed the innocent boy you were when I sent you away. I hardly knew you when you came back. What happened, Cobie, what happened?'

'I grew up,' he said roughly, 'and so must you. It might be of comfort to you to know that it was not because of your rejection of me that I fled to the South-west shortly afterwards. It was for quite another reason. What changed me happened there, in the Territory, and had nothing to do with my life before I left New York—and you—behind.'

Susanna chose to ignore what he had just told her. 'Oh, I do so want a child before it is too late,' she wailed. 'He will never give me one. You could, Cobie, you could.'

It was the worst thing she could have said to him. He wheeled away from her. 'What! And create one more unhappy bastard! We all have to choose, Susanna, and live with our choices. You chose nearly ten years ago, and for good or for ill, you changed our lives. But I will not sentence another to what I have had to endure myself.'

'No one thinks the less of you...' she began, but, agonisingly, she knew that there was nothing left for her to say to him. Whatever had lain between them was over, but she could not resist telling him mournfully, 'You are so hard, Cobie, so hard, I never thought...'

The face he turned on her was one of such suffering that she recoiled from it.

'No, Susanna. If I am hard, it is better so. I could comfort you here and now, but think, what would be the end of such treachery?'

He sat down again, and said prosaically, 'The tea is still hot enough to drink. Let me pour you another cup.'

She was shuddering and trembling. 'I should like to go home, Cobie. I can't stay with you now. I think that I never want to see you again.'

What to say? What to do? Nothing. No words could suffice. Again, of two ills which is the lesser? It would be useless to say to her, You will be pleased one day that you did the right thing, for nothing could console Susanna in her present misery...

He held out the tea cup to her.

'Drink your tea, Susanna, better so.'

Desolately, she took it, and drank it to the dregs, which were symbolic of what time and chance had made of her life.

Cobie was back with Dinah, trying to banish the memory of Susanna's face when she had left him that afternoon.

He looked at Dinah's hopeful one instead, and thought, I was right not to betray my wife, even if I do not love her, whatever we feel, or do not feel, for each other, but oh, how I wish that I had not been faced with such an agonising dilemma.

One thing at least I have gained: I am easy with my bride—which I would not have been if I had given way to Susanna's misery—and who knows, my bride may soon be ready to be easy with me.

Chapter Nine

That night, preparing to go to bed, with both Hortense and Pearson in attendance, so grand had she grown, Dinah was thinking about her husband and her so far non-consummated marriage.

She thought that he had been remarkably considerate in not making her his true wife immediately, when he had already decided to put upon her the burden of transforming her so rapidly from gauche, dowdy Dinah Freville into a *Parisienne* beauty.

On the other hand, it might not have been consideration at all, far from it. He might have simply been deferring the evil day when he had to take to bed an untutored girl whom he had married for reasons she did not understand, but which she was sure, did not include a desperate desire to…to… Her imagination would not supply her with a decorous word—only a vulgar one!

One thing she was now sure of. At some point he would make a move towards her, but that did not mean that if she decided that she was tired of waiting, he would rebuff her if she went to him and… She blushed at the thought but she now knew him well enough to be aware that he would never do anything as unkind as that.

Should she, or shouldn't she, go to him? Her sense of humour, one of the things about Dinah which had attracted her husband, set her thinking, I need a daisy, and instead of plucking off the petals and saying 'He loves me, or he loves me not', I should be asking 'Shall I? Or shan't I?' But there aren't any daisies off the Faubourg Saint Germain for me to pluck. Perhaps I ought to wait until I get home, or go to Moorings where the fields will be full of them!

Yes, that was it. This alien city, so artificial, even if so beautiful and cultured, was not the place where Dinah Freville ought to become Mrs Cobie Grant in fact as well as in law.

She was unaware that her husband, still disturbed by the scene with his foster-sister, had come to the same conclusion. He would wait until they were back in London, where she would be surrounded by the things which she knew.

He thought, with a great deal of wry amusement, that she would be only the second virgin he had initiated into love. The previous one had been over thirty, ten years older than he had then been, and that, like Susanna, she had asked him to be her lover—for one night only. He had agreed, because he owed her his life, and he had betrayed no one by doing as she wished.

It was the first time for many years that he had thought of Jane, who had been so unlike Dinah, and he wondered what had become of her. He shook his head and dismissed the past. Yes, they would return to London shortly—and what would happen—would happen!

Sir Ratcliffe Heneage decided that he disliked Mr Jacobus Grant intensely. Before Grant's marriage to Dinah Freville, on the night when Grant had broken Rainey, he had lost all and more of the money he had won from him at poker and baccarat in those early weeks when Grant's luck had been so bad. Money which, like Rainey, he couldn't afford to lose: he was bankrupt in all but name.

He didn't believe in Grant's bad luck any more. An American friend, over from the States, had told him what a tiger Grant truly was on Wall Street. He knew nothing about Grant's ability, or otherwise, at cards, but he couldn't believe that he was other than a tiger with them, too.

'Grant's uncanny,' he had said. 'He seems to know what you are thinking. He's a ruthless devil. What he wants, he takes, whether it's money or women. He sails close to the wind in everything he does.'

In consequence Sir Ratcliffe Heneage no longer believed that Grant had destroyed Rainey by good luck or by accident. He also thought that Grant had used the cards he, Sir Ratcliffe, had marked for himself, to do so. Looking back, there had been several previous occasions when odd things had happened at the table: times when Grant had lost when he should have won.

Had he been using his marked cards to lose, in order to lull everyone into believing he was an easy mark and make a killing when he wished to do so? Sir Ratcliffe rather thought that he had since there was no chance that Grant had ever had an opportunity to mark the cards himself.

Grant had taken Violet Kenilworth from him, too, just when he thought that Violet was about to capitulate to him—and he hadn't even had to try. Violet had just fallen flat on her back in front of the Yankee pirate! His friend from the States had told him that that was par for the course as well.

Which was all the more remarkable when you thought that he had ended up by marrying that frump, Dinah Freville, who was both plain *and* portionless. Particularly when gossip had it that he had almost blackmailed Rainey, after that disastrous session at cards, into allowing the marriage.

His friend had said, when told of this, 'Well, if that's so, Grant knows something about the girl that the rest of you don't.'

'What's to know?' Sir Ratcliffe had said coarsely. 'A plain poverty-stricken bitch, useless in bed, one supposes. Now…her sister…' and he licked his lips.

His friend had also told him something else. Gossip had it that Grant and his foster-sister were close. 'Very protective of her, I understand.'

Sir Ratcliffe had said nothing but he had thought a lot. He had been living a life more continent than he had done for years, his favourite sports denied him. Ever since Madame Louise's had been raided he had been fearful of visiting any night house… Who knew which one might be raided next? On the other hand, when and if Hoskyns found for him the child who had run away—why, that would be a different matter…

Susanna Winthrop was just the sort of woman he had a taste for. Not too buxom, figure almost boyish, and with pretty deferential manners. If Violet Kenilworth had a fault it was that she was too loud, too demanding. His own wife, with whom he had not slept for many years, although she shared his home and public life, being seen with him on all official occasions, was a pale, defeated woman whom he had married for her money—all of which he had spent.

Now Susanna, on whom he had had his eye since he had lost Violet and the little boys and girls in quick succession, would make up for all of them. She liked pleasant gentle men, that was plain, and he would be as pleasant and gentle as a man could be—to begin with, anyway.

He had approached her the other night, after Grant had returned to Paris, and commiserated with her on his absence, and she had been so gracious to him, that before the evening was over they had been conversing together as though they were old friends.

He had been invited to the Hertfords' reception and she would be there, she had told him. Someone had said that Grant and his wife were back from Paris. So much the better. He would like Grant to see him winning Susanna Winthrop—it would add to his enjoyment.

It certainly didn't add to Cobie Grant's.

He had walked up the giant stairway, Dinah on his arm, amused at some of the stares they attracted. Dinah was wearing a dress of pale lemon silk, cunningly cut to give her a slightly more ample figure than she actually possessed. Hortense had dressed her hair in a new fashion, simple, but effective. It was high on her head, to show the lovely line of her neck, made even more effective by her newly learned proud carriage.

She wore no tiara this evening, but a topaz star, with a giant diamond at its heart, was placed above the noble line of her forehead, held there by a narrow band of silver lamé. Her ear-rings were diamond and topaz, as was the necklace she wore, and the bracelet around her left wrist. None of the stones were large, or ostentatious, but the effect was dazzling. Her slippers this evening were of topaz and silver damask, peeping below the straight hem of her elegant Paris gown.

Her fan was a feather one, dyed to match her dress. She remembered Cobie and the Marquise exclaiming over it when they were choosing her whole ensemble: scarf, slippers and long evening gloves. Her jewellery had been bought later.

'Smile,' he said in her ear. 'You are creating a minor sensation. The Marquise deserves the Ribbon of the Legion of Honour for transforming you at such speed.'

'And what do I deserve, Cobie Grant?' she whispered back to him. 'Tell me that.'

The smile he gave her was wicked, Cobie Grant at his most winningly provocative.

'Wait until we get home, Madame wife, and I shall take pleasure in showing you.'

Dinah shivered. She thought that she knew what he meant, and she spent the whole evening in a lather of excitement, hidden under the surface gloss Paris had created.

'Don't try too hard,' her husband had told her before they had set out, and he had seen her white face when she had joined him in the drawing room.

She had whispered to him, 'I'm frightened.'

'There's no need to *say* anything,' he had whispered back to her. 'Just smile and murmur ''Exactly so'' and hold yourself as Madame taught you. Don't forget to put your fan before your face and smile over the top of it if you feel nonplussed. Men don't expect pretty women to be able to talk.'

Dinah was acid. 'What do they expect from pretty women, then?'

He had picked up her shaking hand and kissed it. 'It will be my pleasure to teach you—soon.'

Now it seemed that soon was almost upon her. She had no time to worry about it, though, for here was Violet coming towards them, magnificent in old rose and cream, but the eyes which she cast on Dinah were inimical.

'Well, well,' she drawled when the civilities were done with. 'That's Louis Pontadour, is it not?' waving a hand at Dinah's beautiful gown. 'However did you persuade *him* to dress her?'

'Money, of course,' returned Cobie, his smile taking the sting out of his words. 'One look at Dinah, though, and he was proud to have her wear his creations.'

'Fancy that,' remarked Violet nastily.

The anger she felt at the sight of a transformed Dinah

was so great that she could hardly prevent herself from showing it. 'I suppose that any improvement, however small, is to be welcomed. You no longer look like a housemaid out for the day, my dear. Such a relief.'

Living with Cobie, even if their time together so far had been brief in the extreme, was beginning to have its effect on Dinah. She now knew that the double meanings in his conversation, which she had remarked on before their marriage, were no accident.

She opened her fan, saw Violet's eyes narrow at the sight of it, yawned behind her lemon-shaded lace gloved hand, and said sweetly, 'Yes, Violet, dear. My next aim is to look like the cook, and after that, I may aspire to the housekeeper. You must tell me how you achieved it.'

'Good God,' said Violet to Cobie. 'Have you given the kitten claws *already*? And talking of kittens, have you seen Susanna Winthrop this evening? No, I thought not. She has become totally occupied by Ratcliffe Heneage while you have been enjoying yourself in Paris.'

'Really?' said Cobie, his perfect calm still present on the surface, but beneath it he was paddling as fast as an apparently unruffled swan paddles in still water. 'A new friend, one supposes.'

'Oh, much more than that,' returned Violet. 'After all, that husband of hers is a dull dog, of which I am sure that you are aware, knowing them so well. Why shouldn't she try to make her life a little livelier?'

'Why not?' agreed Cobie warmly. 'I'm happy to hear that she is present tonight. With, or without, Sir Ratcliffe. I had thought him your admirer, Violet dear.'

So had Violet. She had dropped him for Cobie, then Cobie had had the bad taste to marry Dinah. She had turned around to pick up Sir Ratcliffe again but, lo and behold, he was after that dull stick, Susanna Winthrop, God knew why.

Another disaster for which one day she hoped to make this presumptuous American pay. But she said nothing further, only drifted away to watch her sister and her husband become the sensation of the evening.

A spectacle watched by Susanna Winthrop with even more dismay than Violet. She was determined not to let her foster-brother know how hurt she was, how every time she saw him was like a knife through her heart. It was as though all the love she had felt for him since she had first seen him—a small baby in Marietta's arms—and which she had suppressed for ten long years, had turned at once into hate, like milk curdling in a jug.

Now she was smiling up at Sir Ratcliffe, who was behaving towards her with the kind and careful assiduity of a man determined to make a conquest. More than one person remarked on them.

Halfway through the evening she and Cobie met. He had left Dinah for a moment to speak to a friend. He could see her sitting still and upright, doing, he noticed with his best inward grin, exactly what he had suggested to her before they had left home. Her fan lifted slowly before her face; she was talking and laughing as though she had been showing such *savoir-faire*, such self-control, for years, instead of for only the last month.

Susanna tried to smile at him. For the first time in her life she found herself speaking to him as though to a stranger, making small talk.

Pain lanced through Cobie. He had watched her with Sir Ratcliffe, watched how she was behaving with him, not at all like the cool woman he had always known. She was acting for his benefit, he knew. Look, she was saying. Other men find me attractive, and so I find them pleasing. This man, whom I know you dislike, I am deliberately finding attractive.

It was unwise, he knew, but he had to say something to warn her since she could have no notion of what a cruel swine the man was. He was sure that in her present mood she wouldn't heed him, but the necessity not to allow her to run from one unhappiness to another was strong in him. He now knew too much about Ratcliffe Heneage to keep quiet.

'You are enjoying yourself, Susanna?'

'Very much so,' she told him defiantly. 'I suppose you are, too. You always make sure you do!'

He inclined his head, and said gravely, 'In order to enjoy one's self properly, Susanna, it is necessary to choose one's partners carefully.'

Her laugh was shrill. 'Having turned me away, do you now presume to choose my companions for me, Cobie? I find Sir Ratcliffe an amusing and well-informed man. Do I see your wife looking for you? That is where your responsibilities lie now—not with me.'

There was nothing for it. He said, a little desperately, 'If you must choose someone, Susanna, choose some-one less unsavoury than Sir Ratcliffe Heneage...'

She gave him her shoulder. 'I don't understand you, Cobie. The man is a Minister of the Crown, a friend of the Prince of Wales. He is connected with most of the great families in the land. He is charming and civilised. Can you say as much?'

Every word she threw at him now was designed to hurt. He had lost her. He bowed as though to a stranger.

'I never thought that we should come to this, Su-sanna. I only wish you well. I shall not try to advise you again.'

'I should hope not. Now, if you will forgive me, I see Sir Ratcliffe coming. After all you have said of him, I am sure you do not wish to meet him. Your wife may be looking every inch the woman you are making of her, but she must still need your support. Content your-self with that.'

She turned her back on him, and walked away. More

than one pair of eyes had seen the exchange—and how it had ended. No one knew that something which had been part of Cobie's life for more years than he could remember had dropped dead on the floor of the Hertfords' ballroom.

Dinah had seen all that had passed from a distance. The sixth sense which she was acquiring through living with him told her that however calm and charming he was on the surface while he laughed and talked for the rest of the evening, her husband was deeply disturbed below it. Her new instincts, awoken by the Marquise's training, told her to say nothing.

She had no time to think further. The Prince and Princess of Wales had arrived, and the Royal command was that he wished Mr Grant to present his new bride to him. So there she was, curtsying, and having her small hand taken into the Prince's large one to lift her, while he said, 'No need for that, my dear,' in his guttural voice—his German, they said, was better than his English.

She was not so overset that she didn't register what Cobie had already told her, that despite his easy manner he was no fool, and knew and understood men and women and what moved them. She knew, too, about Violet's liaison with him. Was the Prince about to understand her? What would she do if he took a fancy to her? What would Cobie say and do? She could not see him behaving like a complaisant husband, like Kenilworth for instance, happy to see his wife a royal favourite.

That she pleased the Prince was plain. He complimented Cobie on her, told him that he and his wife must visit them at Marlborough House, his London home.

'See to it,' he said peremptorily to the grey man who was always at his shoulder. Envious glances followed the Grants when he finally released them.

'Your success in society is now assured,' Cobie whispered in her ear, 'for anyone of whom the Prince has approved—and he *has* approved of you—has a secure future, provided that they never breach protocol.

'You are not going to breach protocol, are you, Lady Dinah? However, a word to the wise. Royal favour has its disadvantages as well as its advantages—you must expect jealousy from the many on whom he does not confer his special accolade. Success has two faces, and one of them is not pleasant.'

Dinah had known so little success in her life that she hardly needed warning against it. The evening passed like a dream. So many grand personages came up to speak to them, after the news of the Prince's favour to the Grants had become known, that she began to feel weary. Being a social success was even harder than she had thought it might be.

They were leaving at last, paying their farewells to Lord and Lady Hertford, their hosts, walking down the grand staircase again. Now they were on the red carpet laid before the front door, beneath the canopy over it, put up so that they might reach their carriage untouched by the elements, and in as much comfort as possible.

Even at this early hour in the morning, there were a small number of spectators, standing respectfully back, watching them. She felt Cobie stiffen, then heard him laugh to himself when his eyes swept over them.

He handed her into their carriage, murmured, 'Excuse me, my dear,' and walked over to a burly man, standing on the edge of the group, who, Dinah saw, tried to dodge back, out of the light.

In vain. She watched her husband put a hand on his shoulder, speak and press something into the man's hand before he returned to her. She looked at him questioningly. He shook his head, and said, with the double meaning strong in his voice, 'Nothing, my dear. A *pour-*

boire for a man who needs a little help to speed him on his way.'

Constable Alf Alcott found watching Cobie Grant a time-consuming and tiring business. The man himself seemed tireless. He also knew that he was being watched, winking at Alcott on more than one occasion when he frantically tried to retreat into the shadows.

This evening he had followed him to a grand house, and stood outside waiting for him to come out again. He had complained to Inspector Walker, 'What's the point of all this, sir? He's not doin' nothing but enjoy himself. There's better things for me to do than this, surely.'

'Such as, Alcott, you lazy devil? If I want you to do this, then this is the best thing that you can do. No one else is bitching about their work, you lazy so-and-so. Get on with it.'

His quarry had come out at last, his wife on his arm, his top hat on his head, his white silk scarf about his neck. *He* hadn't been standing in the street for all hours, not he.

Boredom and weariness had made Alcott careless, he knew. His man had seen him, had handed his wife into his carriage and had walked over to where he stood— no hope of escape.

'Why, Constable Alcott—it *is* Constable Alcott, isn't it? I do believe that you could do with a good drink and a bite to eat. Here's a little something to help you on your way. I'm sure that they don't pay you properly at Scotland Yard for all the painful hours you spend in the cold.'

He pressed what the grateful Alcott later found was a golden sovereign into his hand. 'Good luck to you, Alcott, in whatever enterprise you are at present involved,' and the sarky swine was waltzing back to his lady.

It was a waste of time watching him. Alcott dismally knew that his man would have no difficulty in losing him if he were really up to something.

He tried to tell Walker so the next morning. The Inspector was having none of it.

'He's making monkeys of us, sir,' he said as respectfully as he could. Bates, standing just behind Walker where his superior could not see him, nodded his head in silent agreement.

'He is, guv, look,' said Alcott a trifle desperately. 'Look what he gave me last night. Tipped me, he did.' He pulled the sovereign from his pocket to show Walker. 'Thinks we're a joke, he does.'

'You're the joke,' Walker told him through stiff lips, 'allowing yourself to be seen.'

'Then put someone on him who he doesn't know. Maybe they'll have more luck.'

'I haven't got anyone else, Alcott. Get back to your duties, and report to me what he's up to today.'

Grumbling beneath his breath, Alcott stamped out. The only consolation he had was the sovereign in his pocket.

'Bribing Alcott, now, is he?'

Bates, listening to this, coughed, and said respectfully, 'It ain't just Alcott, guv.'

Walker roared, 'What the devil do you mean, Bates?'

'Well, you know as how the missus is expecting. I got home two nights ago to find she'd had a parcel delivered. Mysterious, she said it was. Weren't no mystery to me when I read the note inside. A layette it was for the babby. Beautiful. Compliments of Mr Dilley, it said. I told her it was from a friend I had made. She said that he must be rich. A sempstress, my wife was, knows about such things. What's his game, sir? Tell me that.'

Walker couldn't tell Bates what Mr Dilley's game was, for he had no idea himself.

Seated opposite to Dinah on the drive home from the Hertfords' ball after baiting Alcott, Cobie watched her head droop, and her eyes close when tiredness finally claimed her.

In repose her face was already displaying the delicate beauty which he had thought he had seen latent in it at Moorings, and which, once he had made up his mind to marry her, he had decided that it was his duty to reveal to the world. Left to Violet and a wretched marriage he was sure that it would have died aborning, and with it would also have been stifled her bright and lively mind. He had told her father that he would cherish her, and so he would.

A thought struck him. Was that love—to want to cherish someone, to care for them, to watch them blossom? Were love and lust connected? Did he lust after Dinah? The answer must be no; even if he were able to perform his marital duty by her he would neither love, nor lust after her, but he would simply do what every animal does for its mate—please her, and bless her with a child. He was sure that Dinah would think having a child would bless her.

Violet Kenilworth had children, but he had never seen her with them. They were brought out for her, once a day, for her to speak to them briefly, acknowledge that they were hers—and hand them back to their nurse, governess, or tutor.

No child of his would be so treated, he would make sure of that. Nor would he lie to them, as he had been lied to—which was why he was so honest with Dinah, for to deceive her would be to lay up trouble for the future...

He laughed soundlessly to himself, for was he not deceiving her over some of the most fundamental parts of his life? She knew nothing of what he was doing in the wider world outside, from his major financial exploits all the way down to his mildly criminal ones.

No matter...he leaned forward as she slipped sideways in her sleep and eased her into a more comfortable position. He had not even made her his wife, and here he was, dreaming of children!

They were home again, and she was still soundly asleep. He climbed out of the carriage, and then leaned into it to lift her tenderly out, to hold her against his heart, to carry her inside, followed by a sleepy footman, his valet hovering in the hall.

He shook his head at Giles to dismiss him, and made his way upstairs, Dinah still in his arms. She was half-awake now. She said, sleepily into his chest, 'Cobie?' as though she were questioning him. He thought that she might be dreaming that she was a child again, being carried upstairs, perhaps by the father whom she loved, and who loved her.

Cobie passed the door of her room, and kicked open his own. Candles had been lit—he had so instructed before he had left. The new electric light was too glaring for what he had in mind. The room was full of shadows. For a moment he saw himself, another shadow, in a pier glass, holding Dinah to him, before he laid her on his bed.

She gave a little sigh, put her hand under her cheek, and turned confidingly towards him where he stood over her.

'Goodnight,' she said sleepily. He wondered to whom she thought that she was speaking.

Cobie ripped off his tie and unbuttoned the constricting shirt at his throat before pulling off his tight black coat. There were times when he could hardly bear the conventional constraints of civilised urban wear and urban living, and tonight was one of them.

'We should be alone, under the stars,' he said aloud, 'away from everyone, and beneath a sky full of flaming banners, all of different colours, and there I would teach you the delights of love-making.'

Nostalgia for his lost life in the American Southwest filled him to such a degree that he could almost smell again the scents of the desert, see the mountains, deep mauve against a pale mauve sky...ribbons of varicoloured light beneath a rising moon...

And then he was sitting beside his child wife, the sounds of London life all about him, the Arizona desert far away. She had not heard him speak of what he had once known so well: she was lost in her own dreams, in which, on so many nights, Cobie Grant, unrecognisable, a pistol in his left hand, visited her, and said, 'Remember this, Dinah, appearances often deceive.'

He disappeared, and she was alone in a strange place unlike anywhere she had ever seen. She was lying on the ground, strange shapes all about her; deep mauve mountains were etched against a pale mauve sky in which the moon rode high. Banners of light, in all colours of the spectrum, waved beneath it, and someone was gently speaking her name...

She was lying, fully dressed, on a bed. But she was not on her own bed, she was on Cobie's and it was he who was speaking to her...in a candle-lit room, full of strange shapes....

For a moment she was disorientated, and then she remembered the Hertfords' reception, coming home, and... 'I must have fallen asleep in the carriage,' she murmured, rising on one elbow and looking up at her husband who was sitting by her. 'How did I get here?'

'How do you think, Dinah?' he asked her, and his voice was soft and tender. He had taken off his black coat, and in his open-necked white shirt he looked more splendid than ever.

'You carried me.'

She sat up, and rested her head against the elaborately carved bed-head. It had come from a palace in Florence, she knew. She should have been feeling worried that she was here, alone with him on his bed in the small hours, and half of her was afraid, and the other half was expectant. She shivered—but not with cold.

Cobie turned away from her, rose, and walked into the shadows. He came back carrying a champagne glass in each hand. He handed her one of them, and put the other on the small table by his bed.

'In a moment,' he told her, 'we shall drink a toast.'

'We shall?'

'Yes. Do you want to hear it, Dinah?'

She nodded, mutely, holding the glass carefully so that nothing was spilled from it.

'Very well. It is to us, and to our marriage.'

He sat on the bed again, and picked up his glass to clink it against her own.

'To us, tonight,' he said.

'Tonight?' she echoed, and shivered again.

Cobie usually read her correctly, but not this time. He thought that her shiver was one of fear only, when instead it was of fear mixed with expectancy. He closed his eyes, opened them again, and put his glass down. He took hers from her: she must have drunk the champagne as he had done, in one prodigious swallow, almost without thinking. Their hands touched and she shivered again.

He put a gentle arm around her, and gave her a brotherly hug, saying to her, in an almost conversational voice, 'Your bitch of a sister frightened you, didn't she?'

Fascinated, Dinah nodded, mute again. She remembered the stream of spite from Violet's lips on the night before her wedding, designed to turn her against the man whom Violet coveted, but whom her despised little sister had won.

'She told you I was a tiger in bed, didn't she?'

This time Dinah felt that she must speak, 'Yes, she did... How did you know?'

'I'm a mind reader,' he said lightly, cursing Violet for making his task more difficult. 'She said that you wouldn't satisfy me?'

How did he know such things? Could he read minds? More than once since their marriage, he had told her when he had thought that people were lying to them, and so far, he had always been correct in his judgments.

'Yes,' she managed through stiff lips.

'I shan't be a tiger with you, Dinah. You do believe me, I hope.'

He put up his hand, his beautiful hand, turned her face towards him and kissed her on the lips, a light kiss, a brotherly kiss.

'I shall try to be as gentle as you would wish me to be, but...loving...Dinah, is often not a gentle thing, you understand me?'

He gave her another kiss, then, when she opened her mouth to answer him, a much less brotherly kiss.

Cobie could feel her heart beating. It was like holding a frightened bird in his hands, the bird throbbing at his touch, fearful, wanting its freedom. He was using his voice to quieten the bird.

Now he turned her fully into his arms. She stiffened for a moment, but she didn't resist him. He put his hands into her hair, and kissed her, more strongly this time, forcing her lips apart gently. One hand trailed down her neck, and to Dinah his touch was like fire running down her body, causing it to tremble and shake.

She was on her back now, and he was half above her. His voice said lazily in her ear, 'We're wearing too many clothes, Dinah, but we can't send for our servants to remove them, can we? What do you propose we do?'

And then, his voice loving her, and teasing her, he whispered, 'You do know, you do understand what we are finally going to do tonight?'

She whispered into his ear, 'Yes. Violet told me,' and she shivered again.

'But not why,' he said, a trifle grimly, but his blue eyes were soft. 'We are meant to enjoy ourselves, Dinah, and from our enjoyment there may come a new life. There might be no new life if enjoyment were missing. You understand me?'

Yes, she understood him, But she couldn't imagine doing what Violet had told her of with anyone, let alone the man who was holding her so closely. And yet...and yet...strange things were happening to her, for she suddenly wanted to touch *him*.

'Shall I...shall I undress for you?' she asked him shyly.

Her husband thought, wryly, that she was saying it as though she were asking, 'Do you wish to tie me to the rack?'

'Don't you think that's my privilege?' he told her gently. 'And, in return, you might do the same for me.'

Dinah closed her eyes.

'If you like,' she told him meekly, a lamb preparing herself for the slaughter.

'Oh, I do like,' he smiled, and rose from the bed, to free her, but only for a moment.

'Stand up, Dinah, my love, and face me. A husband likes to enjoy his wife in every way possible.'

She did his bidding without demur, and then, with as

much, if not more, dexterity than Pearson or Hortense, he slowly stripped her of her ballroom finery.

Only Pearson and Hortense did not caress her with lips and mouth while they did so. Nor did they brush their hands across her body, stroking every part of it, even her secret parts, so that it began to vibrate and sing with such pleasure that suddenly she was barely able to stand, but sighed and sagged against him.

She was naked, except for the jewels around her neck and wrists and on her hands, and, hanging unresisting against him, she felt his clever hands continue their work. Suddenly he laughed, deep in his throat, and swung her around to face the long mirror, and stood behind her, still caressing her.

Was that Dinah Grant in the mirror? Was she that wanton maenad, her hair around her shoulders, a man's hands on, and in, her body. They produced suddenly such a sensation of mindless pleasure that she cried his name aloud, closing her eyes, when the ecstasy took her.

'Open your eyes, Dinah!' he commanded, and she did so—to see his face behind hers in the mirror, pleasure at her pleasure on it.

During, and after, the mindless ecstasy he supported her, for her legs were like water—which he must have known, for he held her so tightly, so lovingly—saying, and his own breathing was short, 'There, that was nothing to be frightened of, Dinah, was it?—and it was only a foretaste. Now we must share our pleasure. But first, *you* must strip and love *me*.'

All conscious thought had flown, and Dinah's fear had flown with it. Her inward trembling stopped at last, the rapid beat of her heart slowed, until she was able to strip him in exchange for him having stripped her. She unbuttoned his shirt, removed it, unbuttoned his elegant black trousers and helped him to remove them, until he stood naked before her—they were Adam and Eve together before the Fall.

Dinah shivered and panted again at the sight of him. He was more beautiful stripped than clothed, and she understood Violet's rage at losing him. She was still a little fearful of him, and of his masculinity which, in all the nude male statues she had seen, had been cunningly hidden from sight. Nothing had prepared her for the sight of a roused man.

Cobie saw her reaction, leaned towards her and, taking her in his arms, so that they stood, entwined, a pair of lovers before the mirror, said in her ear, 'You enjoyed the pleasure I gave you just now, Dinah?'

'You know I did,' she whispered back.

'Do you also understand that, as I pleasured you, I might like to be pleasured *by* you?' and he took her hand and slipped it between them, so that he lay stiff and erect in it.

Dinah gasped at the sensation, for what she held was as smooth and warm as velvet, and instinctively her own hand moved to pleasure him after the fashion in which he had pleasured her, a moment before.

He said hoarsely, 'Yes! Stroke me, Dinah, as I stroked you, ah...' and when she did so, tentatively at first, and then more strongly, he sighed and sobbed exactly as she had done, until she felt the ecstasy take *him*. So now it was *he* who was shuddering, his face in her neck, and it was her name he was calling, and she was holding *him* in the final ecstasy.

After a moment he said, still panting, 'You see what you do to me, Dinah. For all my strength, I am helpless before you.'

'As I was to you,' she agreed, her own breathing short again, for his ecstasy had roused her once more.

He nodded, mute, as she had been, and then, a moment later, he lifted her on to the bed, to lie beside him.

For the first time, she moved towards him, turning to put her arms around him, to feel him warm against her.

The desire to touch him, *there*, to kiss him, was so strong that she found her wanton hands were now at work about his body. He laughed his soundless laugh again, and rolled her beneath him, saying, 'Impatient nymph that you are, your satyr needs a little time to recover. But some gentle loving will revive him, I think.'

Revived he was and, before long, Dinah was calling his name and begging him to do she knew not what, 'Oh, please, Cobie, please.'

With joy in his heart that his young wife had not allowed her fear of him—and of loving—to destroy her, but after experiencing their separate joys was looking to him to provide them with a mutual one, he finally made her his. At last the two became one, and Dinah discovered the pleasure that follows and transcends pain.

'Not tigers,' he whispered, after their mutual ecstasy had ended, 'but cubs, playing together. Making love's not a battlefield, Dinah, it's a playground of happiness, of shared joy.'

So why, after laughing with him in their final transports, was she crying? she asked him a little later. Her tears were salt on his tongue, and he was licking them away.

'Strong emotions, Dinah, resemble one another strongly. Tears and laughter are never far apart.'

Well, that was true enough, she thought, wondering why she had ever been frightened of him. She was a little awed by his ability, not only to overcome her fear, but to lead her into realms of sensation she had never thought to experience.

He had told her that he did not, could not, love anyone. Yet what he had done for her surely had love in it for, novice though she was, Dinah was already beginning to understand that he had subsumed his own pleasure in hers in order to ensure that she should be gently initiated into true womanhood.

Before they finally fell asleep she caressed him. In doing so, Dinah consciously registered what she had barely noticed during their love play: that his back was horribly and brutally scarred. She could feel the welts and ridges beneath her fingers. She said nothing, but when he rose from the bed to slip on a dressing gown with his back to her, she saw it fully for the first time, and the sight horrified her.

Unlike Violet, when she had first seen it, she didn't question him, and again, unlike Violet, she knew, intuitively, because she had never seen such a thing before, that he had been cruelly and brutally beaten. His explanation to Violet that he had been dragged for some distance on his back by a mustang which he had failed to control would not have deceived Dinah.

Her own heart was full of love for him, because of the consideration with which he had just treated her, so different from anything which Violet had suggested might be her fate. How could anyone have been so cruel to him, he who had been so kind to her?

Dinah was sure that, kind though he was, he had been telling the truth when he had said that he did not love her, and she wondered all over again why he had virtually bought her from Rainey. She could only be grateful to him, not only for rescuing her from Violet and penury, but for making her his true wife in such a tender and apparently loving manner.

'Remember this, Dinah,' she told herself, when she too, fell asleep, 'appearances often deceive'—and did not know why she said it.

Chapter Ten

Walker was meeting one of his informers in a small pub off the Strand. His man was a member of the demimonde, who called himself Captain Legge. He was someone who was accepted in male society, who was present at little all-masculine dinners, and was welcome in men's clubs, but who was never invited to such important thrashes as the Hertfords.

Despite that, he knew all the gossip that ran around Mayfair and Belgravia, and some that didn't, but which was often more important. A few weeks ago Walker had asked him to discover what he could about Mr Jacobus Grant, the American financier. There would be a little something for him, Walker said, if he came up trumps.

He was already drinking when Walker arrived, and said, jovially, 'There you are, Will. A noggin for you, eh?'

Walker didn't refuse. He accepted his pint and drank some of it down before saying, 'Well?'

'Very well. What's it worth?'

Walker named a sum. His informant laughed scornfully. 'More'n that. I want at least a tenner.'

'A tenner! You're joking. Scotland Yard ain't made of money.'

'That's the price, chum. I've his life story for you. You're not the only one interested in him and his past. Several people are after knowing all about Mr Cobie Grant, and his goings on, and are prepared to pay me well. But if you don't want to know...' and he made to get up and go.

'Oh, very well. I'll give you your tenner. But you'd better make sure that what you tell me is worth it.'

'Your Mr Grant is a strange sort of cove altogether. He was supposed to have been adopted by Jack Dilhorne, the big man at Dilhorne and Rutherfurds, in the States, up there with the Vanderbilts and Rockefellers. Gossip says, though, that he was Dilhorne's bastard by his wife Marietta Hope, born some little time before they were married. Her father was Senator *Jacobus Hope*—get it?—which seems to bear that out. Also he's the image of Jack Dilhorne, and Jack's brother here, Sir Alan Dilhorne of Temple Hatton, late Cabinet minister, but he's never been acknowledged.'

'Dilhorne,' muttered Walker, thinking of Mr Dilley and Mr Horne, and a man who had laughed in his face and as much as admitted that he was a bastard. 'Go on, this is interesting.'

'He was brought up as a rich man's son. He did well at Yale as a scholar and an athlete. He became a mining engineer, and rumour says that there was a plum job in the firm waiting for him when he graduated. Except that, suddenly, without warning, he threw everything up, went to Arizona Territory and got himself a little post at a tinpot mine in a place called Bratt's Crossing.

'After being there for six months he left quite suddenly and disappeared for over eighteen months before turning up in New York with a small fortune which he made into a big one on Wall Street—he wouldn't touch his foster-father's money, I'm told. He became one of Wall Street's biggest pirates.'

'Where'd he get his money from?' asked Walker, interested in this dime-novel adventure.

'Who knows? My informant says that recently a Pinkerton's man was sent to the Territory, but Bratt's Crossing has been a ghost town for years and there was little to be discovered about what happened ten years ago. It seems that about a year or so after Grant left the mine was blown up in a fracas among thieves. The local rancher, named Blenkiron, who ran it for Southwest Associates, and who had earlier employed Grant, was killed in a shoot-out by two ruffians. His hired gunman, Greer, a noted villain, was wounded in it, but had left the district and couldn't be found.

'With the rancher dead, and the mine useless, there was no reason for anyone to live there. The editor of the local paper was a woman, and she was tracked down, quite by chance. She had married the man who had kept the store at Bratt's Crossing and now owned Blenkiron's ranch. They both said that they had no idea where Grant had gone when he left Bratt's Crossing. He never came back, they said.

'They thought he might have found a job with another mine in the Southwest, but the only one being exploited at the time was at San Miguel in New Mexico. When the agent went there to enquire about him, no one had ever heard of Grant, and didn't recognise him from the tintype they were shown.

'The agent says he thought that the Bratt's Crossing woman, Jane Jackson, was lying, that she knew more than she said, but she stuck to her story. Funny thing, the mine at San Miguel was blown up in yet another quarrel among thieves shortly before the one at Bratt's Crossing, but it wasn't permanently damaged.

'Whatever the truth of it all, when Grant reappeared

again, it was to descend on New York and begin to make his reputation. Not just for making money—he's a devil with the women, they say. His first major killing on Wall Street came when he took over Southwest Mining, and had the president sent to prison for fraud. The mine at San Miguel, which is still being worked, was owned by Southwest—Grant owns it now.

'What was he doing during the eighteen months or so he was missing? Was it all a coincidence that two mines were blown up when he was in the Southwest, and that he took over Southwest after he made his pile—or wasn't it?'

'Perhaps,' Walker said. 'This may be very interesting. But it's of no use to me. Is he honest?'

Captain Legge gave a hollow laugh. 'Honest! Makes a mysterious fortune in the Southwest, God knows where or how, becomes a tiger in the world of finance by sailing close to the wind, turns himself into a multi-millionaire, richer than his supposed father—with whom he has little to do—what do you think?'

'I think,' Walker said, 'that he looks as though butter wouldn't melt in his mouth, and I always distrust gents who look like that. And your man thinks he had something to do with San Miguel?'

'Sure of it, but he can't prove a thing. There were a lot of young hoodlums running around the Territory making fortunes for themselves, and some of them managed to hang on to their money. But I've met Grant several times, here in London, and he'd stick out like a sore thumb in a frontier town, that's for sure.'

Walker thought of dirty Mr Dilley/Horne, who melted into the crowd in a London pub, and who garrotted innocent policemen in alleys, and who seemed to possess a dozen different voices.

Suppose that he had disguised himself before he went to San Miguel? By some means turned himself into the sort of grimy ruffian who terrorised decent people in the Territory? Would anyone ever have believed that such a villain could be clean-cut, civilised Mr Jacobus Grant? And why would rich young Jacobus Grant want to do such a thing, anyway?

'Nearly ten years ago, all this,' said Captain Legge cheerfully, 'and now, after making Lady Kenilworth his mistress, he's married into the aristocracy, and the Prince of Wales calls him friend. What makes you think he's up to his games here?'

'Things,' said Walker darkly, 'things.' He could believe anything of Mr Dilley, with his magic tricks. Anything at all. Even becoming a kind of Billy the Kid might not be beyond him, weird though that might seem.

Dinah Grant knew nothing of her husband's magic tricks. The day after the Hertfords' reception she had said to him at breakfast, her tone as impersonal as his was sometimes, 'Why did you marry me, Cobie? I'm sure that it wasn't because you loved me.'

If he was taken by surprise he did not show it.

He said slowly, 'I married you, Dinah, for a variety of reasons, not all of them creditable. I meant what I told you before we were married. That I thought you would make me a good wife and a mother for my children. In time, you will be both, in the fullest sense, I hope. Be sure that you will always have my respect, even if I cannot pretend to offer you love. I believe that, unlike most women, you would not wish me to lie to you about that.'

Dinah nodded, mutely. She had expected nothing else from him. Had he really meant it when he had told her before their marriage that he didn't think that he could ever love anyone? She thought that he might have said it to soften the blow of his not loving her, but it seemed that he had been telling her the truth.

'It must be hard for you,' she said, 'to know that of yourself. To be unable to love.'

'Better so,' he replied. Was there a trace of bitterness in his tone? 'I would rather that you didn't love me, Dinah. The women who have been foolish enough to love me in the past have usually paid a hard price for doing so.'

The memory of Belita, who had died because of him, was strong in him. The lost look which Dinah had worn when he had first met her, and which had brought Belita's memory back to him so sharply, had gone. But there was also Jane to remember, and Susanna, and Susanna's desperate behaviour since he had been compelled to reject her recently. How much better it would have been if she had never met and loved Cobie Grant!

He did not want love to complicate the friendship which was growing up between him and his young wife. He almost told her so, but decided that she was being brave enough in surviving marriage to him at all, without his being as brutally honest as that. Like Marietta, his mother, he had wondered how Dinah would cope with him.

Well, was apparently the answer!

Dinah thought so too a week after she had really become his wife. She was being serenaded. It was four o'clock in the afternoon, and she and Cobie were in bed—or, rather, were on top of his bed. They had spent the morning and the early afternoon at the Zoo.

'What, never been there?' he had exclaimed in mock horror. He had immediately ordered the carriage, and they had enjoyed a few happy hours walking round and admiring the animals, about which he seemed to know everything important. This didn't surprise Dinah: his apparently encyclopaedic knowledge had lost its power to amaze her.

After that they had been driven to a restaurant and had taken lunch on a terrace overlooking the Thames. He had ordered wine, and drank more of it than she had ever seen him do before. He had insisted that she drink her share, too.

She had never felt so foolishly happy as she did when she was being driven across London, back to Park Lane in the open landau, her parasol up, and her husband opposite to her, saying in a low voice, 'What shall we do now, Dinah? It's a day to celebrate. I know, let's...'

He raised his eyebrows at her and left the sentence unfinished, so that she began to giggle helplessly.

'Read a book of sermons,' he finished, looking severe. 'I think that I may have one in my room.'

He leaned back, looking particularly innocent, an expression which she was coming to know. It meant that Mr Jacobus Grant was contemplating, or doing, something exceedingly naughty.

Oddly enough, she had seen it on his face when they had walked through the Zoo that morning. They had turned a corner sharply, and had almost knocked over a large lugubrious-looking man, who had started back from them, looking embarrassed.

'Oh, I *do* beg your pardon,' Cobie had exclaimed, all polite embarrassment, *that look* on his face. 'We didn't see you coming, did we, my dear? Pray do accept our apologies for any inconvenience we may have inadvertently caused you. A lovely day, is it not? You are interested in the animals, too?' he finished brightly.

The man had seemed more distressed by the encounter than they were. 'Not at all,' he had stammered, and shuffled his big feet. 'I mean...'

'I can particularly recommend the lions to you,' Cobie had gone on gaily. 'It will be feeding time for

them soon, I understand. Not Christians—or criminals—of course. Those distressing little habits ended
some time ago, thank goodness. Don't let us detain
you.'

They had turned yet another corner after they left the
man, who was still dithering, and some impulse made
Dinah look back. He had not moved from where they
had collided with him, but was watching them walk
away, a bemused expression on his face.

Yet another impulse which she didn't understand—
she seemed to have a lot of them when she was out
with her husband—made her ask, 'Did that man know
you, Cobie? He gave you the oddest look.'

'What man, my dear?' he had asked her, turning his
bright blue eyes on her. 'Oh, that man,' he said, following her gaze. 'No, I don't think that you could say that
he knows me,' which was, Dinah thought afterwards,
an odd way of answering her. It was yet another of his
two-edged remarks which no amount of puzzling could
explain.

He wasn't being two-edged on the bed. He was completely, gloriously, straightforwardly naked after a
happy hour spent pleasuring Lady Dinah Grant, who, a
Japanese kimono carelessly wrapped about her, was listening to him while he played, not the guitar, nor the
piano, but a banjo.

She was leaning against the bed-head, he was facing
her at the bottom, tickling her toes with his, and was
singing what he told her was a song from the American
South called 'The Devil Take the Blue-tail Fly'.

The voice which he was using to sing it was deep
and throaty, not at all like his usual pleasant baritone,
and she was lying there feeling deliciously sinful, ach-
ing a little, for it had been a rather more vigorous session than usual. She had the notion that slowly, slowly,

he was initiating her into the wilder shores of passion and, if so, she didn't mind a bit, not she.

'Where did you learn that?' she asked him sleepily.

'At the Yale Glee Club. It was my star turn there.'

It would be a star turn anywhere, she thought, closing her eyes, and letting languor overtake her. *He* would be a star turn anywhere.

'Is there anything you can't do?' she asked him, opening her eyes after he had finished the song in a flurry of major chords.

He nodded his head, and said smartly, 'Have a baby.'

She prodded him, hard, with her toes. 'Not that, silly.' She had taken to teasing him lately, and he seemed to like it.

'I can give you one, though,' he told her. 'It's fun getting there, isn't it? What about a bath? I feel sticky.'

Dinah said, 'I'm sticky, too. I suppose I'd better go to my room, and ring for Pearson to run one for me.'

'I'll run one for you,' he promised, beginning to play the banjo again, and singing soft words which she could not distinguish in the gaps in his conversation with her.

'No need to trouble Pearson—or anyone else. We could have one together.' Now he was playing a music hall song, ending with the words, 'If you want to know the time, ask a policeman.'

Memory stirred in her. 'That's what that man we bumped into this morning looked like. A policeman.'

'Clever girl,' drawled Cobie lazily. 'Exactly what I thought myself. Who was he there to arrest? The lions—or the tigers? You, me?'

Dinah remembered what he had been saying before policemen walked into the conversation, 'Do you mean…have a bath…together?'

'Why not?' he told her idly, running his toes down her calf. 'We could discuss the meaning of life in it.'

'Do you think that he was there to arrest someone? I've never seen anyone arrested.'

Dinah had never engaged in such ridiculous conversations in her life as those she had with her husband. He seemed to encourage her to flit about verbally, not say, 'Oh, Dinah, don't be *silly*,' as everyone but Faa did when she let her imagination rove loose.

'Probably.'

He rose with one agile movement, and made his way to the door which opened on to the splendid bathroom which he had had installed after he had bought his Park Lane home.

'Tell me,' he asked, putting his head around the door after he had started the taps running, 'what is your opinion of the notion of the transmigration of souls? That should do for starters.'

Dinah was still occupied with thoughts about the policeman. 'He certainly wasn't there to arrest me.'

'Who? Oh, the policeman. Come on, Dinah, we mustn't waste all this lovely water, or he will be after you.'

Cobie bent down, scooped her up and, before she could say any more, deposited her, kimono and all, into the deliciously warm bath, before following her in.

'It was lucky that I ordered a big one,' he told her. 'I must have had you in mind... Let me do dreadful things to you, Lady Dinah,' and he proceeded to do them...

There was a great deal of splashing, water flew everywhere, and Dinah found herself squeaking, 'I'm upside down, Cobie, I'll drown!'

'No, you won't,' he said breathlessly, lifting them both a little so that she surfaced to cry, 'Oh, oh, no, don't stop, please...'

'Shan't,' he gasped. 'Exciting, isn't it?'

It was.

More water flew into the air, and by the time he had finished with her Cobie had to put a gentle hand over her mouth to silence her when she shrieked in ecstasy.

Later she said, a little timidly, for it was not the sort of question one ought to ask perhaps, even of one's husband, 'Oh, Cobie, have you ever done that before?' Then she laughed a little. 'How silly I am. Of course you have. What a question.'

'Yes,' he said gently, stroking her damp hair, and kissing her ear.

'With Violet,' she couldn't help asking, thinking, Oh, please, not with Violet.

'No,' he said, holding her close, 'Not with Violet. Only once before—long ago. When you were still a little girl.'

He was remembering Jenny, the madam who had run the girls at the brothel at Bratt's Crossing, and knew that even the man he had become had never valued her properly. For whatever reason, she had given him back his manhood after Greer had tried to beat it out of him. She had skilfully restored his self-respect, and her only reward had been to be half-forgotten until some impulse had made him pull Dinah into the bath with him.

'Long ago,' she repeated, and then, as though some psychic current had passed between them, she said, hesitantly, 'When you...when your back was hurt?'

Surprised, Cobie's hand stopped its stroking. He looked down at his young wife who was beginning to show a measure of intuitive understanding for which he could never have hoped.

'Yes,' he said, slowly. 'It helped to heal it.'

'Oh.' Dinah sat up, her face alight, her eyes like stars. 'You are to lie still now. You must be exhausted, holding me up like that. Now, it's your turn to be loved.'

It was the first time that she had initiated love play

between them, taken the lead. She rolled over on top of him, kissed him gently on the lips, and began to use her hands and body to pleasure him, as he had pleasured her. She took her time, laughing at him, and teasing him, and he marvelled at the change in her from the timid girl he had first met at Moorings.

Then thought stopped, and this time it was Dinah who put her hand over his mouth to stifle his cries.

Pleasure over, they climbed out of the cooling bath water. Cobie pulled dry towels around them and they went to sleep, there on the bathroom floor, the happy, sated sleep of those who have shared great physical joy.

Cobie's valet, Giles, glanced at the clock. His master had told him earlier on that he and Lady Dinah would be dining at Mr Van Deusen's and that he should be ready to present himself at six of the clock. But Giles was discreet. He knew that his master and his lady had gone up to their bedroom when they had come in, and had not come down for the tea which had been laid out for them in the drawing room. Tea in the servants' room had been eaten to the accompaniment of nods and winks.

Six o'clock came and went, and still Mr Grant had not rung his bell. Hortense was sent upstairs to Lady Dinah's room, 'But she is not there,' she said, returning downstairs. 'She must be with him. They will be late.'

'I don't think they'll mind,' sniggered Boots, to be reprimanded by senior staff.

At half past six Giles put his head into his master's bedroom. The bed and the room were empty, and all was quiet. He crept over to the bathroom door, opened it as quietly as he could, and looked in. They were lying asleep on the floor, swathed in towels, water everywhere. His grin, when he tip-toed out, was knowing, but kind.

So, Milord, for that was his nickname for his American master, had been having his wicked way with his lady as vigorously as with his whores, had he? Well, he would have to think of some way of waking him up, otherwise, if Milord's track record with women held good, it might be midnight before anyone would see them again.

Cobie, who since his days as an outlaw in the Territory had always slept lightly, heard the door shut quietly behind Giles. He sat up, looked down at his sleeping wife, who was learning the game of love so rapidly that he would have to run to keep ahead of her, and kissed her awake. 'Time to wake up,' he told her, 'the world is waiting for us.'

'S'all a waste of time, guv,' Bates said. 'He's laughing at us, and he isn't doing anything. Jumped on me with his lady wife on his arm today, he did. At the Zoo. Thinks it's all a joke. He won't do anything while we watch him.'

Walker stared morosely at him. Only that morning the Commissioner had sent for him and had said, severely, 'I know you're still having that feller who bribed us followed, Walker, but you haven't found anything solid yet, have you? I'm giving you an order. You're to let it go.'

Walker considered for a moment telling the Commissioner that he knew who the feller was, but he had no real proof that Horne/Dilley/Grant was doing anything criminal, and gave that idea up.

'Let me have until the end of the week,' he said at last. 'Then I'll forget him.'

Which was a lie, of course. He wasn't going to forget Mr Dilley in a hurry.

'No, Walker. Today. You hear me, Walker. I will be obeyed on this.'

Walker heard him. More morose than ever he went downstairs and gave the news to Bates and Alcott. 'No more unexpected presents,' muttered Bates, 'but no standing about in all hours and all weathers, either.'

He and Alcott were not the only ones who had received gifts. Walker had gone home one night to find his wife cutting up a great pineapple, a rare treat. The message on the basket of fruit which had arrived that afternoon simply said 'From an admirer'. His wife was so delighted that Walker was compelled to accept the pineapple and eat it—gall in the mouth as it was.

'Besides, if he's that clever,' Bates told Alcott before he found out what his new duties were, 'he'd lose us if he wanted to—only he don't want. And for why? He ain't doing nothing.'

He had tracked Mr Dilley round London two nights ago. He was having an evening out with his friend, Mr Van Deusen, and they had visited several clubs and dives in and around the Haymarket, Mr Van Deusen having a mind to sample London's demi-monde. Now, he was going to have a night at home for a change, and forget Mr Dilley who took a delight in trailing him round London, letting him know every now and then that he was quite aware of his shadow.

He wasn't going to be shot of Mr Dilley as easily as that, no, indeed, for when he arrived at the Yard early the next morning it was to find Walker waiting for him, his face alight.

'Something's broken, Bates, and if that damned fool upstairs hadn't pulled us off Dilley's case we might know more than we do. What's happened isn't nice— and what *might* happen might not be nice, either, if I know Mr Dilley. Something tells me he's not going to like what's happened.'

He laughed loudly, rubbing his hands together.

'Well, what has happened?' Bates asked. Walker had a habit of not telling you, keeping you on tenterhooks.

Walker told him the unpleasant news.

Bates nodded, and said, 'No, he's not going to like that, sir.' He hesitated. 'Can't say I like it much meself.'

'No more do I, Bates—so what price him, eh?' said Walker. 'We might flush him into the open yet.'

Cobie was spending the morning at Southwest Mining's sumptuous new offices in the City. He was plainly dressed, little of his society splendour showing.

He was reading a report from one of his managers when his secretary put his head around the door.

'There's a man downstairs wishes to speak to a Mr Dilley. He says that he was told that if he wished to speak to him urgently he could leave a message here. You said that you wished to be informed if such a request were made.'

'Urgent? You're sure he said urgent, Rogers.'

'His exact word, sir.'

'Where have you put him?'

'In the small office off the main hall.'

'Good. Tell him I'll be with him shortly.'

Urgent. He needed time to think what might be urgent. Something told him what it might be, but he pushed the thought away. Useless to speculate: he must be ready for anything.

In the downstairs office the clerk he had hired in his persona as Mr Dilley stared at the man walking towards him. There was something so cold and hard about him, so unlike shabby and cheerful Mr Dilley that he swallowed, and said, a trifle defensively, 'I wouldn't have come, only you did say to do so if it were urgent...'

'Quite right. But I trust you to be discreet on such visits. That is why I chose you. To forget—as well as to remember. And that is why I pay you well. What is it?'

'It's the child, Mr Dilley. The little girl, Lizzie Steele. The one you put in the home whose affairs I look after for you. It seems that she disappeared yesterday. The Salvation Army Captain, Bristow, was waiting for me at the office when I arrived there today. They…the police…he alerted the police…think that they've found her. About six o'clock this morning, they said, a girl child was taken from the Thames. They're pretty sure it's her. He…Captain Bristow…thought you ought… would want to know…'

'She's dead.' Cobie heard his own voice as though it were someone else's. The rage had begun to rise in him. He repressed it and asked, 'That man, Hoskyns, the one whom you've been keeping tabs on for me, since he left Madame Louise's. Have you any information about him?'

The clerk nodded, unsurprised by this apparently irrelevant request. He had begun to know Mr Dilley, and nothing could now surprise him.

'I've had a man on him, sir. He's started up again in a tenement near the river. The old trade. Very discreet— a few fine gentlemen—and some as aren't.'

Cobie nodded. 'Give me a minute,' he said coolly. There was little outward sign of the inward rage which was consuming him. He had learned to control it. When he was younger it had been written on his face like a flag, causing men to fall away from him frightened. Now it was burning hotly inside him, but invisible.

'Where have they taken her?'

'There's a morgue at Limehouse, down by the Thames. They fetched her out of the river not far from there. She'd not been in long, they said.'

Cobie walked to the door and ordered curtly, 'Wait here for me.'

He took the stairs back to his room two at a time, calling for Rogers once he reached the top.

'Rogers! Lend me your old coat, the one you use for working in the basement. Send a note to Park Lane, to Lady Dinah. Present my apologies to her, and tell her that I shall be out on business all day. I may be back this evening in time to take her to Lady Kenilworth's for supper, but if not, she may have the carriage to go alone.'

All the way to the morgue, wearing Rogers's old coat over his own finer clothes, he was cursing inwardly that he had not kept a better eye on Hoskyns—or on the child's stepfather or on Sir Ratcliffe Heneage. He could not believe that her death was an accident. She knew too much. He should have been more careful—sent her into the country, but he had done what he thought was best, leaving her where she felt happy among all that she knew.

Anger at such foolish speculation overtook him. He must think what he would do if his suspicions about her death were correct.

Bristow was waiting for him at the police station, his old face grey.

'Mr Dilley,' he said. 'I knew you'd come.'

Cobie said tightly, 'It is Lizzie, isn't it?'

Bristow bowed his head. 'Yes, I've seen her.' He hesitated. 'It will be rather a shock, Mr Dilley...she had been most brutally...treated...before she died.'

'No doubt,' said Cobie. He looked about him when he entered the police station. He knew that since early yesterday he had lost his shadows. He wondered sardonically if he were about to acquire them again; if Walker were somewhere near. Scotland Yard would have been informed immediately of the brutal murder of a child. But in the face of Lizzie's death that whole business with the police seemed stupid and far away.

He followed Bristow to where other policemen stood about. He was introduced to a weary-looking Inspector Jordan as Mr Dilley, the benefactor of the home where Lizzie had lived, who had come to make sure that she was the victim, although the home's superintendent had already identified her.

For once Cobie was so far removed from his normal self that he was not aware that he was being watched. Not only by Bates or Alcott, but also by Walker, who stood hidden behind a half-open door in the morgue, staring at him while he looked down at Lizzie's poor, broken body.

She had been kidnapped, there was no doubt of that, and then she had been taken to a house—Hoskyns's, probably—to be used by one of his clients, killed in the using, and then disposed of in the river. To be found much sooner than might have been expected.

Cold bastard, thought Walker, watching Mr Dilley's impassive stare, unaware of the red rage that was burning inside him. He saw that Mr Dilley was wearing his fine clothes beneath his shabby coat. He watched him turn away abruptly and heard him say to Hedges, the superintendent of the home, 'How did this happen?' and his voice was ice.

'She went out for a walk with some of her friends, after school,' Hedges told him numbly. 'She disappeared quite suddenly, it seems. They were playing by the river when they realised she had gone. After looking for her they came home. They thought she might have run ahead of them, but she hadn't. We went out to look for her—we thought she might have lost her way. Last night we told the police. This morning a lighter picked up her body from the river.'

Last night he had been amusing himself with Dinah while Lizzie died a cruel death.

He said to the Inspector, 'Has no one any idea of

where she might have been taken after she was kidnapped? It is obvious from her condition what happened to her—what was done to her.'

'None,' said Inspector Jordan, who had stood by while Cobie had identified Lizzie. 'Besides, she might not have been taken to a bordello, sir. She might have been delivered to a private house. It's not the first child's body we have fished from the Thames in this condition.'

'So I believe.' Cobie's voice was still ice, almost as though it hurt him to speak.

'Familiarity, of course, breeds contempt. But the kidnapping must have been organised by someone who knew what they were doing, it was done so neatly, and I doubt that she was taken far. In how many houses in London are children for sale, Inspector?'

The policeman said, a little stolid, 'We do what we can, sir.'

Cobie turned away, saying before he did so, 'I know. It's not your fault. As you say, you do what you can. More than I do.'

Walker was still watching his quarry. He was strangely unlike the mocking man who had driven himself and his men mad for the last few weeks.

One of the policemen standing by him said, 'That's the chap what rescued her from Madame Louise's, the Salvation Army man said. Put her in a home he helped to finance. Must give him a nasty turn to see her like that. Must have thought she was safe.'

Walker remembered what Mr Dilley had told him about rescuing a child.

Now he had a new worry. If Mr Dilley had been willing to pay out a fortune to have Madame Louise's place closed and put out of business because he had discovered that children were being bought and sold there, what would he do to the man, or men, who had killed Lizzie Steele?

He remembered Bates telling him of his near garrotting, and Mr Dilley's threat that he would kill those who tried to thwart or cheat him. He must ask permission for him to be watched: for twenty-four hours a day, if possible.

Cobie, still in the rage's thrall, talked with the Inspector, with Bristow, and with Hedges. He told them that he would pay for Lizzie's funeral, and tried to reassure the superintendent that it was not his fault that Lizzie had been kidnapped.

Finally, everything having been arranged, he left with his clerk. 'You will show me where this house which Hoskyns runs is situated,' he ordered him. 'Does Hoskyns live there?'

The clerk nodded. 'Over the shop, you might say. Our man made a plan of the place. Got inside once by sampling the regular trade. Knows where the children are kept, and some of the older girls. They and Hoskyns live in the attics.'

'Good.' Before he left his clerk at his dingy office, he collected the plan of Hoskyns's house to study at his leisure. It was not yet lunch time, and he was already deciding that if he were going to strike at those whom he thought were behind Lizzie's death, he would do so quickly while they were still congratulating themselves that she was out of the way.

He had already decided not to inform the police that he had found Hoskyns's new bolt-hole, and allow them to do his work for them. He suspected that since Sir Ratcliffe—and others—had obviously been warned of the raid on Madame Louise's, despite his wish that they should not be, it was likely that Hoskyns also might be tipped off in time to turn his house into something respectable.

It was not that he thought that Walker would cheat him: no, it was those mysterious superiors above him who would perform that trick. It would be safer to act on his own—and take the consequences, if there were any.

Thanking God that his shadows had disappeared, he drove to Half Moon Street, praying that Mr Hendrick Van Deusen would be at home—which he was. His luck was in, if Lizzie's had been out. Luck! He must remember that it was not automatic, but must be ensured by careful planning. He had reached the stage where the whole world appeared clear and plain to him, and planning was easy.

Mr Van Deusen led him into his drawing room, and Cobie could see at once that the Professor knew that he had come to ask a favour. Something in his stance, perhaps, some memory of dangerous days long ago.

'Professor,' he said abruptly, 'I have come to ask you for back-up. May I count on it?'

The Professor made no effort to ask why or what for. He simply said, 'Say the word, Jake, you know that you have only to say the word.'

'Right. Now listen,' and he began to speak rapidly, ticking points off on his fingers, the Professor nodding, occasionally putting in a word.

Later, all arrangements made, having been seen with Mr Van Deusen in various clubs and haunts of pleasure from early afternoon onwards, Cobie was in one of his secret temporary homes situated in an alley not far from where Hoskyns lived.

There was a change of clothing there—and something more. In the space between the ceiling and the roof he had hidden one of his six shooters, its holster and belt, and a small box of ammunition. It was a Colt .44, not a .45. Many Western gunmen, and Cobie had been one of them, preferred the .44.

He changed rapidly. He fetched out the gun, strapped the holster on to his left hip, tying it down with a piece of rawhide. It would be hidden beneath his shabby frock-coat. Out of habit he began to practise his quick draw—not that it would be needed in Limehouse! Indeed, he hoped that the gun would not be needed at all.

In his sleeve he carried a shiv, a small knife as sharp as the razor it resembled: its sheath was strapped on to his right arm under his coat. Last of all he picked up a dirty black silk muffler, to be worn round his neck, since the day was too warm for another of his trusty tartan woollen ones.

Finally he took out his agent's plan of Hoskyns's bordello, and began to study it again, carefully reading the notes in the agent's meticulous copper plate hand, so much at odds with what he was writing about.

It was a bright early evening when, grimy, anonymous, one of the crowd of lost souls who roved London's dockside area, he turned into a pub not far from Hoskyns's house, where he could watch for a suitable moment to make his play... A carriage was slowly tracking him. It was waiting not far from the pub to pick him up when he left, but it wasn't the police on his trail this time. Inside, Mr Hendrick Van Deusen, late the Professor, scourge of the law and outlaws alike, sat in it, reflectively smoking a large cigar—as was his usual habit.

Hoskyns was counting his money. Last night had brought him what the Yankees called a bonanza. The pickings in this place were not so good as those at Madame Louise's—but it was all his own, and the police hadn't found it yet. The house didn't open for business until eleven o'clock, the cover of darkness being all important so far as the major part of his business was concerned.

After his accounts were finished he went around, checking everything, before his small staff arrived. He was lighting the oil lamps, when Nemesis struck. One moment he had the taper in his hand, minding his own business, the next he was being strangled, unable to call for help. Consciousness came and went, he was being manhandled along the landing, into his own room.

He was thrust into a chair. He was blindfolded, his hands were tied behind his back, his legs to the chair legs, to hold him secure. His keys had been taken from his pocket, he had felt them go, and his assailant was saying in a hoarse voice, 'We're locked in, Hoskyns, and we shall stay so, until you tell me what I want to know.'

The blindfold was being removed, which wasn't much help—the man opposite to him was unrecognisable in a tight woollen helmet, or balaclava as it was sometimes called, which left only his eyes showing, and none of his hair.

'No, you don't know me, Hoskyns, but I know you. Now, tell me, and I might spare your life if you do, who ordered the girl child to be kidnapped yesterday, who used her for his pleasure, and who killed her—and why. I take it that you saw that she was thrown into the Thames.'

'As God's my witness...' Hoskyns began.

'God? Who's He? Say the devil rather. As the devil's your witness you were going to lie to me. But you're not, Hoskyns, because if you don't tell me the truth I shall finish you off, here and now, with my little knife.'

He waved the shiv at Hoskyns, and with cruel deft fingers began to unbutton his jacket.

'Shall I do it now, Hoskyns? This is a house of pleasure. Tell me why I shouldn't take mine.'

'I don't know nothing of no girl child, I don't,' Hoskyns screamed. 'I run a straight business.'

The knife hovered over Hoskyns's throat. He tried to shrink away from it.

'Sit still, man. I know you lie. You procured the girl for Sir Ratcliffe Heneage at Madame Louise's, as you had doubtless procured many others. She was stolen away from you, Hoskyns, wasn't she, before he could take his pleasure with her? Don't tell me that you know nothing of girl children. You knew that one, and you saw her dead last night, didn't you? You don't know what a straight house is, Hoskyns.'

He ran the knife down Hoskyn's torso, which set him screaming again.

'Now, Hoskyns. Spoil my pleasure. Tell me the truth. Who had the girl child last night—and who killed her afterwards?' This time he drew blood.

Hoskyns screamed thinly on realising that the devil before him meant what he said.

He began to babble. 'Him. The man you said. Heneage. Mad furious he was, that she got away from Madame's. It were dangerous he said, to have her on the loose. We tracked her down for him. Oh, Gawd, I never thought he'd kill her for his pleasure, I swear, I didn't. But he said…'

He fell silent, sobbing, tears and snot running down his face.

The knife was hovering again. The masked man said, his tone mocking, 'You tempt me, Hoskyns, you really do. What did he say…? Quick, before I gut you and rob you of your life.'

Between sobs it all came out. 'He said that he had killed two birds with one stone. He'd killed the girl for his pleasure and destroyed her evidence at the same time. I swear I never thought he'd do for her…'

'You lie, Hoskyns, you lie,' said Cobie. 'Of course

you thought... But since you've told me what I want to know, I'm going to give you half a chance, which was more than you gave Lizzie Steele. I'm going to set fire to this place, but before I do, I'm going to untie you, and give you a chance to escape. A slight one, but a chance.'

He was untying the rope around Hoskyns's legs, leaving his hands tied behind his back, when Hoskyns, moved by rage, and fear, swung round and bit at Cobie's hand when he pulled the cord free. Almost casually Cobie knocked him down, on to the dirty floor.

'Less of a chance,' he flung roughly at the man on the ground, 'but still a chance.'

Cobie had already decided that Hoskyns's evidence against Sir Ratcliffe—and others—would be given no credence by the authorities, nor would that of any of the children—even if they had known the names of the men who had abused them, which was unlikely.

They were all what were sometimes called 'men of straw'—people of no account when set against the great and the mighty.

He ran from the room, using Hoskyns's keys to open the door to freedom to a group of small boys and girls cowering in the corner of the dingy attic which was little larger than a closet. They stared at him, at his strange and wild appearance. He had picked up an oil lamp from the landing and was holding it high above his head.

'Out,' he ordered. 'Your jailer's gone. Run away, and ask for help at the Salvation Army hostel, the one across Waterloo Bridge—they'll look after you. Trust no one else.'

For a moment none of them moved. They shivered away from him, cowed, unable to believe what he was saying. Cobie hesitated. A thought struck him. He moved on to the next room and unlocked the door to

that. This time a group of young girls, sullen and rag-
ged, none of them older than sixteen, faced him.

'Who the devil are you?' asked one bold girl, who
held her arm out to prevent the rest from making an
undisciplined bolt for freedom. She was well spoken,
and he wondered what dreadful circumstances had
brought her to this cut-price bawdy house where the
worst of perversions and vices were on sale.

'The devil,' Cobie replied, unhesitating.

'Aye, Lord Satan,' said the bold girl cheekily. 'It
would need the devil to free us from here, seeing that
it was he who brought us here.'

'Well, I've come to set you free. The little ones next
door are too frightened to leave. We must help them,
before Hoskyns's bully boys arrive to do for all of us.
I've told them to go to the nearest Salvation Army hostel—see that they go there.'

He ran down the stairs towards the front door, the
children and the girls after him. Above them, Hoskyns
panting and shouting, had recovered sufficiently to
stumble clumsily to his feet and begin to make for
safety.

Once Cobie and his following were all downstairs he
threw the oil lamp up towards the first landing. Almost
immediately the flames from it began to eat the decay-
ing wooden banisters: the whole house was rotten with
age, and stank of mould, so that the fire spread rapidly.

The girls and the children rushed screaming through
the front door, hopefully in the direction of salvation—
all except the one who had been their leader. She had
returned to the kitchen which he was setting alight with
another lamp, and had taken a carving knife from the
drawer.

He stopped his urgent work to ask, 'Why that?'

'It's for him,' she said wolfishly, 'the devil that

brought me here, and held me down for others to enjoy. I want him—unless you've killed him already.'

'No,' Cobie shook his head. 'I let him go, he told me what I wanted to know, and even the devil finds it difficult to kill in cold blood.'

The real truth was, that he could not add to the toll he had already taken without fearing what yet another killing would do to him.

She laughed, and pointed towards the bottom of the stairs. 'Here he comes.'

It was Hoskyns, screaming, his hands still tied behind his back, making for the door. He had almost reached safety. When he saw the girl he shouted at her, 'Help me! Help me!'

The girl laughed at him. 'Aye, as you helped me,' and, the knife in her hand, careless of the flames licking about them, she was on him, to thrust the knife into his heart, so that he fell at her feet, where she kicked at him.

The house was rapidly turning into an inferno. Cobie caught the girl by the arm when she kicked at the dead man again.

'There's no time for that, and you've had your revenge. Come away, or the flames will have us both.'

'What do I care, mister? Where shall I go? To find another like him? Who will look after such a thing as I have become?'

He caught her up, even as she spoke, and ran with her in his arms through the flames to the kitchen door. There were people outside, drawn by the fire; some were shouting for the Fire Brigade, others for the police.

Several tried to help Cobie and the girl. He thrust them away, and shouting, 'She's not hurt,' he pushed through the crowd, who were so eager to see the fire's conclusion that they ignored him.

Safely away from the gathering mob he put the girl

down, and croaked at her, 'If I tell you where to go, and put you in a cab with proper directions to get there, will you do what I ask?'

She stared at him. 'You said that you were the devil. Can I trust you?'

'As much as you can trust anyone. I am sending you to a home for lost children. Tell them that Mr Dilley sent you. Do not tell them you are from Hoskyns's house. Tell them anything but the truth—you seem to be able to look after yourself.'

'So you say. Yes, I'll trust you.'

'Good.' He took her by the arm and ran her further away from the fire which was now lighting up the whole river bank: a fit funeral pyre for the man who lay in its heart.

They were back on the Embankment. In the middle distance he could see Hendrick Van Deusen's carriage. A cab plying for hire came up to them. He raised a hand to stop it, opened the door to push the girl in and, once she was safely sitting down inside, he wrenched off his woollen helmet so that his bright hair fell about his face.

'Take her to the Salvation Army Home in Sea Coal Street. Quickly.'

The money he handed the cabby was twice the fare. The cabby tipped his whip at him, and drove away at speed.

Cobie watched them go. The aftermath of the rage was strong in him. Nausea and pain fought for supremacy with bitter remorse. He shrugged and began to trot towards the carriage where the Professor was waiting for him.

He knocked on the side of it, to be admitted, and immediately began to change into his fine clothes. The Professor was trying to help him, raising bushy eyebrows when he took Cobie's six-gun and belt from him.

Unseen, his coachman drove them steadily towards the West End, to Belgravia—where children were bought and sold in more luxurious surroundings than any Hoskyns could offer.

The Professor said, 'Busy minding everyone's business again, Jake?' and he gestured towards the light in the sky.

'You might say so.' Cobie was struggling to do up his shirt, not helped by his erratic sight—the post-rage migraine strong in him.

'Any more notches on the old six-shooter?' The Professor's voice could not have been more sardonic.

'Half a notch. The actual killing was done by someone who had an even better reason than I had to finish the beast off.' He fell silent.

'Where to now?' The Professor asked no more questions. If Jake wanted to tell him of what had passed, he would. If not, not.

'Somewhere where I can be seen with you again, and I can find temporary oblivion.'

The Professor was cheerful. 'Oh, I think I can promise you that…'

Behind them the flames reached higher and higher into the sky, to fall back until now it was only the moon which illuminated the firemen and police who struggled about among the hot ashes—to find Hoskyns lying among them, a kitchen knife in his heart.

Chapter Eleven

'This would happen just when we had no one following him.'

Walker's tone was more one of disgust than anger. It
was three o'clock on the following morning and he and
Bates were standing in the still-warm debris of Hoskyns's house.

'Oh, come on, guv,' said Bates, who thought that
Walker was being uncharacteristically wrong-headed
about Mr Dilley. 'You surely don't think he had anything to do with this.'

Walker said nothing for a moment. He had been
fetched from his bed to deal with a case of arson and
murder since Hoskyns's charred remains had been
found in the ashes, the knife in his heart. He had also
been told—to his chagrin—by the Commissioner that
Hoskyns had been one of those who had escaped arrest
at Madame Louise's and that 'higher authority' had allowed him to open his new house unhindered.

'Of course it's him,' he said at last, for it was no
business of Mr Dilley's to do the police force's work
for them—even if those at the top were betraying the
poor hard-working coppers at the bottom. 'You saw his
face yesterday morning, didn't you?'

Bates recalled Mr Dilley's impassive expression, his stillness while standing over the dead girl. 'I didn't think it bothered him much,' he said truthfully, remembering other people confronted with such deaths, raving and crying vengeance. 'Cool about it all, wasn't he?'

'You're a fool, Bates,' Walker said. 'That's what showed him to be dangerous.'

'Well, if you think as 'ow it's 'im, what do we do next?'

'Good question, Bates,' and Bates wasn't sure whether or not his superior was being sarcastic. 'We'll go and find out what he's been doing since he left the morgue. I'll lay odds that Mr Dilley will have an alibi, but I'll break it as sure as my name's Walker. I'm not having him carrying on his murdering games on my patch.'

'There's some that would say that he's done us a favour, killing such a villain,' Bates observed. 'And how did *he* know Hoskyns had started up again? We didn't, until the fire brought all the informers running up to tell us about it and make suggestions as to who done it. One of his rivals, they think…sir.'

'Then they think wrong. Now, it's off to Park Lane to find out where he's been, what he's been up to.'

'At this hour, guv?' Bates was looking at his watch. 'It's only just gone three. Jumping on the quality in their own homes in the middle of the night. Aren't we in enough trouble?'

'I'll take that risk, Bates. And even if we get nowhere, I want him to know that he hasn't fooled me.'

Dinah had been disappointed when Cobie hadn't arrived back in time to escort her to Violet's supper party. It was a small family one, and Violet might grumble at his absence, but she would welcome Dinah, with or without an escort.

The welcome would be because, unaccountably, eighteen-year-old Lady Dinah Grant was becoming a personage in society to be reckoned with. The Prince had more than approved of her, and the delicate wit which Cobie had admired from the moment that he had met her was gaining a wider acceptance. It would not do to be seen to be unfriendly to the sister whom she had once despised.

'Where is he, then?' Violet demanded of Dinah imperiously in the drawing room, before they adjourned for their informal meal.

'On business, he said.'

Dinah was brief. Cobie often was, and she was beginning to copy his ways. The less you said, the less you needed to explain.

'At this hour!' Violet snorted her disgust and disbelief.

Dinah chose to improvise a little. 'I believe,' she said carefully, 'as I told you before, that Americans often do business in places other than their offices—places where…good women can't go.'

'I know that.' Violet was more imperious than ever. She said nastily. 'I'm surprised that he's taken up with all that again so soon after your marriage. Still, men!'

It had surprised Dinah, too, and saddened her a little. She had been given a Kenilworth cousin to take her in to supper, and, after Cobie, she found him dull. She found the whole occasion dull.

Rainey said to her, after supper, 'Husband not here. He's not neglecting you, I hope?'

What did she say to that, remembering the delirious night they had spent together, the way he had kissed her before he had left that morning—and the promise he had made of more fun when he returned in the evening. Nothing, of course. Let Rainey, Violet and the others make what they would of his absence. They had been happy enough to sell her to him without knowing how he would treat her.

All the same, it was a disappointment to discover that he was not yet home when she finally returned there. Her bed seemed a lonely place without him beside her. She wondered what it could be of such importance that he had broken his word to her. She knew, without him telling her, but from all that he said and did that, palter verbally with the truth as he might when speaking to other people, in all the personal things which concerned them, he had, so far, never been less than honest.

Well, there was always a first time. She fell into an uneasy sleep, her arms around the pillow, not around him.

A knock on the door aroused her. To her surprise it was not yet day, although the first faint light of the early summer dawn was straying through the curtains.

It was Pearson, wearing a brown cloth dressing gown over her night-wear.

'Oh, Lady Dinah, Mr Chandler's sent me. It's the police. They want to talk to Mr Grant, but he hasn't returned home yet. They said they'd like to talk to you, instead.'

He was not back yet! That thought struck her before the strangeness of the arrival of the police. Could it be that something had happened to him? Panic rose and swelled in her, clogged her throat.

'Do you want to see them, Lady Dinah? Shall I tell them to come back in the morning? It's not fit for you to receive them at this hour. Whatever would Mr Grant say?'

'He's not here, and so he can't say anything,' retorted Dinah briskly through stiff lips. 'Go and tell Chandler I will be with them shortly—in the drawing room. Then come back and help me into my tea gown, a pair of slippers, and do my hair up. That should make me respectable enough to speak to any number of policemen.'

Thus dressed, looking as though she expected the tea tray in at any moment, as though it were after four in the afternoon and not nearly four in the morning, she swept into the drawing room, announced by a strongly disapproving Chandler.

There were two of them waiting for her, both hard-faced men in plain clothes. Her anxieties grew by the moment. *Say he is not dead? Say he has not had an accident? I couldn't bear it. Not now.* She knew suddenly that the love combined with hero-worship which she had felt for him from the first moment she had seen him at Moorings had turned into a grand passion—something of which she had read, but had never hoped to experience.

If they tell me that he is dead, I want to die. I cannot live without him.

The Marquise's training held, even in her growing distress. They were standing. She motioned them to chairs. They refused to sit. The taller, older, better-dressed one, said crisply. 'Forgive us this intrusion, Lady Dinah, but we had hoped to interview your husband...'

Hands clasped nervously together, she interrupted him before he could say any more. 'You have not come to tell me of an accident to him, then? He isn't... hurt...is he?'

'Oh, no, Lady Dinah. We have come to ask him a few questions about something which occurred last night. We think that he might have been...a witness. The butler says that he hasn't come home yet. Is that usual, Lady Dinah? Does your husband frequently stay out all night?'

He was alive, and that was all that mattered.

'Indeed, no, Inspector. This is the first time that he has done so since we were married.'

Walker inclined his head. It had been his idea to speak to Mr Dilley's wife. He had known that she was young, but not so young as she had proved to be. Bates had argued with him, had said, 'She'll know nothing, guv. Won't be able to tell us anything.'

Well, she had told Walker something. Whatever Mr Dilley's feelings for his pretty young wife were, she loved him, no doubt about it. Fear had been written on her face until relief that he was safe had followed it.

'Is that all?' Dinah asked him, seeing that he remained silent, thinking that they could have spared her both her fright, and her hasty dressing. 'If that is so, Inspector, you will excuse me.'

'You would not object to us questioning the servants, Lady Dinah?'

Dinah's beautiful eyebrows rose. 'Not at all, Inspector. Although I cannot think what you hope to learn.'

This came out so much in Mr Dilley's manner that Walker knew at once how potent his influence was on the girl before him.

'Police work is built up on the acquisition of unconsidered trifles, Lady Dinah,' he offered her, making his tone as deferential as he could.

They moved towards the door, and into the entrance hall, Dinah to go to her room, Walker and Bates to the servants' hall. Neither was to get there quickly.

The big front door was being unlocked. Voices could be heard, and stumbling steps. The door was flung open, incontinent, and three men stood there.

Or rather, two men stood there. The third, abstemious, temperate, sober Cobie Grant hung between them, unable to walk without assistance. Oh, he had made a night of it, no doubt of that! Even at a distance he reeked of liquor, deliberately so, to hide the smell of fire which had been strong upon him.

Supporting him was Mr Van Deusen, patently not quite sober, but not as far gone as Cobie, and another man, Bellenger Hodson, whom Dinah only knew by sight as yet another rich American newcomer to London society.

Cobie stared drunkenly at the three of them.

'What the devil, Dinah, my love…why are you entertaining the police at this hour?'

Even in the state he was in, the mockery which always riled Walker was strong in his voice.

Before Walker could answer Mr Van Deusen spoke, saying apologetically, 'Sorry about this, Lady Dinah. But we have been combining business with pleasure with Hodson here, and I'm afraid we all got rather enthusiastic after the deal was completed, particularly your husband—he's not used to strong liquor, you see.'

There was some truth in this. They had done an impromptu deal with Hodson after meeting him in a gaming club to which they had been driven after he had picked Cobie up. Once there Cobie had deliberately drunk himself into a state where he couldn't think clearly about anything, particularly Lizzie Steele's death, and what had just happened at Hoskyns's house.

Mr Van Deusen was roaring on. 'We told him that we'd get him home safely without you knowing. We never thought you'd be up at this hour—bad luck, that.'

Walker, gritting his teeth, certain that Mr Dilley was going to slip through his hands again, said woodenly to Mr Van Deusen, 'Are you saying he's been with you all night, sir?'

'Certainly, Inspector; in fact, Mr Grant has been with me since shortly after noon yesterday. Business first, you understand, then pleasure. Ain't that so, Hodson?'

Hodson, himself pretty far gone, nodded agreement.

Only to the last part of the statement, of course, not the first—but Walker was not to know that.

'Let's get him to bed, Inspector,' pleaded Mr Van Deusen. 'I want to get there myself, you see.'

Cobie was now hanging, a dead weight between them, his eyes rolled up into his head. He was by no means quite so drunk as everyone thought he was, but to appear to have lapsed into unconsciousness might hold the Inspector off for the time being.

Dinah suddenly took charge. She said firmly, 'By all means, let us get my husband to bed. I'll ring for Chandler, and he can rouse one of the footmen to help get him into it. And you two,' she said to Mr Van Deusen and to Hodson, 'may stay here for what remains of the night. We have beds enough for an army.

'As for you, Inspector,' she said severely, rounding on the discomfited Walker and the inwardly grinning Bates, 'you may delay your questioning of my husband and his friends until they are in a fit state to answer you. I suggest Scotland Yard at three o'clock tomorrow afternoon. In the meantime, I propose to return to my bed. Goodnight to you all,' and she was gone in a preposterous flurry of *crêpe-de-chine* skirts.

But not before, when she swept by him, her husband had opened his eyes and rewarded her with his sweetest smile.

Oh, she knew *that look*, she did! What had he been getting up to now? She knew that he had been getting up to something, he and Mr Van Deusen. She trusted neither of them an inch. Not an inch!

Cobie sat on his bed the next morning—his body, his head and his hand were one vast ache. Worse, when he tried to think, everything hurt even more. He rose, stripped off his night gown, stared at his drawn grey face in the mirror, ran stone-cold water into his bath, and in one swift shuddering movement immersed himself in it. Everything, including his brain, clenched. He had a visual experience of total recall: Lizzie Steele, lying dead and mutilated in the Limehouse morgue.

He closed his eyes, uselessly, to shut out the inward sight, then rose, streaming from the water, having dipped his bright head in it, to seize a towel and dry himself as though he were punishing someone.

He couldn't honestly take the blame for Lizzie Steele's death—after all, he had saved her once, and had tried to arrange for her to be saved permanently, but it was on his conscience just the same. Still immature, he told himself morosely, still haven't grown up, won't recognise my own limitations: Hendrick is right—still trying to rearrange the whole world to my liking. He remembered Susanna telling him that once, years ago.

The sardonic realism which lay behind everything he said and did, jeered at him ruefully, Well, she's a fine one to talk, taking up with Ratcliffe Heneage of all people—Lizzie's destroyer. And how many others has he destroyed? And, yes, how can I destroy him?

Back in San Miguel, in New Mexico, it would have been easy enough to go as far as killing him—even though the idea filled him with revulsion. But how to do such a thing here, in more civilised London—even if he wished to? There must be other ways of stopping him.

The wary cop, Walker, knew that he was responsible for last night's blaze. He was also sure that it was Mr Dilley who had killed Hoskyns—which he had, in a way,...he had put him where the poor young tart could finish him off. That reminded him—he must check whether she, and the children, had ever reached the places of safety to which he had sent them.

It was plain that Walker was quite unaware of Sir

Ratcliffe's involvement in the matter. It was likely that he did not even know that he was one of the mighty for whom the night houses were protected, so that they might take their obscene pleasures in safety.

On the other hand, however, if he did find out that someone near to Cobie Grant were to die mysteriously—and through Susanna, alas, he was near to Heneage—then he would be after Jacobus Grant as determinedly as the terrier who pounces on a rat in order to capture it and worry it to death.

He was dry again and felt cleansed now that the stench of fire and alcohol had been removed. He climbed on to the bed and sat cross-legged and naked on it, eyes closed, first thinking, and then, thought erased, letting his inward self, not his mind, rove free as he had been taught to do by the Indians in the desert.

Reason told him that he need not kill Sir Ratcliffe to destroy him. There were other ways of destroying a man in a society as sophisticated as the one he was living in in England. He could ruin him financially, and then he could ruin him socially. That would leave him in an even worse torment, for it would be a death indefinitely prolonged, instead of being the swift and sure route to oblivion a bullet, or a garrotte, would give him. But how?

Slowly, as always while meditating, his mind stopped its busy work. Time and chance would offer him an opportunity which he could not yet see, and meantime it was pleasant to do nothing, to be nothing, to forget the malaise of last night's drunken bout and Lizzie's dreadful death which had caused it.

To rise and to float free, somewhere near the ceiling, looking down at the figure on the bed, lost in a nirvana which was, he was sure, partly self-hypnosis, but none the less pleasant and life-renewing for that…

* * *

Dinah, the memory of the previous night strong in her, had given orders that he was not to be disturbed. She had overruled a supercilious servant, whom she had caught on his way to Cobie's room, coffee and a pick-me-up being borne before him on a silver tray.

'Not now. Leave him. I'm sure that he will ring when he wants you.' How in the world did she know that?

The man had given way unwillingly, and now she was about to be the busybody. Noon had come and gone, and she had promised—although in his drunken state he might have forgotten—that he would be at Scotland Yard by mid-afternoon. Surely he was not *still* asleep. She had had little experience of drunken men, she owned, but this drunken man must be awakened and made aware of his responsibilities.

Later she was to laugh at herself and think how far she had come in such a short time, that she could make such decisions—and carry them out.

She knocked on the bedroom door. Not a timid knock, nor a defiant one, either.

By now Cobie was nowhere at all, a state he usually achieved only after some little time, but which always heralded the end of the semi-trance into which he had not so much accidentally arrived, as consciously taken himself. In it, he heard the knock on the door, had the sensation of falling, and then was acutely awake, all his senses alert, the pains of his hangover dispersed. He felt himself sink on to the bed again, wondering how long the trance had lasted this time.

'Come in,' he called: it was probably Giles, ready to shave him.

It was Dinah who entered, however. In his heightened condition he registered how charming she looked, how carefully she had dressed herself, in one of her Paris walking gowns, straight-skirted, deceptively simple, a deep beige which should have extinguished her, but didn't. She held herself with confidence, her round shoulders gone.

Dinah took him in, sitting there, cross-legged and naked. His wet hair had dried and had sprung up in unruly curls around his head. His face now showed no signs of last night's excesses. His blue eyes were grave on her, but he was looking at her as though she were miles away, in a place where Dinah Grant was an intruder.

'I'm pleased to see that you are awake,' she said carefully to the remote creature on the bed. 'I ought to tell you that it is now past one o'clock, and I must remind you that, last night, in your names, I told the Inspector that you and Mr Van Deusen would visit him at Scotland Yard by three o'clock this afternoon. It was forward of me, I know, but it was the only way I could think of to rid us of him as quickly as possible.'

'And very well done, too, Lady Dinah Grant,' he told her gravely, 'and it would be remiss of me not to carry out your most reasonable wishes. I take it that you will now inform Giles that I am ready to be dressed for the day—I mean, the afternoon. I had not thought it to be so late.'

He was rarely as formal as this with her, and if he wished to be so, then so be it.

Dinah inclined her head. 'Indeed. And I will order the carriage to be ready. I cannot do as much for Mr Van Deusen, you understand. He was not so far gone as you were last night, and insisted on returning to his own home, but he did say that he would see you at Scotland Yard.'

Cobie was off the bed in one of his cat-like movements, and was pulling on a dressing gown. He walked over to where she stood, put a hand under her chin, and kissed her on the lips, gently, and passionlessly.

He said, his face, for the first time alight with his usual humour, 'What a treasure of a wife you are, my dear. No reproaches for the husband who failed to come home to take you out last night, failed to give you the pleasure he had promised you afterwards, and then turned up in the small hours, in a state for which I must apologise to you most profoundly. I don't deserve you.

'I can only say, in my favour, that nothing but the most urgent of considerations would have caused me to behave in the way in which I did.'

Dinah said, 'I know that, Cobie,' and said nothing more.

'I believe you do,' he said slowly. 'I see that you are even more of a treasure than I thought that you would be. You deserve a better man than I am. Now, you had better send Giles to me, so that I may be ready to tell the police whatever they wish to know.'

She nodded, and made for the door. He said to her when she began to open it, 'Don't you want to know why the police wish to question me, Dinah?'

To his amused and astonished pleasure, she gave him back one of his own smiles, before saying, 'Oh, Cobie, I'm sure if you wish me to know you will tell me without my having to ask you.'

The sound of the door shutting failed to hide the shout of laughter he gave at this considered, two-edged answer—proof that Lady Dinah Grant was not averse to learning from her husband's example.

Walker regarded the two men before him unfavourably. He had begun by seeing them separately, Bates with him, to hear what they had to say when they had not heard the other's explanation. He was sure that they were lying when they claimed that they had been together since the early afternoon of the previous day, and had never been apart before they had arrived to find him and Bates waiting in Park Lane.

Their accounts had almost tallied. The 'almost' in

that sentence annoyed him most of all. Had they tallied exactly, he would have suspected that they had rehearsed what they were telling him. They had certainly not had time to prepare any alibi since he had seen them early that morning. He had ordered that each of them should be watched until the pair of them left for the Yard. Both of his men had reported that they had not met again until they had arrived in Walker's office: Mr Van Deusen twenty minutes before his laggard friend.

While, amazingly, Mr Hendrick Van Deusen looked much the worse for wear after the previous evening's excesses, Mr Jacobus Grant appeared even more splendidly innocent than usual, his air of slight disdain—as though Walker had not seen him disgustingly drunk not so many hours earlier—as hard to bear as ever.

He left them in separate rooms: Mr Grant contemplating the silver top of his cane as though he were consulting a crystal ball for guidance, Van Deusen smoking his usual cigar, not seated, but leaning easily against a wall.

'A ripe pair of villains,' he told Bates disgustedly, after questioning Hendrick.

'What, him, too?' exclaimed Bates, thinking that Walker's wits were slowly unravelling under stress. 'Van Deusen looks a right harmless old codger to me. Just a fat Yankee.'

Walker's face darkened. 'Does he so? Well, I think differently. And that ain't fat, Bates. It's muscle. Like *his*, like Dilley's. They've got away with it this time. They were drinking with half the aristocracy at their last port of call. Yes, they were on the Embankment about the time of the fire. They wondered what was going on. No business of theirs, they said, because they were going to make a night of it without the women. They must think me a prize fool!'

He brought his fist violently down on the table. 'I *am*

a prize fool, Bates. I can't pin a thing on either of them. Make a wrong move with Yankee plutocrats whom the Prince favours, without decent evidence to back me up, and Will Walker's without a job.'

He ruminated a moment, biting his thumb, before roaring abruptly, 'Send 'em in, Bates. I want to see them together.'

Bates thought that they looked an unlikely pair of villains: what with Mr Grant's innocent golden beauty, and Mr Van Deusen's appearance of middle-class, middle-aged solidity. He had to remind himself of dubious Mr Dilley and his magic tricks and to consider that appearances often deceive—a favourite saying of Will Walker's—one which he, unknowingly, shared with Cobie Grant.

'You've not changed your minds?' Walker queried nastily. 'You're not about to tell me the truth?'

Cobie said languidly, his cane now behind his back, 'We're telling it to you, Inspector—so how can we change our minds? It seems a pity that we have to pay for a night on the town by enduring all this. I could have done with an easy afternoon, Inspector, after last night's hard work.'

He gave the Inspector what his wife thought of as 'that look'.

'I know that *you* had a busy night of it, Grant, Dilley, Horne, whatever your real name is,' snarled Walker. 'Very busy, indeed. I'm not sure how much your fat friend was involved in burning down a bawdy house and murdering its owner—but I *am* sure that he's given you an out by his lying evidence.'

'Oh, that's a bit extreme,' murmured Van Deusen. 'No proof, have you, Inspector? By the by, I do resent being called fat. Well built would be a better description.'

'Fat or thin,' said Walker grimly, 'I'm letting you

both go, but I warn you, I'll have the pair of you yet—
and if you did murder Hoskyns, Grant, I'll see you
swing for it, however long it takes.'

Mr Van Deusen felt rather than saw Cobie tense. He
was not surprised when his friend began to speak in a
voice that reached all the way back to San Miguel, and
before that to a hillside where Van Deusen's life had
been saved by a boy whom he hardly knew.

'I'm so glad to hear, Inspector, that you have got your
priorities right. That you are prepared to devote your
life to chasing the murderer of a pimp providing children for sexual sport. Is it possible that you might devote a fraction of it to finding the man who killed Lizzie
Steele—or doesn't she matter in the great scheme of
things?'

For one delirious moment Bates thought that Walker
was going to strike at the mocking face of the man
before him. He saw Van Deusen's watchful eye on
Walker while he struggled to control himself.

'Out,' he whispered at last. 'Out, you damned Yankee
swine, before I forget myself. Bates, see them off the
premises, and Grant, watch your step. One false move,
and I'll have you.'

Dinah was enduring Violet's pinpricking nastiness.
'It didn't take Apollo long to become bored with drinking nursery tea, did it?' her sister said, smiling, and
eating and drinking Dinah's very much not nursery tea.

'Up yet, is he? I hear that he and that Yankee friend
of his spent last night making merry in every gaming
hell in London.'

'Oh, yes.' Dinah smiled back at her half-sister, offering her the sugar bowl. 'More sugar, Violet? You
seem to be in need of it.'

The Marquise's training was standing up well, she
thought. At this rate she would soon not only be rivall-

ing Violet in verbal nastiness, but beating her at her own game.

'Yes, he *was* late home, and yes, he is up. Off on business again. He can't be idle. He has to look after his own fortune, Violet. He didn't inherit wealth as we all did—or didn't, in our case.'

It was no longer easy to put Dinah down, to see her cringe, to watch her shoulders growing rounder, and the betraying brightness appear in her eyes. *His* influence, no doubt. Violet didn't like Cobie Grant the more for that. She decided to try sticking in another dart.

'That sister of his, Susanna Winthrop. Someone was telling me that the rumour is that when they were in the States, years ago, they were more than foster-brother and sister. I don't envy you keeping a watch on *his* wandering eye.' She looked across at Dinah to see whether her dart had struck home.

Apparently not. Dinah idly took another macaroon, and said cheerfully, after disposing of it, 'No difficulty there, Violet. I've had so much practice in seeing you all keeping watch on your husbands' wandering eyes. And speaking of wandering eyes, when did we start talking like kitchen maids, Violet? Is it the latest thing in the Prince's set? If so, you must coach me. I wouldn't like to sound not completely *à la mode*, Cobie might not approve.'

She didn't believe that rubbish about Susanna Winthrop. On the other hand, she knew that there was a strong bond between them. No, it was merely Violet, mischief-making as usual.

Violet rose and prepared to take her leave. Dinah, looking aethereal in a pale amethyst tea gown—his choice, no doubt—was proving boringly unbaitable. She suddenly wanted to ask the unaskable, jealousy seizing her by the throat. 'Tell me, is he a tiger in bed with you?' but some shred of caution remained to have her say briefly, 'I'll see you this evening at Marlborough House, then. The Prince seems very taken with him.'

This was yet another reason for holding her tongue. Tum Tum wouldn't like it if she were to be cool to those whom he favoured, and unaccountably he was favouring not only Cobie Grant, but his delicate young wife.

Violet had hardly disappeared in a cloud of scent before Cobie returned from his visit to Scotland Yard.

'Tea!' he exclaimed gratefully, and sank down into a large armchair. Dinah thought that he looked tired. 'Was that Violet I saw leaving?'

Dinah handed him his tea, Fortnum's best Chinese. 'Yes. She came to scratch, but I think she tired of missing the target and left early.'

He made no answer, simply sat there, drinking his tea, a look of total abstraction on his face. She began to speak to him, but changed her mind at the last minute. Ever since she had seen him hanging between Mr Van Deusen and Bellenger Hodson in the early hours of the morning, she was sure that something was troubling him, and troubling him greatly.

Not that anything showed, other than to the keen observer she was becoming. Outwardly he was still in his usual state of calm control. But his manner that morning, in his bedroom, had been that of a man who had journeyed long and far away from her—and, she suspected, from everyone else.

He must, she thought, possess the sixth sense she had heard discussed by those interested in psychic phenomena, because he suddenly looked across at her, and said, oh so smoothly, 'What's worrying you, Dinah?'

Now what could she say to that? You are, Cobie. I am sure that you are engaged in something secret, something hidden from the world, and Mr Van Deusen is in the secret with you. I am not sure that I really know you at all, that anyone really knows you—except perhaps Mr Van Deusen…and what does that tell me—about your past and his?

Instead she replied, seamlessly and without delay, so that he could have, she hoped, no idea of her inward questionings of him, 'I was thinking about the Inspector who called this morning. I know I said that I would not pry into your affairs, but I wondered why he disliked you so much.'

She had surprised him again, and he must go carefully. On no account must she be burdened with the knowledge of what he was doing, of his secret life, of his determination to destroy Sir Ratcliffe Heneage for what he had done to Lizzie.

He gave her his charming smile. 'I ran across him over a business matter, and I fear that I was not perhaps as tactful with him as I ought to have been. I think that he may also dislike all fine gentlemen, which may probably have reinforced his dislike. For all of which I am sorry.'

Nothing which he had said was truthful, but neither was it entirely untruthful, and if he knew when people were lying to him, he also knew when people were aware that he might be deceiving them, so he knew, immediately, that Dinah was aware that he was equivocating.

Yes, Dinah knew. She felt a bitter regret. She wanted to say, 'I would like you to tell me the truth, Cobie, however unpalatable it might be. I may be young, but I am not a child. I would like to think that you could trust me.'

Instead she replied thoughtfully, 'Yes, I suppose that such a person might resent someone like you—who appears to have everything.'

Which, all in all, was as equivocal as anything he had

ever said to her, and if she was aware of what she had done—so was he. He wanted to bow to her, to confer on her some accolade—but the habit of many years of secrecy about not only his doings, but his feelings, was strong in him.

After he had gone, having favoured her with an almost absent-minded kiss on the top of her head—the sort of kiss one might reward a child with for being clever, thought Dinah acidly—she sat down and examined her own feelings.

It was time, she thought sadly, to come to terms with how she felt about him. Before she had married him she had hero-worshipped him, until he had been unkind to her—which had had something to do with Violet, she was sure. Cobie had once walked through her dreams like a distant adventurer in some romance she had read. Now that they were married, and she was his passionate partner in the game of love—for that was all it was to him, she was sure—she knew something else, something highly inconvenient.

He had begun to turn Dinah Freville from a raw girl, gauche and unsure, into a beautiful and assured woman, but he had also accomplished something else. In the doing he had caused her to fall passionately in love with him, so much so that when he was away from her she could hardly wait for him to return, could only envy and dislike all the other women to whom he had made love; worst of all, beside him every other man paled into insignificance.

For the first time she could understand Violet's jealousy of her for having won him, and the envious looks of virtually every other woman in society.

She tried telling herself that she was being foolish. He was only a man, after all, flawed and fallible as all men were, even the gods of legend whom he so much resembled. It was useless, particularly as she was becoming increasingly aware that she was beginning to share some strange bond with him.

That morning, when she had seen him on the bed, she had known that he had travelled far away from her. The other evening, after they had made love, and she was in a state which she had never achieved before, where her body had disappeared, and her mind as well, and only sensation was left, she had touched him, and for a second he, the bed, and the room had disappeared.

She had arrived again in the strange land which she had only visited in her dreams. There was a great sky overhead, coloured with all the hues of the rainbow. It was hot, and the moon was casting strange shapes on to a desert floor.

Suddenly, the desert vanished, and she was running down a narrow alley, away from someone—she had no idea who... then that vanished and she was in a room, about to look down on something, and something inside her screamed *no*...

And she was back on the bed with him, and he was saying, a little anxiously, 'Dinah, are you feeling ill? For a moment there you seemed to have lost consciousness. I have been too rough with you, tonight,' and his voice was full of remorse.

She had sat up, and said vigorously, although her head was swimming a little, 'Oh, no, Cobie. It was wonderful. So wonderful that I lost myself for a moment, that was all.'

For some reason she didn't want to tell him of her visions. Now, remembering, she thought, But were they *my* visions? Or were they his?

He had kissed her, she remembered, gently this time, laughing a little at her artless delight in their lovemaking. But the visions stayed with her, and they served to tie her even more completely to him. For whatever he felt for her, for Dinah, her husband was her whole world.

Chapter Twelve

'I only came to warn you to be discreet.'

The grey man who stood in the bow window of Sir Ratcliffe Heneage's study spoke with his face averted, looking down into the street below. 'My masters would not care for an open scandal, you understand. They will protect you—within limits—for a reason of which you are well aware.'

Sir Ratcliffe tried to pretend ignorance. He said as coldly as he could, 'I can't say that I understand of what you speak.'

'No? I am quite sure that you do. You have been neither discreet nor careful lately. The last bolt-hole which you chose for your pleasure was an unwise one. Unlike Madame Louise's, it was not protected.'

'Madame Louise's protected!' There was suppressed anger in Sir Ratcliffe's voice. 'How protected was that? It was only by great good fortune that I was not present when she was raided.'

'Not good fortune,' returned the anonymous grey man. 'You were sent a specific warning to stay away that week, a warning of which I am well aware—for I sent it. Had we known then that it was your careless folly in allowing a child to escape which brought about the raid, you would not have been warned.'

'Not my folly,' replied Sir Ratcliffe through gritted teeth. 'Hoskyns's folly.'

'For which he has paid with his life. It was he who procured the child for you in the first place, and he who kidnapped her for your pleasure a week ago. My God, man, it was your vile habits and Hoskyns's desire for revenge which resulted in the child being taken, dead, from the Thames.'

He saw Sir Ratcliffe's face change, 'You were not aware that the child's body was found almost immediately? That Hoskyns is dead, and that his brothel was burned about him—arson, undoubtedly?'

Fear gnawed at Sir Ratcliffe. 'You are sure of this?'

'Do you take me for as big a fool as you are? Of course I'm sure, and sure, too, of who rescued the girl child in the first place, and put her in a home run by the Salvation Army. He set the fire, and almost certainly killed Hoskyns when he discovered that her death had come about in Hoskyns's house. You'll be his next target, be sure of that.'

'The police,' said Sir Ratcliffe hoarsely. 'They will surely not condone murder and attempted murder. If you know who killed Hoskyns and might kill me, why is he still at large?'

'Because although they are sure who the man is, the police can prove nothing. My information is that he was tricky enough to arrange matters so that there is no clear evidence against him. He was seen elsewhere again and again that night. I am here to warn you to go warily…' He paused. 'Such evidence as exists is unofficial, and was gained by devious and unauthorised means.'

Sir Ratcliffe said roughly, 'Be plain, man. Tell me his name.'

The man in grey shrugged. 'That I cannot do. I can

only tell you to be cautious. I would advise you to live a pure life, but I doubt that that is possible for you. In any case, it might not be enough to save you.'

'Anything. I will promise anything.' He was frantic, the more so because he knew, deep down, that once the desire to please himself was on him there was little he could do to check himself. He added desperately, to try to pacify the man before him. 'I know that I have been careless, but not again, I promise you.'

The grey man stared at him, dislike written on his anonymous face. 'I hope you mean that,' he said, 'I really do. You have been so grossly careless in your behaviour that I, personally, find it hard to believe that you will behave yourself in future. Be warned. Your masters and mine will tolerate much from you, but they will not tolerate conduct which puts the good name of this country, and its government, at risk.'

There was nothing for it but to swallow the bitter pill of a reprimand delivered by a man of lower station than himself, and privately decide that he would do his damnedest to find out his pursuer and dispose of him whatever the faceless ones behind his interlocutor might say or do.

Unaware that Walker had passed his suspicions to the Commissioner, who had complainingly passed them on to a higher authority who had at last taken Walker's report seriously, Cobie continued to behave as apparently innocently as possible.

He *was* aware, however, that he had greatly underestimated his young wife. Oh, she was learning fast, was she not! He had expected her to grow and mature after marriage, but not at the rate which she was currently displaying.

What he had not expected was that she would immediately guess that he and Hendrick had been up to some mischief on the night of Hoskyns's death. For her own sake—and his—she must never know what he had done. The thought that she might become a target for Sir Ratcliffe, if he discovered who was after him, set him shuddering—and deciding that the sooner the man was dealt with, the better.

He had not taken Hendrick into his confidence, either, nor had Hendrick demanded to know why he had burned the brothel down, and—possibly—disposed of Hoskyns.

'No, don't tell me, Jake, what you're up to now,' he had said when they left Scotland Yard. 'The less I know, the less I can inadvertently give away. All I can say is, be careful, and if you need your back guarded again, you know where to find me.'

What Walker did not know, and what the Commissioner did not see fit to tell him, was that although higher authority had taken his report seriously enough for it to end up with the grey man, that same authority had told him to tell Walker quite otherwise, and that his surveillance of the man he suspected was to cease.

'Gawd,' said Bates to Alcott, after Walker had broken the news to them, 'he's in a right old temper about being told to lay off Grant. Bit my head off, he did, about that there book you lent me. He found me reading it when I was suppose to be writing up my report on that fence we nicked. Would have thrown it away if I hadn't told him it was yours.'

It was after being informed by the Commissioner that he was to forget Grant and all his works that Walker had discovered Bates surreptitiously reading a paperback book which had been imported from America.

'What the devil are you up to now, you lazy dog?' he had roared, snatching the book from Bates's knee. 'Get on with what you're paid for, and I'll dispose of this.'

'It's not mine,' said Bates fearfully. 'Alcott lent it to me.'

'So he's reading this rubbish, too, and in work time, I suppose. What have I done to be gifted with such rare idiots?'

He flung the book down on his own desk after reading the title on a cover illustrated by a lurid drawing of one man shooting down another in a desert setting behind a title which read *The Wild, Wild West.*

No sooner had he done so than he remembered something which Captain Legge had told him: that Cobie Grant had spent part of his youth in outlaw territory in New Mexico. It was information which he had kept to himself, for it didn't seem to assist his current investigation of the villain he knew Grant to be.

He picked the book up again and began leafing through it. Most of it was old stuff about Davy Crockett and the Alamo, Wild Bill Hickock and Buffalo Bill, of whose Western show even Walker had heard.

The last chapter was entitled 'Boy gunmen of the West: Billy the Kid and others, plus the mystery of Jumpin' Jake Coburn and his taking of San Miguel'.

San Miguel! Wasn't that the township in New Mexico which Legge had told him that Cobie Grant might have visited? Intrigued, he turned to the end of the chapter, to learn that Coburn had been a young man of about twenty who had turned up one day in New Mexico from God knows where. He had become the chief henchman and shootist of one of the outlaw bands which took refuge in a valley there appropriately named Hell's End. The band had been led by the infamous Blake Underwood. There Coburn had robbed banks, blown up a train, and gone on to kill Big Ben Hawke, the outlaw who ran San Miguel, the town nearest to Hell's End. He had taken it over and run it himself before riding away one morning, never to return, and never to be heard of again anywhere.

His origins and his destination were alike mysterious. He had disappeared as effectively as though he had never lived. It was thought that he might have died in the desert. Oddly enough, the writer ended, like Billy the Kid, he was supposed to be a left-handed gun.

Left-handed! Grant was left-handed—or perhaps a better word would be ambidextrous. His Christian name was Jacobus. Was he ever known as Jake? Half of Coburn was half of Cobie, and Jumpin' Jake would be a highly suitable-nickname for the way Grant carried on when he wasn't being a good imitation of a languid English aristocrat and was running around being Mr Dilley instead!

And twenty—this had all happened ten years ago when Grant would have been twenty—and was known to be in New Mexico. It all fit—or did it?

Walker stared at the woodcut of a hairy, young, pony-tailed tearaway with a Colt in his hand which adorned this unlikely tale. Was he going mad, to see Grant in every nook and cranny into which he looked? Bates and Alcott plainly thought he was, and now the Commissioner obviously considered him to have lost his common sense where Grant was concerned.

Nevertheless…Walker shook his head. It wouldn't do any harm for him to treat Grant as warily as he might have treated the young hooligan, Coburn, if he had ever had the misfortune to meet him. In the meantime, damn the Commissioner, and damn everyone else—he, Walker, would continue to investigate Grant, in his own time, if not the Yard's.

Sir Alan Dilhorne had invited the Grants to his splendid palace in Piccadilly for a little dinner. Sir Alan, Cobie's unacknowledged uncle, was enjoying what he had told them was his last London Season. His beautiful wife had died two years ago, and it was time, he said, that he retired to Yorkshire for good.

What amused Dinah more than anything else, remembering the condition they had been in the other night, was how sober Cobie and Mr Van Deusen looked, how delightfully respectable. She smiled to herself a little while recalling how she and her husband had spent the afternoon…

Once again Mr and Mrs Grant had not been At Home. Instead they had repaired to the bedroom where Cobie, somewhat recovered from his depression after Lizzie's death, had entertained her with music after the more earthy delights they had enjoyed were over.

As well as Cobie and Dinah, Sir Alan had invited Hendrick Van Deusen, and Bellenger Hodson and his wife. Mr Van Deusen, always avid for knowledge, had discovered that Sir Alan's father had been transported to Australia where he had won for himself a massive fortune and created a dynasty.

In the drawing room where they all sat, waiting for dinner to be served, he stared curiously at a painting of someone called Sir Beauchamp Hatton, done in the 1780s, which hung in a place of honour over the hearth. The remarkable thing about it, from Mr Van Deusen's point of view, was that it might have been a painting of his friend, the erstwhile Western gunman and outlaw, Mr Jacobus Grant, so like was he to the handsome and arrogant man who had lived over a hundred years ago.

Sir Alan had registered Mr Van Deusen's curiosity. Mr Van Deusen, for his part, had already noticed that, despite his years, Sir Alan missed little of what went on about him. In that, his friend Jake resembled him greatly.

'I see that you are admiring my Gainsborough,' Sir Alan said. 'It is one of two which he painted of my wife's ancestor, Sir Beauchamp Hatton. The other, larger one hangs in my place in Yorkshire. Do not be deceived by his beauty. There was nothing effeminate about him: he was a hard man, who could be cruel on occasion.' Was it a coincidence that he had looked across at his unacknowledged nephew while he was speaking?

And what was the connection, Mr Van Deusen wondered, between Sir Beauchamp, Sir Alan and Cobie Grant—who was so amazingly like both of them? He thought that it might not be wise to ask, given the erratic behaviour of the aristocracy at that period—and now, too, for that matter.

Instead he began quizzing Sir Alan gently about his father, the transported convict: a man of whom he was obviously proud and of whom he was quite willing to speak.

'We used to call him the Patriarch,' Sir Alan said. 'It was only half a joke. He was a most remarkable man.'

He saw that he had his audience's attention, and added, 'Not long before she died, my mother told me the truth of her marriage. It seems that, being gently born, but desperately poor, he rescued her from penury by marrying her. But given the disparity in their years and their station, she being a gentlewoman and he a transported thief, something he never hid, he delayed making her his true wife until some time after they were married. Indeed, I gathered from my mother, although she gave me no details, that he had tricked her into marriage. Despite his trickery it became a true love match, rare then—and even rarer now.'

He paused, lost in thought: his mind had retreated nearly sixty years into the past.

'She had an air of your wife about her, Jacobus,' he said slowly, and wondered why his nephew should have given him a look, an oddly subtle look, which he recognised—a look he associated with the Patriarch.

The old man had been devious, devilish devious, as was this young one, who resembled him so greatly in both looks and character. He remembered something which his brother Jack had said a little bitterly of his unacknowledged son, 'When I am with Cobie it is as though the Patriarch was back on earth again. If anything he's even trickier and more ruthless than the Patriarch ever was.'

So the line held true. None of Sir Alan's sons or grandsons bore the look of, or resembled in character, the Patriarch, but his bastard grandson did. What was more, something which he had just said had amused that grandson.

'My father made his own law,' Sir Alan said reflectively, 'which I believe to be much more difficult in these over-civilised days. It was easier for him because, in a frontier society like Australia nearly eighty years ago, the law was a more fragile thing. As I understand it was, until recently, in the American Southwest.'

'Indeed,' said Cobie, drinking his own solitary glass of brandy, another trait he shared with his devious and temperate grandfather, and marvelling, that like him, he had tricked his wife into marrying him. 'But I fancy that a determined man might follow his own line, don't you, sir?'

'At some risk,' returned Sir Alan heavily, 'and it were best to remember that, young Cobie. My father was lucky. Sometimes those who soar too near the sun are not.'

Mr Van Deusen looked from one man to the other, and said, with a knowing grin, 'A case of the pot calling the kettle black, one imagines.'

Sir Alan laughed. 'True, old age brings caution to us all, I must not forget that. I rather took after my father in youth. But here, in England, the power of the law is greater than it is either in Australia, or the United States.'

Cobie, his brandy finished, took this as a warning: the third. 'What I tell you three times is true.' First the Salvation Army Captain, next Hendrick, and now my uncle. I must never forget that Sir Alan had sat among the mighty in Britain for nearly fifty years and, that being so, is probably still in touch with them. He probably knows more than he cares to reveal.

So he would heed the warning, and would be cautious, but he intended to have Sir Ratcliffe Heneage's scalp, even if the means of taking it had not yet been revealed to him. Patience, he told himself, and Chance, Machiavelli's Chance, the horse I have ridden before, will come to me to be ridden again.

'You will, of course, visit us at Moorings, immediately the Season ends. Kenilworth is insistent on it.' Goodness knows why, was her inward comment.

'We shall then join the Prince at Sandringham. Shortly afterwards the whole party, including the Prince, will travel on to Markendale, our place in the North,' Violet said to Cobie and Dinah when she met them at the Leominsters' ball. 'I shall expect you to join us there as well.'

The Leominsters' ball was always one of the most prestigious events of the London Season and had been for nearly a hundred years. The present Lady Leominster greatly resembled her famous predecessor who had reigned over high society in Regency times and who had bullied everyone from high to low. Cobie had once joked to Dinah that there must be something in the air of Leominster House which turned the wife of its owner into a dragon.

The dragon had shrieked at Dinah, 'My dear, you are

this Season's darling—and all the result of marrying that handsome husband of yours, I am told!' It was the kind of personal remark which only she could get away with.

'So he informs me,' returned Dinah slyly, earning another shriek, plus a rap on her right shoulder from the Countess's fan.

Dinah had been reading a newly published collection of Regency letters which had included many describing the extravagant conduct of her hostess's predecessor. She could only conclude that her hostess had read them, too, and had modelled her behaviour on what had been written there.

'You see, Dinah,' Cobie had explained to her before Violet had swept up to them in the hope of sharing some of her once-despised sister's fame, 'if you want to be hailed as a true eccentric who must be allowed to say what one pleases, you must be as *outré* as possible. Half-measures in your behaviour will merely ensure that you are despised.

'Behave like Lady Leominster and one or two others in society and you become a kind of dreadful icon to be adored. If you lived in London's East End such conduct would earn you the admiring comment, "Ooh, you are a one!" Here we drawl, "Typical Lady L., that. Whatever will she say next!"'

'And you should know, Cobie,' Dinah could not resist saying. 'You should know.'

'Oh, naughty,' he whispered in her ear. 'Remind me to reprimand you properly when we reach home tonight. I can't do it here—I might frighten the footmen.'

This last remark had Dinah blushing and laughing, so that Violet raised her eyebrows, but dared not say anything dismissive to society's latest pet. And what a turn-up that was!

'Of course we shall visit Moorings, and Markendale,

too,' Cobie said before Dinah could open her mouth. 'Won't we, my dear Dinah? Wouldn't miss either of them for the world. I do hope that you propose to invite Hendrick, too. He and Dinah can hide in the library and read Gibbon's *Decline and Fall* together.'

It was Dinah's turn to hit someone with her fan—as she had fantasised at the Marquise's in Paris—and that someone was her husband.

'And what, sir, will you be doing? Perhaps I ought not to ask.'

'Watching over the pair of you,' he returned, 'to see that you do not neglect your studies.'

Dinah's smile at Cobie was one of pure glee. 'Don't you mean that I ought to watch you and Mr Van Deusen so that I can be sure that *you* are both behaving yourselves?'

Violet stared at the pair of them. What surprised her most was not that Cobie was teasing Dinah, but that she was teasing him back. It was like watching a tennis match, she decided, a verbal one. They seemed to be doing it all the time these days.

'I ought to tell you,' Violet said, 'that I really came over at the Prince's request to ask you to join his party. He's in the yellow drawing room—he doesn't dance much these days, and he seems to have taken a great fancy to you, Cobie.'

She didn't add that the Prince had also praised Grant's pretty young wife. 'Never thought that she'd turn into such an unusual beauty. She didn't look like that when she lived with you, Lady K.'

If there was a slight reproach hidden in his words, Violet had chosen not to heed it. Instead, she made a performance of ushering Cobie and Dinah to the salon where the Prince was holding state among a small and select group of his friends.

'Ah, Grant, there you are. I knew that Lady K. would

have no trouble in finding you.' If there was another double meaning hidden there, his hearers chose not to heed that, either.

'Take a chair, Grant, and you, Lady Dinah, come and sit next to me. Such fresh young beauty does an old man's heart good.'

He was indicating a small stool beside his armchair. Dinah bowed and, plumping out her skirts when she sat down, did as she was bid.

'Excellent. Now I have a question for your husband—and it is not about how he has transformed you—I'm sure that we all know the answer to *that*. No, it's a serious one, about business—and I don't mean the business of Princes, I mean the business of surviving on Wall Street and in the world of commerce. Answer me that, sir.'

Cobie had been shown to a seat opposite to the Prince who appeared to be in the most jovial of good humours that night. He bowed slightly from the waist before offering his royal questioner his sweetest smile.

'Oh, that is an easy question to answer: by the exercise of a great deal of low cunning—with an occasional admixture of the higher sort.'

The Prince threw his head back and laughed: turning to Dinah, he asked her a question. 'Tell me, Lady Dinah, is that the kind of *bon mot* which he favours you with? And what do you say to him when he comes out with such remarks?'

Dinah's smile for him was as sweet as Cobie's.

'Why, sir, I pay him back in his own coin—as, for instance, to what he has just said, I might reply, "Then, Cobie, that being so, I am sure that you will not object to me following your example the next time we go shopping together."'

The Prince waved his cigar in the air, and led the

general laughter. 'Oh, bravo, Lady Dinah. And you, sir, is she telling the truth? Do you go shopping with her?'

Cobie's smile was as much for Dinah as the Prince. 'When we were first married, yes, but once I had instructed her in the high art of overspending on everything, I soon found that she needed no further instruction. She was well able to excel in it on her own.'

Again the Prince's guffaw led the laughter. Was it really as easy as this to gain a reputation for being a wit? thought Dinah bemusedly. She could see that both Violet and Rainey were staring at her as though she had grown two heads— Sir Ratcliffe looked as if he thought that she had sprouted three!

The Prince was still concentrating his attention on them. 'I hear that you have many other talents, Grant, besides a facility for making money. Once the Season ends, we shall be going to Sandringham, and you and Lady Dinah must do me the honour of joining me there—for the whole week, if you please. I am determined to put you both through your paces.

'After that I am off to Markendale Hall, Kenilworth's northern place, and I have given orders that you are to be invited there as well—if Lady K. has not already done so.'

Violet said, a little desperately, Dinah thought, 'Oh, I have already issued them an invitation, sir, and they have accepted it.'

'Good, excellent. I shall look forward to enjoying your company, Grant. In the meantime, since I understand that you excel at cards also, I command you to join me in a rubber of whist—as my partner, of course.

'Lady Dinah, I instruct you to lead your friend, Mr Van Deusen, to the library where you may inspect Leominster's superb collection of Rembrandt's etchings and drawings. At least, I've been told it's superb, haven't seen it myself—not my sort of thing at all, but if what I am told is true, then I'm sure that you will both appreciate it. I shall order coffee and wine to be served for you there. Beauchamp will be your escort and look after your wants.'

He waved an airy hand at the small grey man who stood behind his chair saying, 'Of course, sir, as you wish,' to everything which his master ordered.

'When they have finished their inspection, Beauchamp, pray bring them both back here so that Mr Van Deusen may be presented to me. From all I hear, he sounds to be well worth knowing. Particularly, of course, if Mr Grant values him as a friend.'

Cobie, amused by all this Royal favour, wondered how much silent teeth-gnashing was going on while he and Dinah were moved up the chess board of life to the squares where the favourites of Princes stood.

He had been watching Dinah's reactions to the honours conferred on them, and her slightly sardonic expression was a joy to him. He had a brief flash of memory. A few days after he had sent the bold girl to his Sea Coal Street home, he had visited it, to find out whether she had actually gone there.

Bristow had been present, and had given Cobie a warm greeting. It appeared that most of the children he had rescued from Hoskyns's brothel had arrived at the refuge near Waterloo Bridge, where they had been cared for, and that the bold girl had found her way to Sea Coal Street.

'She's in the kitchen, with my wife,' the Superintendent, Hedges, told him. 'Do you wish to see her?'

'Yes,' said Cobie. 'I should like to know what your plans are for her future.'

'Well, Mr Dilley, she was a bit wild and troubled at first, but good food and kindness softened her a bit. The doctor helped, too. My wife discovered that she was badly bruised, and sent for him. He examined her, told us that she was clean—you know what I mean, I'm sure—and that she needed loving care. Seeing as how she was older than the rest of the kiddies, my wife thought that we might try to train her to be a parlour maid. Our present one will be leaving us soon. She, the missis, thinks that she will suit since she seems eager to learn.

'She won't tell us anything about her family, so we can't send her back to them. In any case, they might not want her. We hope that you approve of what we are doing.'

'Very much so,' said Cobie.

He rose when the bold girl was shown in by the Superintendent's wife.

'This is Miss Mary Connor,' she told Cobie.

The girl stared at him sullenly. He was wearing his masher's outfit.

Cobie offered her a slight bow, and, 'How do you do, Miss Connor.'

'You rescued me,' she said, at last. 'I suppose I ought to thank you. Connor's not my name, but it will do. Why are you here?'

'To see that you are safe—and are reasonably happy.'

'As happy as I shall ever be, I suppose. Why do you care about me?'

'You'd rather I didn't?'

She laughed suddenly. 'I like you. You're not a canting parson, are you, trying to save my soul? I like them, too,' and she inclined her head towards the Superintendent and his wife. 'Yes, I'll be their parlour maid. It will be a better life than the one I led in Hoskyns's attic, that's for sure.'

'Good,' he said, and took her hand to kiss it. She stared at him again. Surely men only did that to ladies in society and not to humble kitchen-maids?

'I wish you luck in your new life, Miss Connor, and

I shall keep an eye on your progress, you may be sure of that.'

This, and the kiss, brought her first smile—a watery one, to be sure, but still a smile.

Like the dead Lizzie her expression and manner had reminded him of the defeated Dinah Freville whom he had first met at Moorings. He had been pondering on this odd piece of insight while he walked along Sea Coal Street on his way home when a hard voice broke in upon his musings.

'I thought that I might meet you here, Grant. Doing your charitable bit, are you? How do you square it with your other, less legitimate, interests?'

It was Walker, looking at him with an expression which could only be described as malevolent.

Cobie smiled at him. 'Are you on duty, Inspector, or are you chasing after me in your spare time? I cannot think what you hope to discover.'

'You can't?' Walker's brows rose, and although he didn't know it his expression was a mirror image of the one his quarry sometimes used to upset his enemies.

'I might find out what you got up to at Hoskyns's bordello, mightn't I? And check whether it was in any way similar to your goings-on in the American Southwest where you seem to have been running around under yet another name. Criminal coves using more names than one deserve to be followed. The only trouble I have is to decide by which one I am going to call you when I nick you for Hoskyns's murder, as you may be sure that I will, however long it takes me.'

Cobie thought quickly, So, the wary copper is no fool. The question now is, by what means has he discovered my murky wild western past? Has he uncovered Hendrick's as well? If he hasn't, I must be sure not to say anything that would put him on Hendrick's trail. The less Walker knows, the better. He now knows too much already.

'I really cannot imagine what you can be speaking of, Inspector. I trust that you have not been reading too many dime novels. They rarely bear any relationship to the truth of the events which they purport to describe.'

His manner when he came out with this was so aloofly majestic that it would have done credit to a hanging judge on the bench. It did little to improve Walker's frayed temper.

'So you say, so you say,' he growled. 'Not that I'm after you for what you got up to ten years ago, but it does offer a few pointers to what you might be getting up to today, doesn't it?'

'Hardly,' said Walker's quarry, still apparently unmoved. 'Allow me to save you some further skulking in corners in order to catch me at my wicked work. Tonight I am to be found at the Leominsters' ball, where I hope to meet the Prince of Wales. Tomorrow my wife and I will be among the guests at a boating party up the Thames which will take in a picnic at Hampton Court. There, that should give you the next thirty-six hours off since I can scarcely be supposed to be organising some kind of criminal operation in full view of half the members of London society, can I? That world is not one where such ventures can be openly followed, now is it? It has little to do with Sea Coal Street and the East End.'

'No, indeed,' snarled Walker. 'I agree with you there, but it's what you get up to when you're not in full view that troubles me.'

Cobie gave a weary sigh. 'Delightful though this exchange of courtesies is, Inspector, you really must allow me to continue on my way. I have urgent business awaiting me in my City office. Like many of my society friends, you appear to forget that I have to earn my own living, and that doing so takes up a great deal of my time. I wish you luck in all your ventures, and oh, by the by, do remember me to Bates and Alcott, I quite miss their friendly faces.'

He could almost feel Walker's scowl boring into his back when he walked away. The pity of it was that he respected the man and his office, but since he had started off on the wrong foot with him, they were doomed to remain at cross purposes. Cobie admitted ruefully that this was his own fault since he had under-estimated Walker and his determined honesty.

No, it wasn't Walker's honesty he mistrusted—it was that of those above him.

He was back in the present again. The present where he was sitting down at the whist table, cutting the cards, with the Prince of Wales for a partner seated opposite to him.

He was only a few miles in space from Sea Coal Street in London's Docklands, but, in the great scheme of things—as he had suggested to Walker—he was a whole world away.

Chapter Thirteen

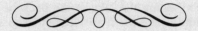

'I thought that we were being invited to a house party, not a family party,' Dinah remarked to Cobie on their second day at Moorings.

'Mmm, so did I,' he said.

He was standing before the long mirror in Dinah's bedroom, checking that he was the perfect image of an English gentleman about to enjoy himself in the country.

Unlike most of the English upper class, however, he was spending his nights in his wife's bedroom rather than the one which he had been given as his own—or in someone else's wife's.

'I prefer this, don't you? It's easier,' he continued, turning to look at Dinah who had been as careful as he had been in preparing for the day before them.

'Oh, yes. In all honesty I was growing a little tired of constantly being one of a crowd—even if that crowd is the one surrounding the Prince of Wales. I want to visit Markendale, of course—it's supposed to be very beautiful and grand, Violet has never seen fit to have me there before—but the price I shall have to pay for it is to join the social round again. The same holds true of our visit to Sandringham—honour though it is.'

'True,' said her husband, 'but I have the feeling that you will find some pleasant bolt-holes away from the crowd. If you don't, HRH will arrange some for you—like he did at the Leominsters!'

They had a happy laugh together at that.

Later in the day Dinah took her book into the park, and was enjoying it on an iron bench in the shade of a small gazebo facing the lake at the back of the house. She did rather miss Mr Van Deusen, who had joined Bellenger Hodson for a short stay in Brighton, and whom they would meet again at Sandringham. Otherwise she was pleased by the solitude created by the only other members of the house party: Violet and her husband, and Rainey, who was only too delighted to be living at someone else's expense.

He was finding the income which Cobie had given him rather constricting. He had been warned that under no circumstances, if he exceeded it, would he be given a loan by his brother-in-law.

Dinah's solitude was not to last long. She was presently joined by Lord Kenilworth who was taking a stroll round his grounds in the warmth of the mid-afternoon.

'You will allow?' he asked in his pleasant voice, before seating himself by her.

She closed her book. 'Of course. I have been reading for quite long enough.' Which was not the truth, but was the kind of polite lie which Madame had taught her to employ when in company. 'To oil the wheels of life,' she had said.

Dinah had had very little to do with her brother-in-law before she had married Cobie, and had thought him rather dull and a trifle slow. She was beginning to discover that he possessed an acute mind behind his lazy manner. Lord Kenilworth, for his part, was finding Lady

Dinah to be not only a pleasant child, but also a clever one.

He was beginning to understand why Grant had married her, and had taken the trouble to improve her looks. He supposed that she had got her brains from the unacknowledged father, and was now being trained not to show them overmuch, but to use them all the same.

'You might like to know—I don't suppose that Violet has informed you yet—that we have invited your mother to stay with us until we go on to Windsor. Now that Violet's father is dead I don't think that we need to keep her in permanent exile, do you?'

'Oh, how kind of you,' exclaimed Dinah. She was shrewd enough to know that the invitation had been inspired by Lord Kenilworth rather than Violet, and also shrewd enough not to let him know that she was aware of that.

He waved an idle hand. 'Not kind, sensible rather. These grand feuds are rather silly, don't you think? Time to forget the past. Particularly when the result of it is such an ornament to Society as you are.'

This was going a bit far, thought the dazzled Dinah; nevertheless she smiled her thanks at him.

He waved them away, too.

'I'm pleased to learn that your husband accepted our invitation to Markendale. I rather feared that his business in the City might keep him in town, but he has assured me that everything is under control at the moment. In any case, if anything should go wrong, it would not be too difficult for his staff to contact him. He said that he would not miss seeing Markendale's treasures for the world. And then, of course, there are the local races.'

'Ah, yes, the races,' agreed Dinah politely. She had never been to a race meeting in her life and had not the slightest notion whether they were among Cobie's many interests. She thought that the Marquise would be particularly proud of her today!

'One problem, though,' he said confidentially, 'is that the Prince has asked me to invite Sir Ratcliffe Heneage to be a member of the party at Markendale. I don't fancy the man, I wouldn't have had him in the house, but I couldn't refuse to obey them when Beauchamp came up and told me of Tum Tum's express wishes. I couldn't refuse him, could I?'

Dinah was puzzled. 'Why didn't the Prince just ask you himself? Why did he send Mr Beauchamp?'

Lord Kenilworth barked out a short laugh.

'No, no, my dear. Beauchamp is the Prince's grey man: the private and trusted servant who does his master's work for him—the dirty work which his master doesn't want to do himself. Tum Tum knows I don't care for Heneage, so he didn't want to order me in person to invite him—easier to send Beauchamp, and avoid any embarrassment putting me out might cause him personally. Although why he should want Heneage at Markendale, I can't imagine.'

Dinah's initiation into the Machiavellian politics of the great was going apace. How clever Cobie must be to manoeuvre through all this as easily as he did!

Rather daringly she decided to ask Lord Kenilworth a personal question.

'You said that you didn't like Sir Ratcliffe. Do you like my husband, Lord Kenilworth?'

'I wouldn't have had him here if I didn't. I'd have refused to invite Heneage to Moorings whatever the Prince's orders. Markendale now, that's different. More of a museum than a family home. I only have my real friends here. I regretted having asked him this spring. The man's a bounder, and I've decided that Moorings is now closed to him. Besides, there's something about your husband which intrigues me, don't you know. He's a clever fellow and commands my respect.

'I heard that you told Rainey and Violet that you think he's dangerous—which they pooh-poohed. Very shrewd of you, my dear, very shrewd. He showed his true colours a bit, didn't he, when he did for Sir Ratcliffe and Rainey at cards? Besides, he didn't make his fortune sitting about being Goody Twoshoes, did he? Indeed not.'

His laugh at his own wit was so jollily hearty that Dinah joined in with him. 'Not if what he told the Prince of Wales at the Leominsters' was true,' she replied.

'Um, heard about that from Sykes. He and Lipton were cut up at whist by your husband and the Prince— a real treat for Tum Tum: he's not the greatest card player in the world, you know. His real talents lie elsewhere.'

Yes, there *was* more to Lord Kenilworth than one might have thought. It was to be hoped that Violet appreciated that—and him. He and Dinah talked on companionably. He told her that her mother was expected on the morrow.

'I knew her years ago when I was first on the town. Violet's very like her.'

That was true.

'I'm not,' Dinah said sadly.

He smiled at her, and said, 'You are like no one but yourself, my dear sister-in-law, and if, as they tell me, you take after your father, then he must be a most remarkable man. You make me wish that I were twenty years younger. You will forgive me if I leave you: I have urgent letters to write.'

With that he kissed her hand, rose and strolled away.

Dinah stared after him. Now, what was all that about? She did not have long to ponder on the puzzle Kenilworth had suddenly presented her with, because another man, who posed an even greater one, was the next to join her.

Cobie appeared, also carrying a book. 'There you are, my dear. I've just met Kenilworth who told me that you were hidden away here. I was detained by the ineffable Violet, and spent some little time trying to fend off suggestions that we might carry on where we left off the last time I was at Moorings. I pointed out to her, as gently as I could, that I was then a free man, but that now, alas, I have a pretty young wife to care for. That being so, I knew that she, Violet, would not really wish me to break my marriage vows to her sister, either now or later.

'You are, perhaps, not acquainted with a rather good poem by the late A.H. Clough, where he says, among other wise things, ''Do not adultery commit. Advantage rarely comes of it.'' It is one of my few maxims for good conduct—not that I have always followed it in the past!'

No, Dinah did not know the poem. What she thought that she knew was that whatever Violet might hint, Cobie was setting her mind at rest, by assuring her that he was not about to renew his brief liaison with her either in the present or in the future.

'I also have to tell you, although I suspect that Kenilworth may have forestalled me, that he has insisted on your mother being invited to Moorings. I gather that he told Violet, very firmly, that bygones must be bygones.'

'Yes, he has told me, Cobie. But is it *you* that I really have to thank? Because if it is, it is yet another debt of gratitude which I owe you.'

'Wise child,' he said—and would say nothing more, until he stretched himself out on the grass in front of her, and began to read to her from his book. It was the satiric epic poem *Don Juan*, by Lord Byron.

'Just to complete your education about the goings-on in society,' he told her, before he began. 'Nothing changes over time but the clothes and the trappings we wear, you know. Men and women remain the same whatever the age they live in—and however much they try to deceive themselves.'

Dinah said daringly, '*You* deceive people, Cobie. I do know that.'

His smile at her was a rueful one. 'Yes, I am aware that you do. But I try not to deceive myself, and that is the important thing, Dinah. One must never believe one's own myth—that way self-destruction lies.'

He fell silent for a moment before continuing to read.

I would do well, he told himself later, to remember what I have just said the next time that I confront Walker—or Sir Ratcliffe for that matter.

Dinah's mother arrived on the following day as Kenilworth had promised. Cobie drove Dinah to the station to collect her and her little maid.

Moorings Halt looked exactly the same as it had done when Dinah had arrived there in the early spring.

The cat lay in the sun, the flower-beds were carefully tended, the porter still sat in his little sentry box. The only thing which had changed was Dinah Freville. Changed by the man who stood beside her who was helping his mother-in-law down from the railway carriage and accepting her kiss on his warm cheek.

'Hello, my darling, how good of you both to come to collect me,' exclaimed her mother, kissing Dinah, while Cobie transferred her luggage from the platform to the waiting carriage.

'What a lovely day!—and oh, how charming you look!'

She whispered conspiratorially into Dinah's ear, 'His doing, I suppose?'

'Definitely,' murmured Dinah, smiling.

Violet, of course, was on her best behaviour when she welcomed her mother to her home and took care to address her formally as Lady Rainsborough, before calling her mother, something which she had not done for many years. Kenilworth had, for once, put his foot down before her mother arrived.

'I expect you to be civil to your mama and to your sister, at least while they are at Moorings,' he had told her. 'Nothing is to be gained by being otherwise. You do understand me, my dear? I will have my way in this.'

Yes, Violet understood him. Of all things, her husband had fallen for the charms of his sister-in-law. If she threw any darts at Dinah, she would have to do so when he was not present. All, therefore, to Dinah's amusement, was sweetness and light. It was as though her mother had never run away with the tutor and borne an illegitimate child, as though Violet had never had an *affaire* with Cobie, and as though the illegitimate daughter had never married a Yankee of dubious origin after he had blackmailed her brother in order to be allowed to do so.

All in all, it was rather like being part of a Jacobean tragi-comedy without there being any dead bodies on the stage to frighten the footmen—something which Cobie had recently said in a different context!

It was, though, delightful to pass the time in idleness at beautiful Moorings, which unlike Markendale was not too hugely grand. In their different ways both Cobie and Dinah were enjoying this brief interlude where they were not required to act, as they were when they trod on life's wider stage.

For Cobie it was a time to lie in the sun, his panama hat over his eyes, and think. About everything. About his extraordinary social success which had resulted in him being named the friend and favourite of a Prince.

About Sir Ratcliffe and of how he had escaped punishment and was still roving the world, enjoying himself—apparently secure in the knowledge that, once again, he was free to indulge himself in his disgusting vices.

He owed it to Lizzie to see that her murderer would not escape punishment, although how he could bring him to some sort of justice Cobie could not at present foresee.

He thought about the dogged Walker and his blatant honesty—but he was not so honest that he would not engage in any ploy which might net the criminal which he had decided Cobie was! We are more alike than he knows, Cobie thought wryly—we both make up our own rules.

To control the present was difficult enough: to control the future was harder still. In that unexplored land which changed even as one breathed, there were always so many branching possibilities to consider. Perhaps best not to consider them at all, but simply to grasp the skirts of Chance when she, frivolous goddess that she was, chose to swing by him in her merry, mindless dance among the scrambling mortals from whom she took her pleasure.

He dismissed both Chance and Sir Ratcliffe and thought instead about Dinah. To his astonishment, and little had ever astonished him since his time in America's Southwest, his feelings towards her were undergoing a rapid, and daily, change.

He had rescued her out of pity: there had been nothing of love, or lust in his mind when he had done so. Yet…yet…day by day, living with her, watching her, even before she had come to change and blossom, something strange had begun to happen to him.

What were these new feelings? At first he had thought that it was simple protection that he felt: protection for someone who, although charmingly innocent, had proved to have a sharp and incisive mind. Was that what had attracted him—that he could give her the opportunity to let that mind rove free? He had initiated her into the pleasures of the bed and she had rapidly become as adept as he, but it was not simple lust which he felt for her. No, it was more than that.

For all his cleverness—perhaps, indeed, because of it—he could not give his feelings a name. Was this, then, love? If so, it was something which he had never felt before, and if it were, he knew that he had never loved Susanna as she had loved him. Or, if he had, it had been the untutored love of a boy, not this complex feeling which Dinah evoked in him.

He sat up, violently, pulled his hat away from his eyes, and stared across the beautiful garden to where Dinah was walking and talking with her mother.

No, he didn't want it, no. He did not want to be overcome by what he had deliberately renounced. For to love was to be obligated, to be in some way tied to the person loved, and he did not want that. He had spent ten years creating and preserving his solitude, and to love Dinah was to breach it, and destroy in a moment every brick in the wall which he had built around himself to keep others out...and himself secure.

Long ago on a hot morning in the desert he had confronted the possibility of a cruel death at the hands of a man who was determined to make an example of him to deter others who might wish to free themselves from the bondage in which he and his master held them.

It was love and friendship which had brought him to that pass, and he had vowed then, that if he survived, he would never be at anyone's mercy again. He would live by and for himself, and no one else. If he helped others, it would always be on his own terms...

But what had he done, all unwittingly? He had bought himself a wife, almost by accident, and in doing so was discovering that he had altered the nature of his whole world, that his personal future, once carefully mapped out, had changed completely. He had lost the key to the map of his life and was wandering on strange roads, not sure of his destination.

Cobie shook himself and lay down again. 'Much thinking hath made him mad,' had once been said—by whom? Perhaps he ought to try—for a time—not to do so. Slowly, slowly, he transported himself into the mindlessness trance again, but he knew, that when he awoke from it, his problems would still be there waiting for him...

Dinah was having a heart-to-heart talk with her mother among the scents of the herb garden where, earlier in the year, Cobie had reluctantly done Violet's bidding and had been cruel to her. It seemed another life, not a mere few months ago, that she had left the haven of her mother's cottage, fearful of her future. She could not then have imagined her present situation as the admired wife of a man who had deserted Violet to marry her.

And if she still had no notion why he had done such a thing, that was no longer a matter for worry. He had done so—and that was that.

'You are happy?' her mother was asking. 'You look happy.'

Dinah thought for a moment. 'Yes, I suppose I am. Not completely so, but then, who is?'

She was thinking of Cobie and of her wish that he would come to love her as she loved him. Of course, it might be thought, if one were being logical, that she loved him because of what he had done for her. It would then follow—or would it?—that she might have to do something for him to make him love her. What in the world could she, powerless Dinah Grant, late Dinah Freville, ever be able to do to help the self-sufficient man who was her husband?

She could hardly say all that to her mother.

'True,' said her mother. She added shrewdly, 'Violet tells me that you are the success of the Season—and him, too. Now, one might have expected his, but yours is the more surprising—although not when I look at you now.'

'Ridiculous, isn't it?' Dinah said, laughing a little ruefully. 'I'm not entirely sure that I like it. People standing on chairs to stare at me. I'm not really such a knock-out, surely.'

'You're different,' said her mother, shrewd again. 'Society always wants something different.'

'And strange,' agreed Dinah. 'I suppose I might have been even more remarked on if I'd possessed two heads!'

'That's it,' said her mother. 'That's the sort of thing you can get away with now. Violet tells me that your picture postcard is on sale in newsagents' shops. I'm surprised that you consented to that.'

'I didn't. Some photographer took me at Henley Regatta without my permission—I was wearing my hat with the snowdrops. The next thing we knew was that it was on sale entitled *The English Snowdrop*. Cobie thought of making a fuss and having it withdrawn, but he changed his mind and let it go. Besides, he said that it would make Violet fume to know that there was another Freville sister celebrated in the beauty stakes— she had thought that she was the only one.'

'Good for him,' said her mother. 'Violet needs a bit of taking down now and then—it's good for her. Rainsborough and I spoiled her when she was a child—not a wise thing to do. I didn't make the same mistake with you.'

'No, indeed,' said Dinah, laughing again. 'Firm, but loving, that's what you were—just like Cobie.'

'And you are happy with him? You should be...'

'Seeing what he's done for me? No, if I love him it's not because of that. It's for a dozen other reasons.'

'And the Prince. Violet also tells me that the Grants are high in his favour. Does he behave himself with you?'

'Oh, yes. You see, the women he particularly favours are all much older—and larger—than I am. He sees me as a daughter, I think. He admires Cobie because he is an American who does things, but manages to look and talk like an English gentleman. In essence we're a couple of freaks.'

Her mother began to laugh. 'Oh, I see why you're a success, my dear. Now, if you will forgive me I will go indoors. Since I grew older, too much sun troubles me, but if you wish to remain outside, I quite understand.'

Impulsively Dinah kissed her mother on the cheek.

'I'm so glad Violet invited you. Yes, I will stay outside a little longer.'

She watched her mother walk away, before strolling down the very path in the Knot Garden on which she had stood with Cobie on that distant March day.

She could see him lying on the small lawn, in the shade of a willow, his hat over his eyes. She would not disturb him. She had already learned that there were times when he wished to be alone—as she wished to be now.

Dinah sat down on the grass and looked about her. Like Cobie she began to muse on life, and on the problem of what she felt for him—and he for her. She had no doubt about her own feelings; for all his faults—and she was wise enough to recognise them—she loved him—and passionately.

But did he love her? That was the difficult question.

Perhaps it was simply that he pitied her—and, pity was surely kin to love—but she wanted more than his pity, she wanted from him the equivalent of what she felt for him. Something told her that, if she were patient, then it was possible that she might win his love, either by *doing* something for him—or *being* something for him, she was not sure which.

Patience, she told herself, all my short life I have been asked to exercise patience, so it should not be difficult to exercise it again.

Dinah looked about her. On the edge of a bed of thyme a solitary, late daisy nodded. She remembered what she had thought in Paris: that there were no daisies in the Faubourg St Germain. But here at Moorings, where she had suffered, and where she had met the man whom she loved so fiercely that it was almost painful, there was a daisy—one.

The last daisy.

Was it an omen? She would take it as one.

Dinah plucked it, and before she knew what she was doing, and after she had looked across at him, supine in the sun which he so closely resembled, Apollo himself, she began to strip the petals from it, one by one.

She whispered as she held each one for a moment in her hand, before letting it fall, oh, so gently, into her lap, 'He loves me, he loves me not.'

The litany continued until she plucked the flower's last petal, saying with quiet triumph, 'He loves me.'

Oh, yes, he would, he surely would.

Dinah's lips moved in a silent prayer that her wish would be granted while the last petal drifted slowly to the ground...to be taken away by the light breeze.

In the distance Cobie stirred, his trance broken by he knew not what. He drifted slowly back to life, thinking—what was he thinking? No, he was feeling...what?

He brushed a daisy's petal from his cheek. The light

breeze which blew across the garden had gifted him with it. From nowhere two thoughts crossed his mind before the sleep, which often followed the trance, claimed him.

Is it possible that I could learn to love?

Is it possible that I could love Dinah—who is eminently loveable?

*   *   *   *   *

Will Dinah gain Cobie's love?
Will Cobie finally corner Sir Ratcliffe
before Inspector Will Walker corners him?

Watch for the next novel in

THE DILHORNE DYNASTY

by Paula Marshall,
coming soon.

MILLS & BOON®

Makes any time special™

Mills & Boon publish 29 new titles every month. Select from...

Modern Romance™   Tender Romance™

Sensual Romance™

Medical Romance™ Historical Romance™

MAT2

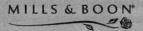

MILLS & BOON®

Historical Romance™

A TRACE OF MEMORY by Elizabeth Bailey

A Regency delight!

The Earl of Wytham is suspicious when a
bedraggled woman accosts him in his woods
claiming to have lost her memory. His first thought
is that this is yet another ingenious matrimonial
ploy. But when her beauty and her vulnerability
become an increasingly alluring mix, can they resist
their longings, because each unfolding memory
suggests that she could belong to another man!

LORD FOX'S PLEASURE by Helen Dickson

The Restoration of Charles II
...secrets, intrigue and conquests...

The Restoration of the monarchy meant a time to take
stock for wealthy landowner Lucas Fox. The pleasure-
seeker wanted a wife and it was the proud, impulsive
Prudence Fairworthy who caught his eye. But with
her suspicions over his motives and the mystery
surrounding his past, Lucas knew she would not be
easily tempted by marriage. But there was untold
pleasure to be found in the art of persuasion...

On sale 1st June 2001

Available at branches of WH Smith, Tesco, Martins,
Borders, Easons, Sainsbury, Woolworth
and most good paperback bookshops

0501/04

FREE!

2 Books
and a surprise gift!

We would like to take this opportunity to thank you for reading this Mills & Boon® book by offering you the chance to take TWO more specially selected titles from the Historical Romance™ series absolutely FREE! We're also making this offer to introduce you to the benefits of the Reader Service™—

- ★ FREE home delivery
- ★ FREE gifts and competitions
- ★ FREE monthly Newsletter
- ★ Books available before they're in the shops
- ★ Exclusive Reader Service discounts

Accepting these FREE books and gift places you under no obligation to buy; you may cancel at any time, even after receiving your free shipment. Simply complete your details below and return the entire page to the address below. **You don't even need a stamp!**

YES! Please send me 2 free Historical Romance books and a surprise gift. I understand that unless you hear from me, I will receive 4 superb new titles every month for just £2.99 each, postage and packing free. I am under no obligation to purchase any books and may cancel my subscription at any time. The free books and gift will be mine to keep in any case.

H1ZEB

Ms/Mrs/Miss/Mr ....Initials...................................

BLOCK CAPITALS PLEASE

Surname...

Address...

....

....Postcode ....

Send this whole page to:
UK: The Reader Service, FREEPOST CN81, Croydon, CR9 3WZ
EIRE: The Reader Service, PO Box 4546, Kilcock, County Kildare (stamp required)